LOST AND FOUND

Best wishe!

Duncan

A David Mallory and Lara Rios Story
DUNCAN ROY

 FriesenPress

One Printers Way
Altona, MB R0G 0B0
Canada

www.friesenpress.com

Copyright © 2022 by Duncan Roy
First Edition — 2022

Illustrations by Greg Garand

All rights reserved.

No part of this publication may be reproduced in any form, or by any means, electronic or mechanical, including photocopying, recording, or any information browsing, storage, or retrieval system, without permission in writing from FriesenPress.

ISBN
978-1-03-912784-5 (Hardcover)
978-1-03-912783-8 (Paperback)
978-1-03-912785-2 (eBook)

1. FICTION, MYSTERY & DETECTIVE

Distributed to the trade by The Ingram Book Company

For Janet
with love

In the course of a lifetime, we lose things. Some of them we don't miss because we didn't value them in the first place. They drift away like the fluff from a summer dandelion, unconsidered and unregretted.

But some of them we don't miss because we don't know they'd gone. We can live a long time without discovering that they have vanished, only to stumble across the loss at some inconvenient and painful moment when we are unprepared.

Then again, the most precious things we find are not those that we acquire through careful searching. They are the things that we trip over by accident or create out of random elements. Precious truths distilled from unlikely ingredients, a human alchemy urging pure gold from base materials.

CHAPTER 1

I

The few good friends I have will tell you that I'm not the most sociable person. They might go on to say that I seem happy on my own, and if they'd had a couple of drinks, they might add that I can be a bit of a curmudgeon.

It's true. Given the choice I'm happier at home with a book, but my work has required many job-related social outings, so I've learned how to survive. Sometimes I get so wrapped up in the act that I even enjoy myself.

The trouble is, I think too hard about the conversations when all that's really required is to relax and go with the flow. Nothing profound is discussed at birthday parties, and no world problems are resolved at bar mitzvahs. It's just banter about sports, the weather, children, and holidays.

I know I take myself too seriously. It's something I've been told more than once.

When I do go out, I'm always surprised by the way people introduce themselves.

"Hi, I'm Lola. I'm an interior designer."

"Good evening. My name's Graham. I work with Bachman Insurance."

It's as if our day jobs have become the most compelling part of our identities, as if "accountant" was a surname, "architect" a personality type, and "lawyer" a belief system.

Well, my name's David, but I haven't found a title that fits what I do for a living right now. I suppose "educational consultant" would come close, but it doesn't really fit with what schools hire me to do.

I'm the first person a school calls when a scandal pops up. The headmaster gets too friendly with a student, the bursar buys a second home in Malibu that he couldn't possibly afford, the chaplain has a drug habit.

I made my reputation with the St. Eustace grade-tampering case.

The school's new head was desperate to improve the school's reputation, but the kids it attracted weren't getting any smarter. Second-tier colleges and vocational schools were the usual destination of St. Eustace grads, and the academic dean smelled a rat when twelve of the graduating class were admitted to Ivy League schools. He bypassed the head, whom he suspected was involved, and went straight to the board chair, who happened to be a former student of mine. He knew I could use the work and called me in.

My mandate was to investigate but under a thick cloak of confidentiality. That's my speciality. I get to the bottom of anything, pass my findings on to the person who's paying me, and make sure the affair stays out of the headlines.

In this case the headmaster was having an affair with the woman who managed student records. He persuaded her that altering the grades was OK in the cause of institutional advancement.

It took me about five minutes to change her view on that, and she spilled the beans. The board chair had my report within the week. It was almost the end of the academic year, and the head was quietly replaced by an interim before the students returned in September. Not a word appeared in the media.

The board chair was pleased with my work, and over the next few years my name was dropped in bars at exclusive golf clubs and in the steam rooms of ritzy gyms. I guess I created the niche, and it's been good to me. I charge a daily retainer plus expenses, and now I get calls from prestigious schools all over the world.

I should note that I only work with independent schools—private schools, some people call them. The press loves it when a posh school for the children of the good and the great gets itself into trouble, and reporters spare no effort to drag everyone involved through the gutter. Reputation is everything to these schools, hence the need for confidentiality—and my services.

I'm good at my job because I worked in independent schools for forty years. I was head of three of them. You would certainly know the name of one, perhaps all of them.

There isn't much related to the human condition that I haven't seen. Also, I have a high tolerance for ambiguity, which comes in handy when you're trying to unravel a situation and point to the truth in the full and certain knowledge that your findings may be buried under a thick layer of legal accommodation and hush money.

I wouldn't be doing this job but for the fact that my wife, Joanne, left me for her accountant the year after I retired from my last headship. We had both been earning good money for the better part of three decades, and retirement looked comfortable or better, but the divorce changed that. I'd just celebrated my fifty-seventh birthday when I hung up my shingle as a consultant and got a couple of jobs right away. One was advising a school that was starting up a franchise in the Gulf. The other was doing a search for an advancement director, but the jobs didn't pay much, and worse—much worse—they were really dull.

One of my many character defects is that I get bored easily. The St. Eustace gig came along hard on the heels of the other two, and I knew I had found something special, something that used my talents and experience and had that frisson of mystery and intrigue that meant it would never be boring. I suppose I'm part detective, part therapist, and part actor. Joanne says I'm manipulative. I don't agree, but if I am, I'd consider it an asset in my current line of work.

What else would you like to know about me? Well, I was born in London, but my father worked for the Foreign Office, so we lived all over the world: Buenos Aires, Pretoria, Delhi, Los Angeles. I met Joanne at university in Scotland. We fell in love, and I moved to Canada to be with her when I was twenty-four, abandoning a job at Sotheby's and a career in fine art.

We lived in a small village in Southern Ontario. Joanne worked in banking and supported us while I spent a year at the University of Toronto doing a postgrad education qualification. I taught history for a decade at two private schools before moving into school leadership. I turned out to be good at that, and after headships in Melbourne and Lima, I ended my career at a marquis school in Vancouver.

We'd lived in school housing for thirty years. Joanne got the house in Ontario, which we had kept for retirement, as part of the divorce settlement. I decided to move to the beach house in South Florida that my parents bought when my dad retired. I'd rented it out for the five years since Mum died, but now I needed a roof over my head, and a tropical beach sounded OK.

The house wasn't grand. Three bedrooms, two bathrooms, a huge kitchen, and a living room with floor-to-ceiling windows looking out onto the big deck and the ocean. It was located on A1A in Highland Beach just north of Boca Raton.

Most of the neighbours who, like my parents, had bought in the 1970s had sold to property developers who bulldozed the old homes and built luxurious Moorish palaces and ultra-modern glass-and-chrome boxes for the newly super rich who were bleeding down from the northeast. My place looked unfashionably modest and restrained, but the property was worth a fortune if I ever wanted to sell. But, as I said, I needed a place to live.

II

It was a Monday in early October and still humid and stifling as I walked in from the garage to the dry coolness of the house. The weather would change in a couple of weeks, and a few million people would head to Florida for the winter. The house was sparsely furnished. As I'd gotten older, I felt burdened by all the stuff we'd accumulated. It was one of the points of tension between Joanne and me. She loved to be surrounded by her possessions.

I bought a queen bed with a firm mattress. There was a California closet in the bedroom where I kept my clothes. A leather sectional sofa and a couple of comfortable chairs occupied the living room, and some deck furniture was visible outside the windows.

I'd hung nothing on the walls except a framed photo of my granddaughter, Jessica. She's eighteen and just starting an engineering degree at Cambridge. I love that girl more than anything that is left in my life. I stand in front of the picture as if it's a mediaeval icon, and I always come away with a smile on my lips.

My son, James, and his wife had separated, and they lived on different coasts in Canada, but Jessica seemed unaffected. We travelled a lot together right through her early and mid-teens, and we know each other very well.

The only luxuries in the house were two things that I had inherited from my parents and had kept because they had loved them. An oak refectory table sat in the large kitchen. It was fifteen feet long and was surrounded by ten press back chairs. My mother, who loved to entertain, had found the table at an antique store in Nova Scotia before I was born. It had formed a centrepiece in our itinerant lives, following us as we moved from posting to posting. My mum burnished it with beeswax, and I never saw her happier than when she was sitting at the table surrounded by friends or family.

In the garage was a 1963 Mk 2 Jaguar that my father had doted on. It was a gorgeous shade of opalescent blue with red leather upholstery. Sitting beside it was the small sun-bleached Japanese sedan that I use most of the time.

I'm not sentimental, but the table and the Jag keep me in touch with a different time and help evoke memories of how things had been. They have power for me.

I shed my clothes and had my second shower of the day. The shower was the only major improvement that I'd made to the house. It was a big glass walk-in with grey-blue slate walls and floor and a huge rain shower head.

My childhood in London involved twice-weekly baths in tepid water. In contrast, the sensation of a powerful hot shower still makes me smile.

I surveyed the closet and pulled out a pale blue Canali shirt, a lavender Hermes tie, and a pair of Guess jeans. I got dressed and then slipped on a lightweight Boss jacket in a heather mixture and the pair of Gucci loafers that Joanne had bought me for the last birthday we'd spent together.

I had moved away from the Gieves and Hawkes suits that I'd worn when I was a headmaster, but I still felt more comfortable when I was a bit over-dressed. The jeans were my concession to Palm Beach County.

I lowered myself into the Honda, opened the garage door with the remote, and headed out. The afternoon sun filtered through the palms lining the short driveway. I pulled onto A1A heading south toward the small office I rented on the corner of Federal Highway and Spanish River Boulevard. The office was in a one-story strip mall that also contained a post office, North Dixie Fitness, and the One Stop Smoke Shop.

That part of East Boca was working class, and I liked it a lot better than the brash wealth on display just a couple of miles south where oceangoing yachts jostled each other around the fringes of Lake Boca, and the Russian mafia laundered its money flipping properties in Riviera Shores Country Club. I ventured down there occasionally when I wanted a great cocktail or a special meal, but East Boca was comfortable and easygoing, and I could afford the office rent.

Although I've spent my career dealing with the rich and famous, I think I'm fairly low maintenance. When I moved to Florida, I spent a bit of money on flying lessons up at Lantana airport. It was something I'd always thought about doing, and the moment seemed right. I did the forty hours of ground school and sixty hours of flying and got my private pilot's licence. I've been pretty busy since, so I don't get up much. Apart from flying lessons, I live frugally, and I've actually been able to save quite a bit of money. You'd say I was doing OK.

Emerante Beauvais smiled at me as I walked in the office door. She held the landline receiver under her chin and raised her hand in a small wave as she listened to the caller. Emerante, who is known by everyone as Emy, is my only employee, and she does a bit of everything. She answers the inquiries, looks after the accounts, arranges most of my travel, and has never refused when I've added another task to her growing portfolio. I'm sparing with superlatives, but Emy is the best assistant I've ever had. I pay her well, and she seems happy with her work.

She had answered the ad I placed in the *Palm Beach Post* five years ago. Back then she'd just turned twenty-five and was going through a difficult time. She had two young children, and her husband, Raymond, had just been diagnosed with advanced prostate cancer. He was forced to quit his job, and because they had no medical insurance, Emy had to look for something.

Raymond died the week after Emy began with me. The children had started kindergarten, which made things easier for her in a way, but I knew that Emy missed them every minute for those first months.

Perhaps the fact that both our situations had recently changed in important ways allowed us to share more personal things than we might have done otherwise.

Her parents were still in Haiti and couldn't offer her any support. I think Emy sees me as a cross between a grandfather whose advice is worth considering, an employer whom others seem to seek out, and a man-child who needs looking after. Whatever the reason, our professional relationship is enhanced by a degree of warmth and understanding that makes the office a pleasant place to be.

"How was your weekend, Mr. Mallory?" she said, replacing the receiver. "How was the Red Cross fundraiser?"

"It was awful, thank you, Emy. The sound system broke, the woman sitting next to me at dinner started the conversation by asking if I wore anything under my kilt, and I think the valet scratched the Jag. Still, once again, the temptation to show off in public worked a treat, and a great deal of money was raised."

"Poor Mr. M. Never mind. I think I have something interesting for you. That was the head of the Shelburne College in Cape Town on the phone. He's in Miami for a conference next week, and he would like to meet you for lunch. He says he has something that he needs your help with, but he wouldn't give me any more details. I said I would ask you and call him back today. Cape Town is six hours ahead of us. He gave me his office number and his cell number."

"Thank you, Emy. Call him please and see if he can make it for lunch at the Bazaar on Collins at noon next Wednesday. How was your weekend?"

"It was sweet, Mr. M. Thanks for asking. The twins want me to thank you for the picture book. I had to read it to them twice on Saturday night and three times on Sunday."

Emy's smile was a mile wide. She was wearing an emerald-green sundress that I hadn't seen before along with a pair of green leather pumps. A subtle line of red lipstick ran across her lips between her white teeth and brown skin. She was a beautiful young woman, strong and clever, and I was sure that good things lay ahead for her.

"Did you find any time for yourself," I asked.

"I went up to Delray on Saturday afternoon with a girlfriend. Her mum looked after Marie and Jean, and of course, we went to church yesterday."

Emy and the children never miss a Sunday at the Friendship Baptist Church, a fundamentalist congregation popular with the Haitian community. I had gone there for her husband's funeral, and the experience had stayed with me. There was live music, a pastor who spoke in tongues, and congregants who fell down in the aisle in holy rapture. It was as far from the Anglican Church of my childhood as I can imagine, but if I was ever to reclaim my faith, I think I would favour the joyful chaos of Friendship Baptist over the hushed sanctimony of St. John the Divine.

III

There was a little paperwork to take care of from my last case in Costa Rica. Warring factions on the board of an international school in San Jose had thrown out the new head, and they needed a peacemaker. It was an easy fix, and I might not have taken it, but I loved the country, and it was an excuse to spend a couple of days with my old friend Adrian Mendes Cruz, the best birding guide in the Monteverde Cloud Forest. As usual, he had found us a Resplendent Quetzal.

There was nothing of substance in my calendar for the rest of the week, so I decided to take a few days away. I asked Emy to check into flights to Cape Town in case the following week's meeting led to anything. I suggested she take Wednesday off, and then I headed back out to the car.

It had been standing in the sun for an hour, and the steering wheel was too hot to touch. I started the engine, turned the AC up high, and walked around the corner to the Publix supermarket. I didn't lock the car; it would be a desperate thief who would choose my 1999 Honda Civic.

I picked up some field tomatoes and fresh basil along with a baguette that was still warm and a bottle of Moselle. By the time I got back to the car, the interior was a better temperature. I tuned in the BBC World Service on satellite, engaged the gear, and headed back up A1A to my house.

In the kitchen I sliced the tomatoes and tore up some of the basil leaves. I made a vinaigrette, cut a chunk of the bread, and arranged everything on a plate. Then I balanced the plate on my laptop and headed out onto the deck. I put the things down on the wooden table that lay in the shade of a large sea grape. Back in the kitchen, I got some ice from the freezer, popped a couple of cubes in a glass, and filled it with Moselle. I rarely drink at lunchtime though, sometimes I make up for it in the evening, but that day it felt right. I took a sip and surveyed the beach that ran away from the edge of the deck to the sparkling ocean. The afternoon sun was torn into sparkling petals on the water, and it was almost painfully bright to look at. The beach was empty apart from an older couple walking hand in hand at the water's edge. I resolved to go for a long swim when the sun was lower.

Although I have been "on stage" a lot with my work and can, when required, appear to be the life and soul of the party, I'm happiest on my own. While some head to a resort for relaxation, I look for remote places. I used to be very low maintenance, but now I prefer a bed and a hot shower, though I can take a few days without if the reward is sufficient.

I opened my laptop and clicked on the bookmark for Darville Hall on Great Exuma, a place I had been several times before. When most people think of the Bahamas they think of Freeport or Nassau, but I have come to love the tranquility of the out islands, and of these my favourite is Great Exuma. Darville Hall is an old house just outside of Georgetown. Sheltered by palms and casuarina, it sits on a rocky headland looking east over Elizabeth Harbour toward Stocking Island and the Atlantic. Most visitors to Georgetown are sailors from Europe, Canada, and the US. They like to winter in the cays, sailing around the hundreds of islands and dropping anchor in the sheltered bays.

I made a reservation with Bahamasair for the 4:00 p.m. flight from Fort Lauderdale through Nassau. Then I called Bessie Rolle, who looks after the house. There aren't a lot of conventional tourists in Georgetown, and Darville Hall is usually available even at the last minute, as it turned out this time. I asked Bessie to arrange for Eldon to pick me up at the airport and to put a few basics in the fridge, which she is always happy to do.

I'm happy on my own, but I'm also happy in the company of Lara Rios, so I called her next and invited her to join me. Lara is in real estate and can do most of her work from her smartphone. She sounded happy at the prospect of time together.

I met her at a black-tie fundraiser last year, and the fact that we developed an intimate relationship within a few days surprised me more than a little.

After my divorce and the previous decades of monogamy, I didn't feel very confident about starting a new relationship, but conversation with Lara was easy, and we shared some interests—art, wildlife, wine. After our second lunch date, we skipped dessert and went to bed. Lara is fifteen years younger than me and looks younger still. I was nervous, but she took charge, and we both enjoyed ourselves. Lara and I see each other as often as our schedules allow, but we are pretty relaxed, so sometimes two or three weeks will pass if I'm overseas or she is wrapped up in a big deal. We don't know each other well yet, but I hope that will change.

I changed, packed a few essentials, locked the house and set the alarm, then drove the Honda down I95 to the airport. It's only thirty minutes in good traffic, but the traffic is never good, so I gave myself an hour. I parked the car in the daily parking lot, grabbed my bag from the trunk, and walked across the street to departures. It's a strange airport with multiple functions. Cruise ship passengers milled about in garish shirts, Haitians headed home with big tote bags of supplies, and there were even a few business people in formal attire who preferred Fort Lauderdale to the mayhem of Miami International.

I checked in at the Bahamasair counter behind which a young man with a broad smile instantly reminded me of the carefree Bahamian vibe and of the reason why I loved escaping to the islands. I cleared security and saw Lara sitting close to the gate. Whenever I see her, I feel my blood pressure drop a few points. This time was no different; I felt a smile on my face as I walked up behind her.

"Hi, Lara," I said, touching her shoulder. She turned to me.

"David. I'm so happy to see you. How are you?"

Lara has a special voice. It still bears the inflections of her Colombian childhood, and it was deeper than her petite stature would suggest. It's so warm and mellifluous that I often get lost in our conversations because her voice carries me away on a different thought. Her hair is dark brown, and she wears it shoulder length, but the thing that strikes me every time we meet are her sparkling green eyes. I've never seen their like. I know she likes to play tennis, and she goes to the gym three mornings a week, so she is in really good shape, and she takes care with her wardrobe. That day she was wearing a French blue sleeveless dress and carrying a pale-blue cardigan.

"You look beautiful, Lara. I'm so happy that you could come." I leaned forward and kissed her cheek.

CHAPTER 2

I

I was happy to see David. He's a kind man, and I enjoy being with him. He can be a bit of a perfectionist, especially with his work, but I know he likes me making fun of him about it, and I can usually get him to relax.

David doesn't stand out in a crowd. He's a little less than six feet with what one would call a medium build. He still has most of his hair, which is pale brown and shot through with silver. But when you look at him more closely, you notice that he is quite striking. His eyes are a vivid pale blue, and he has laugh lines that crinkle when he is amused. His skin is lightly tanned, and he has a wide, winning smile that he doesn't show often enough. He keeps himself in shape, and he looks pretty good for a man about to turn sixty.

David has been good for me. I've been through a difficult decade in which the death of my sixteen-year-old son Alejandro stands front and centre and casts a dark shadow over my life. For the first several weeks after the funeral, every part of every day was consumed with his absence and my guilt. A year later there were a few brief times in each day when I might find beauty in something or might smile at a friend's remark, but then the cloud would reappear, and I would feel guilty again for having forgotten him even for a moment.

I told David about it at our first meeting. We were seated together at a dinner in support of the Haitian earthquake victims. The people on the other side of the table were braying about golf and Republican politics, so we were in our own little conversational bubble. Obviously, it was rather a heavy topic for a first conversation, but David didn't try and change the subject, and he listened to me in such a complete way that I believed he understood. A week later I embarrassed myself by dissolving into tears after our first time in bed together, but David held me and stroked my hair, and a lot more was said in that intimate silence than could have been achieved with words.

I know that David likes our lovemaking, and I'm sure he is quietly pleased that I'm aroused by him. He's quite a bit older than me, and I could tell that, at first, he was nervous about making love to a younger woman. Perhaps that's why he takes such care to make me happy. So, I'm lucky to have found him, and I think he feels the same. We've made no commitment, but I know we would both be sad if we couldn't see each other.

II

The plane to Nassau was a regional jet, but onward to Georgetown we were squeezed into a tiny Beechcraft with twelve other passengers. There was no door to the cockpit, so we could see everything that the pilot and first officer were doing, and through the windshield we were aware of the pitch and yaw of the plane as it was buffeted by thermals and winds.

Out the window the turquoise sea was complemented by the swirl of shining white sand lying just below the surface. "Baja mar," shallow sea, the early explorers called it. With a few exceptions, the water to the west of the islands is only a few metres deep. Immediately to the east though the water turns deep navy blue and dives quickly down to the depths of the Atlantic Ocean.

The airport on Great Exuma consists of a short runway and a cluster of whitewashed buildings. Within a few minutes of landing, we had cleared the friendliest customs on the planet and were nestled in Eldon's Suburban heading south to Georgetown. We sat in the back and held hands for the twenty-minute drive.

We quizzed Eldon on the weather and his family, and he responded in his deep, gravelly voice, turning to us with a broad smile and a chuckle to emphasize important points. Eldon is a respected elder in the small island community. He always wears a white open-neck shirt and khaki pants and is addressed with reverence by everyone in town. He's a good man to know.

The Suburban crunched up Darville Hall's gravel driveway and slowed to a stop under the small *porte cochere* that provided shade from the blazing sun and shelter from the occasional rain. The house had no air conditioning, but it had windows on all sides, was shaded by a huge, old banyan tree, and was kept cool by the steady trade winds. A sweet, musky smell wafted in the windows from the frangipani plantings in the garden, and I was reminded how much I loved to be there. Yellow bananaquits were hopping around in the bougainvillea, and Luther the house cat strode sinuously out of the shade and brushed against my leg in welcome.

I pushed open the French doors that led into the house and put my bag in the big, airy bedroom. Through the window I saw David chatting with Eldon. He looked so happy.

I had a few brief relationships before David, but I knew that none of them were good for me. The men could sense my insecurity and either took advantage of it or ran from it. I had more success with Elaine. She was a realtor for a rival firm, and we met at an open house in Pompano Beach. She was very pretty in a blonde, sculpted Florida way, and she made all the running, taking me for a cocktail that developed into dinner and then bringing me to Delray to show me her new condo where we shared a bottle of Amarone. Over the limit, I fell asleep on her couch but woke the next morning in her bed with her arm draped across my breasts and a peaceful feeling in my heart. Elaine moved away to the west coast shortly after, and we lost touch.

Perhaps I should open up more to David and tell him about Elaine, but I like what we have, and I don't want to risk losing it.

III

I woke up on Tuesday morning with the sun angling in the window and the sound of the water slapping against the small jetty beside the house. A couple of ground doves were calling, and the shadow of a palm frond moved against the curtain.

I looked over at Lara as she lay facing me, her hair sprawled over the pillow and her mouth slightly open as she slept. I saw the gentle rise and fall of her chest and smelled her jasmine perfume, muted by the passage of the night. She looked so vulnerable, and I felt my heart clench as I watched her. We saw each other frequently, but we never really spent enough time together to understand each other's deeper feelings. As I watched her, I wondered whether I had the courage to try and change that.

I wasn't sure that I was the right person for Lara, and I didn't want to hurt her. At times she seemed to agree with what I said or did, not just to be obliging but because she didn't want to show what she really felt.

And me? There was a lot of baggage that I wasn't ready to unpack. If we opened up to each other more, we would discover things that could end our relationship, and I was increasingly aware that Lara's friendship was very important to me.

When Joanne left me, I was angry at first and then very sad. We had lived most of a life together, had raised James, and doted on Jessica. Joanne knew what I was thinking without me saying a word; we were inclined to finish each other's sentences. She was a strong-minded woman, and I don't think she had ever really doubted herself. Her confidence was like oxygen for me; it allowed me to run faster and climb higher than I could have done without her.

Allan, her lover, an accountant, was several years younger than Joanne. He was a good-looking man, and I had always enjoyed chatting to him when we met on social occasions, but he didn't strike me as clever enough for her. He didn't read much, and his idea of foreign travel was a beach resort in Cuba. He had no interest in languages and couldn't even speak French, which is quite an achievement growing up in a country where French is compulsory in school for eight years.

I've been lucky with my health. At my annual medical the doctor always concludes that I'm in pretty good shape for my age. For the last twenty years, however, I have suffered from panic attacks, which can be totally debilitating. They don't occur more than once or twice a year, but they are hard to predict. They seem to occur most often just after I've had a really uplifting experience. It sounds counterintuitive, but I've lived with it long enough to know that it's true for me.

The lighthearted joy of a phone call with Jessica and the beauty of a Chopin prelude have both been precursors of an episode. When they hit I'm overcome with a feeling of impending doom. I break out in a sweat, and my heartbeat reverberates in my ears. I get the feeling that nothing is quite real. The first time I had one I was certain that I was going to die. The doctor gave me some Benzodiazepine to take when I feel the onset, and I carry a couple with me wherever I go. I know it sounds strange, so let me tell you about the first time it happened.

It must have been about a decade ago. I was visiting the Frick Collection in New York where I'd been for a few days interviewing and hiring faculty at a big recruiting fair. The Frick is a small gallery. I prefer small collections because I can develop a relationship with the spaces and the pieces in a way that would be impossible at, say, the Hermitage or the Louvre. A friend had lent me his apartment in the Dakota on Central Park West, and I walked across the park to the Frick on a late-winter afternoon with the sun already low in the sky and a chilly breeze blowing across the Sheep Meadow. Inside, I spent time in front of one of my favourite paintings, Giovanni Bellini's "Saint Francis in the Desert."

The painting's radiance and happiness always draws me into the landscape. Everything is in bloom, all the animals are still, the laurel trees sway, and everything is bathed in the gentle light of the Tuscan sun. The saint holds his pierced and bleeding hands in front of him and gazes in ecstasy at the beauty of creation. It's a moment of revelation. I can get lost in that lovely picture.

Later as I walked down the gallery steps and crossed 5th Avenue back onto the Sheep Meadow, I felt a grey shadow lurking behind me. My skin began to tingle, and my heart raced. Spandex-clad joggers, muffled against the raw breeze, passed me as I walked. A homeless man sat on a cardboard pad under a large chestnut tree and asked me for change. The dark mud at the side of the path was rutted with bicycle tracks. All I could think of was suffering and ugliness, and I moved off the path onto the damp grass. My pace slowed until I was standing in the middle of the park listening to my breathing, unable to tear my eyes away from a squirrel that stood a few paces away, twitching its tail as it nibbled an acorn. I felt all the trees in the park and all the buildings in Manhattan and all the stars in the dark sky crowding in on me. I counted my breaths. When I got to twenty, I raised my eyes and found a light on the roof of the Plaza. I walked toward it.

IV

As I lay back that morning in the dappled light in our bright and airy bedroom on Great Exuma, my thoughts dragged back to a moment that replays far too often.

I was having coffee with Joanne, sitting on the terrasse of a café beside the courthouse where our divorce had just been finalized. We had been to the café many times before, but that day the atmosphere was unique. Thirty-five years of familiarity had been overwritten. We would not be going home together. I felt numb and scared but also strangely brave, so I asked her the question that I had asked myself every night before I fell asleep over the past several weeks.

"What brought us to this, Joanne? What can Allan give you that I can't?"

She looked me in the eye as she sipped her cappuccino. "He's a lightweight, David, but so are you in many ways. He doesn't know the things you do, but you're scared to use what you know. It's a waste. So, it always comes down to me to make the decisions. If things go well, you bask in it. If things go wrong, it's my fault. I don't show it, but I can't deal with the pressure or the guilt. Alan is easy. He's a good lover, and he takes care of me. That's all I want now."

In my mind I could feel the reply that I might make, I could see the words running behind my eyes, but I couldn't seem to say anything. My eye caught the motion of a leaf as it spiralled to the ground. I heard the thrum of a hummingbird's wings. A curly haired child with ice cream on his face smiled up at me as he passed.

It was as if I had taken a drug; my senses were supercharged, and my heart was beating fast but not in anger, in terror. I should have known all this. Did I, in truth, know it but refuse to accept it?

I slipped out of bed, trying not to wake Lara, and padded over to the kitchen to put the coffee on. Through the picture windows I saw the light chop on the turquoise water of Elizabeth Harbour and the casuarinas swaying in the fresh breeze.

I cut up a pineapple and put it with some yogurt and granola into two bowls, poured the coffee, and brought the tray through to the table on the porch. Just the other side of the pink seawall, the waves were getting lively, pushed along by a freshening breeze.

Lara appeared in the doorway. She stretched and yawned and came and sat in one of the bleached wooden deck chairs.

"I could have slept for the whole morning," she said, serving herself some chunks of pineapple and spooning yogurt over the fruit. "I feel so relaxed here, and I hardly dream at all." She poured a few drops of cream into her coffee. "What shall we do today?"

The choices on Great Exuma were limited, but they were all good. We could visit one of the great beaches, eat at one of the three restaurant bars within walking distance of Darville Hall, or take the water taxi over to Stocking Island.

Each of the restaurants was special in its own way. The Peace and Plenty was a pink-washed stone building in the centre of the village with its own dock. It had been around for a century and had black-and-white pictures of the Duke of Edinburgh visiting the place—maybe sixty years back judging by his youthful smile. The food was average, but Lermon, the barman, was an island legend and reason enough to visit. He was affectionately known as the "doctor of libation," and his Goombay Smash made me sigh with pleasure. Eddie's Edgewater Grill was a wooden shack with no pretensions. It served only rum and beer, but it was where one went to hear the locals play on rake-and-scrape nights. JJ's was up a flight of stairs in a cinder-block building by the government wharf. The food was pretty good, and the drinks were cheap.

"What would you like to do, Lara? If we went over to the island, we could walk for an hour on the beach. I like the idea of some exercise."

"Let's do it," she said. "I'll have a shower. You keep an eye open for Rudy."

Rudy is the owner of the water taxi that runs around amongst the local cays. The boat has a bright yellow hull and is visible from a long way off.

In twenty minutes we were boarding the boat, Rudy smiling from ear to ear and giving Lara a hand she didn't need but which she accepted graciously. The boat chugged away from the town dock across the impossibly blue water. The wind was picking up out of the southeast and there was a bit of spray in the air as we motored sedately over to Stocking Island. Rudy chatted on the radio to his buddies in other small boats. The talk was about a storm brewing out in the Atlantic just east of Anguilla.

"She could be a big one, man. My buddy seen it on the satellite, and he don't like the look."

"When do you think it will hit, Rudy?" Lara asked.

Neither of us was that concerned. Life in the tropics wasn't complete without the occasional hurricane. Rudy took a sip from the bottle of local Kalik beer that was an ever-present feature of his water taxi. "Well, my buddy says Chantalle—that's the name of the storm—will be here in thirty-six hours. Maybe Thursday morning. She's picking up speed, but there's a chance she might slip past to the north."

"What will you do with the boat, Rudy?" I asked. "Do you tie up at the wharf or leave her at a buoy in open water?"

"Neither of those, man. My brother and me will take her down the island and tie her up in the deep mangrove by Williamstown. All the fish and the birds go shelter there in a big storm, and they know best. My auntie has the bakery there, and we'll ride out the storm with fresh coconut bread and dark rum."

Rudy broke into the irresistible throaty chuckle that accompanied everything he said. "Should be back by the weekend or when the rum runs dry."

V

I paid Rudy and then he ran the boat in close to the beach where we jumped off into a foot of warm water. We hiked up the beach to the Chat and Chill, a ramshackle wooden hut under some big casuarinas. A couple of locals were sitting at the bar. They nodded to us as we approached. There was a smarter place, the St. Francis, where the yachting crowd went for cocktails at sundown, but we liked the anonymity of the Chat and Chill. We each had a grilled grouper sandwich, for which the place was famous, and they were as good as always.

We talked for a while till the sun started to sink lower in the sky and the heat backed off a little. Then we took the trail that led over to the beach on the east side of the Island. We walked through the long marram grass and up the sloping dunes.

The view from the top always took my breath away. Several miles of pale golden sand lay below. The long Atlantic rollers crashed onto the beach, leaving a kiss of pure white foam before rolling back into the turquoise water of the shallows. A little farther out the water changed colour to a starling French blue and then, as the water deepened even further, to a dark navy. As usual, no one else was around. We held hands and laughed as we ran and slid down the steep face of the dunes.

We walked south for a while till we got to a spot we'd visited before. It lay at the foot of the dunes and was surrounded by clumps of sea oats that swayed in the breeze while two stunted sea grapes with yellow-flowered suriana at their feet gave a dappled shade to the sand on which we sat.

We lay in each other's arms for many minutes listening to the breeze in the grass and the crash of the surf. We stood and held each other's eyes as we undressed and then lay down again, naked on the warm sand. Lara kissed my forehead and moved to straddle me. I kissed her breasts as she lowered her pelvis over me, moving me into her.

We swayed with the gentlest of motions, and Lara rocked her head slowly from side to side as she smiled down at me. This was as much affection as lust, and it was beautiful. I moved my hands over her buttocks and her back and felt the warm sun on her soft, tanned skin. Lara gripped me harder, and I let out a small sound, closed my eyes, and pushed my head back into the sand. Her hair tickled my face and chest as she increased her speed, her stomach sliding over mine. She moved her hands to either side of my head. Then she bent closer and put her lips on my eyelids, her breath warm on my face. Feeling myself about to come, I held back until Lara arrived there with me. We locked eyes as we moved as one to the climax. Then Lara eased herself down onto my chest, and we lay there panting and giggling as the sun dipped behind the dunes.

VI

By the time we finally rolled apart, the sun was off the beach, and I could feel a cool breeze blowing in from the water. I brushed the sand from my body, stepped back into my shorts, and pulled on my top.

I'm pretty sure we surprise ourselves most times we make love. David has told me that it's the most intense he has ever experienced, and I know he's telling the truth because he doesn't know how to lie. I love that he lets me set the pace. I get a charge out of seeing him under me.

We walked slowly back along the line of the sea foam toward the dock at St Francis where we had arranged to meet Rudy. We sat on the dock and dangled our feet into the crystal-clear water as we watched the yellow boat chug its way over from Georgetown. Pipefish swam around the pilings, and a big basket starfish worked its way into the shade of the dock. I turned my head and saw that David was looking at me. His lips moved in a smile, almost sad, but he kept looking at me. I couldn't turn away. It was as if he was downloading his emotions directly to me without words. I reached out and squeezed his hand. We were still sitting like that when the water taxi gave the dock a gentle nudge and broke the spell.

The ride back involved less of Rudy's smiling banter than usual. He told us that the storm had picked up strength and that a warning had been issued for Long Island and the Exuma cays. It looked like a direct hit late the following day, and flights to Nassau and Florida had already been cancelled through Thursday, so we were going to have to ride it out whether we wanted to or not.

On the way back to the house, we stopped in at the Exuma Market to lay in some supplies. Everything on Great Exuma is brought in on the ferry from Nassau. The boat had visited the day before, so the shelves were stocked. Hardly anyone was around, as the yachting crowd had all upped anchor and run for Miami. We chatted with a couple of the local women as we filled up our basket and checked out.

We stopped at the Scotiabank opposite to pick up some cash in case the storm knocked things out for a few days and then walked over to John Marshall's Liquor Store and bought a bottle of gin and a couple of bottles of wine.

David thought it would be good to have a car just in case, so we rented one from Thompsons. Unlike most places in the world, rental cars on Exuma are old and tired. They are imported from Japan and Korea where the governments make it expensive for people to drive older models. They are loaded up onto cargo ships and sold to brokers in the States who sell them on to Bahamians. We dumped the shopping in the back of an old brown Toyota Corolla with sun-faded paint and worn upholstery and then headed home.

Our evening was quiet. David poured drinks; I made dinner. Later we sat on the porch and played a few rounds of Trivial Pursuit using the house set, which dated from the 1990s. It made for amusing memories.

We slept long and well. The next morning, after coffee, we walked around the grounds, putting away the lawn furniture and making sure nothing was lying around loose that could do damage in the storm.

The sky was still clear although in the southeast it was an unusual bluish purple, so we decided to take advantage of the car and drove down island across the wooden bridge onto Little Exuma and had lunch at Santana's.

We ate fried lobster and sipped rum punch on the deck overlooking a small white-sand beach. Santana's is simple, but its claim to fame is that

Johnny Depp and the crew ate there when they were filming *Pirates of the Caribbean,* and the walls are adorned with pictures to prove it. After lunch I took a bread roll and fed the lemon sharks that hung around in the shallows a few feet off the beach.

We drove slowly back north and turned off at an unmarked dirt road that led down to Tropic of Cancer Beach. The ancient Toyota grumbled as it bottomed out in the deepest potholes, but it bumped its way downhill till the water came into view.

We always went there when we visited the island. Anyone who hadn't been there would never find it, and, as usual, only one other couple was walking along the long crescent of white sand that ringed the sheltered bay. We walked in the shallow water and disturbed a few rays that scuttled away in puffs of sand. I unwrapped the sarong that I wore on top of my bikini and kicked my flip flops up the beach before sinking into the warm turquoise water. David joined me, and we lay on our backs, floating weightless, holding hands, and staring up at the sky where a few tiny cotton-ball clouds just made the blue seem more intense.

We stood then and held each other in a long embrace that neither of us wanted to break. We were motionless so long that small silver fish came up and nibbled our legs, which made us both wince and giggle.

David confessed to being "a bit British" when it came to expressing emotions, but as we held each other he brushed a lock of wet hair behind my ear and leaned in close. "I really love how I feel when I'm with you," he whispered.

I pulled back a few inches, gave him a goofy smile, and kissed his nose. Two heartbeats later I realized the last person I had kissed that way was my son, Alejandro.

A shiver moved through my body and I leaned into David and held him tighter. A storm was coming. I could feel it in my heart.

VII

Hurricane Chantalle hit the Exuma cays that evening. By dark, the wind was tearing at the palms, and the rain was hitting the roof so hard that we could hardly hear each other speak.

Unusual for a hurricane, bolts of lightning lit the night, bringing flashes of bright green vegetation to life for a second before plunging us back into darkness.

The generator kicked in at about midnight, meaning the island was without power, but by that time we had gone to bed. Lara lay quietly beside me, her back to me.

I must have fallen asleep for a while because when I woke there was a glimmer of light in the sky, and the wind had dropped to a strong gale. Realizing I was alone in the bed, I swung my feet to the floor, pulled on my dressing gown, and pushed my feet into my sandals. I walked through to the kitchen, but there was no light on and no sign of Lara.

Then I saw her; she was standing outside on the porch in the warm rain with the wind whipping her long hair into her face. I opened the sliding door and went to stand beside her. I couldn't tell if she was crying because her face was wet with rain, but as my eyes became used to the low light, I saw that her face was riven with anguish. She turned and looked at me as if she had never seen me before. She put both hands up to her face and let out a moan that was filled with despair.

"Lara, what's wrong?" I went to put my arm around her, but she cringed away. "What is it? Tell me. I can help you."

She took a breath and started to cry, great rending sobs that shook her whole body.

"Come inside, baby. Please come inside," I said. She let me take her arm and guide her back in.

We were both soaked and left a trail of water on the tiled floor. I draped her in a big beach towel and sat her at the kitchen table while I got the coffee going. We didn't speak until the coffee was ready. I sat opposite her and reached my hand across the table. She took it and looked directly at me; she was much calmer now.

"You must think I'm crazy, and maybe I am," she said. I went to speak but she shook her head. "I went through almost the whole of yesterday without thinking about Alejandro. And in the afternoon at the beach when I realized that, I felt so guilty. I felt I had betrayed him and that I could never forgive myself. Last night I didn't want to live, and the storm was inviting me outside. I don't know why."

"Why didn't you tell me how you were feeling, Lara? You know I care for you."

"You don't deserve my misery, David. What we have is good for us both, and if we dig too deep it's going to be spoiled. You couldn't understand how I feel about what happened with my boy, and you shouldn't have to."

"How about if I want to? We're good together Lara, and I think we could be really good. If we want to build something special, we're going to have to trust each other and be honest with one another. I want to be with you, support you, care for you." The words came out by themselves. I hadn't thought to speak them, at least not yet, but they wouldn't be denied.

Lara looked sad rather than pleased. "We need to take our time. You don't know me well enough to make that commitment, David. There are things I haven't told you, that I'm not ready to tell you yet. I want more than anything for you to be patient and to give us the time we need to see if we can work. You're a good man, and I don't deserve you."

She stood and came around the table, putting her arms around my shoulders and her head against my neck. "Let's go back to bed," she whispered. "I just want you to hold me."

We caught the first flight out on Friday morning. The sky was fresh and bright blue, and there was little turbulence as the tiny United Beechcraft headed due north for Florida, then touched down with a couple of bounces ninety minutes later in Fort Lauderdale. We walked over to the garage, dropped our bags in the back seat of the Honda, and joined the procession on I95.

When we arrived at Lara's place in Boca West, I got out of the car and carried her bag to her ground-floor apartment.

"Can we do that again soon?" I asked.

"We can," she said, then paused. "Thank you." She stretched up and kissed me. "Thank you," she said again, her eyes locked on mine.

From Lara's I headed straight for the office where I was greeted by Emy's radiant smile and a few questions about my time away.

"And Dr. Crocken from Shelburne College called back. He's hoping you're free for lunch tomorrow as he has to fly back to Cape Town on Sunday."

"Yes, that's fine, Emy. Please call him and tell him I'll see him at the Bazaar at noon. And can you call Andres and ask for my usual table please?"

CHAPTER 3

I

I don't go to South Beach very often. It represents the best and worst of what humans can do. The architecture is stunning, the restaurants are sensational, and beautiful people fill the streets, but it is all done in the service of pointless wealth and limitless hedonism. Any craving will be satisfied, any itch scratched. If one can't come up with any secret desires, South Beach will suggest a few that one might like to try.

The traffic was light, and I was a little early as I turned off I95 onto NW 82nd and crossed the intracoastal onto Miami Beach on the NW 79th Street Causeway. I took my time heading south on Collins enjoying the parade of beautiful people. I passed the Eden Roc and the Fontainebleau and pulled up at the swanky SLS hotel just before noon.

I parked the faded Honda in the valet line behind a pink Rolls Royce and a lime-green Lamborghini. The young man at the valet desk smirked as he gave me the ticket. I walked into the hushed cool of the lobby and headed for the restaurant.

When I had to visit South Beach, I favoured the Bazaar. It was relatively quiet, which I liked now that my hearing wasn't so good, the service was first class, and the chef, Jose Andres was a wizard.

"Signor Mallory, welcome. We have missed you." Andres, the maître d', had an encyclopaedic memory and a pleasantly ingratiating manner. "Your guest is already here, and I have seated him at your table. I hope that meets with your satisfaction, Signor Mallory."

"Indeed, thank you, Andres," I said as we moved through the elegant dining room to my usual table, located in a quiet corner overlooking the lawn and gardens of the courtyard.

"Dr. Croken." I offered my hand as a giant bull of a man raised himself effortlessly from his seat, and my hand disappeared into his massive paw.

"Mr. Mallory, this is a pleasure, and I thank you for making the time to see me today. I apologize for the short notice. I hope it was alright."

He spoke in an educated South African accent with a slight roll to the "r" and a flat "i" in "right."

"It's good to meet you too, Dr. Croken. I was keen to see you, and besides, I love an excuse to visit the Bazaar. I smiled at him. His face lit up, and the skin around his eyes crinkled as he smiled back.

"I heard about this place from the head of St. Mildred's here in town. She says the ceviche is the best in the Caribbean. You have good taste, Mr. Mallory."

"It's as good as you could find in Peru, Dr. Croken."

I spoke from authority as I had friends who live in the oceanside Lima suburb of Barranco, whom I visited a couple of times each year. "You won't be disappointed."

We sat down, and I had a chance to examine my lunch companion in more detail as he settled his napkin back in his lap and poured sparkling water into our glasses. He was a big man but muscular and fit, probably in his early forties with a head of blond hair cut short and a deep tan that spoke of time spent outdoors, maybe on the water.

His eyes were a pale grey and sparkled as he looked over at me. He was dressed in a white open-neck dress shirt with a monogram on the collar and a dark-green sports jacket with pearl buttons. It was an older look for a younger man, but he wore it well.

In contrast to his otherwise immaculate appearance, both of his ears were mangled and misshapen with scar tissue. It told me that Dr. Croken was, like many of his countrymen, a rugby player.

"I see you played tight head for quite a while," I ventured. Only rugby forwards playing in this specific position ended up with ears like Dr. Croken's. He looked up and smiled again, bringing his right hand to his ear.

"It's a giveaway, isn't it? Yes, I had a bit of a career."

He didn't seem to want to elaborate.

"But it takes one to know one, Mr. Mallory. So, what was your position?"

"Ah, well, many years ago I played in the back row, but that was in the days when you could be my size and survive. I wouldn't want to be out on the field with the big boys who are playing now."

"Who did you play for, Dr. Croken?"

"Pius, please call me Pius," he said. "Well, I started out at school in Durban, and then I played with the Sharks for three years. I even got a trial with the Springboks. That didn't work out though; they said I was too slow." He grinned. "I was heartbroken. You know every young boy in South Africa wants to pull on the green and gold, but I realize it was a blessing in disguise. It taught me some humility, which I think I was lacking, and it means I can still walk today without a limp or a cane." He laughed to himself.

We ordered foie gras and then the ceviche, which came with pecans, lemon, and hibiscus. We each had a glass of the Sancerre and then coffee with the Cana de Cabra Mousse, which I always choose when I visit the Bazaar. It's honey ice cream with candied orange, caramelized croutons and crème fraiche. Ridiculously good, and Pius nodded his approval.

We still had not discussed any business, so I suggested we take a second cup of coffee over to the small lounge that overlooked the beach and the ocean. Pius lowered himself into a leather armchair and put his coffee on the side table, then leaned toward me.

"I'm assuming you will treat what I have to tell you as confidential and that you will disclose it to no one without my explicit permission."

I nodded as I sipped my coffee. "That's typically the way I work. But if you ask me to break the law, or if I find that you have broken the law, I will walk away."

"Understood. Your name was given to me by Lamar Delfont, the head at Rolfe's Academy. He was most complimentary about your efforts on his behalf."

"Lamar's a good man," I said. "I was glad to be able to help out."

He paused, took a deep breath, rubbed his chin, then began to tell me the story. "Two weeks ago we suffered a tragedy at the school. One of the grade ten boys was found dead. He was a popular boy, a lovely boy—Tom Parkes was his name. He and his brother, Sam, have been at school since they were ten years old. They're twins—identical, in fact.

"The cause of death is proving a bit tricky to pin down, and that's fuelling speculation. Edmund Parkes, the dad, is an old boy, and what's more difficult, he's on the board of governors. He's an odd bird, rough around the edges, but he's been very generous to the school. Lena Michaels, the stepmother, is chair of the one hundred and fiftieth anniversary committee.

"You know how schools are, David. First and foremost they are social institutions. If they don't work on that level, they don't stand a chance of being successful academically. The whole school is grieving, which is normal and good, but we need some answers. The police are calling it an accident, but the community isn't convinced. It's a complicated situation, and having Ed on the board makes it difficult for me to be seen as the honest broker. I'm hoping that's where you can play a role. I need this thing sorted out, and I need it to be done with discretion. Can you help me?"

I let several seconds pass before I replied. The situation was intriguing, I liked what I had seen of Pius Croken, and I thought I could help.

"Yes, I'd be pleased to look at this for you," I said. "I can't guarantee the outcome, but you'll find that I'm thorough. I won't be outworked, and sometimes an outsider can open doors that are closed to others. My calendar is fairly open, and I can move a couple of things around. I imagine you want me on this as soon as possible?"

Dr. Croken's expressive face broke into a wide grin. "You're correct. My God, you're correct. Let's talk details. What sort of compensation will you expect?"

Shelburne is South Africa's most prestigious and expensive private school, so I didn't imagine this was a deal-breaker

"My rate is the same for everyone and hasn't changed since I started doing this. Two thousand US per day plus expenses. Expenses will include a rental car. I'm pretty low maintenance, so I don't need a fancy hotel. If it turns out that I need to spend money to get a result, I'll get your permission before I do so."

"That's fair. I'll have my bursar put that into a contract. For the sake of discretion, we'll charge it to professional development, and we'll refer to you as a special consultant on operations. My executive assistant will arrange the hotel and the car. Do you want us to look after the flights as well?"

"No, thank you. It'll be best if my office takes care of that. I'll try to fly out on Tuesday. The South African Airways flight through Kennedy and Joburg is probably best, so I should be with you by end of the day on Wednesday."

We stood and shook hands, and after a few pleasantries, Pius ordered a cab and moved off through the tables and out into the bright Miami sunshine.

II

It was Sunday afternoon, and Emy had managed to get me on a flight the next day, which would allow some breathing room at the other end. Getting to the bottom of the Shelburne affair would take time. Getting to the bottom of it and keeping it discreet would take longer. I was packing for a month. If it took longer than that I'd buy what I needed in South Africa. I'd been thinking about being apart from Lara for that length of time, and I wasn't enjoying the prospect, so I called her up and asked her out to dinner.

"David, I'm really glad you called." The honey tones of her voice made me smile.

"Sure, I'd love to have dinner. How about we head up to Delray? We could go to the Red Lion. The food's not special, but they have live jazz on Sunday night."

"That's just what I feel like tonight," I said. Then I realized this seemed to happen a lot with Lara. "Great idea. Shall I pick you up?"

"Why don't we Uber? Then you can have a beer, and we can see what the evening brings."

"Beautiful. Shall we say eight o'clock?"

"We shall. If I get there first, I'll try and grab us two seats at the bar."

As it turned out I was a few minutes late. My Uber driver was on his first-ever ride, and his GPS wasn't cooperating. Lara was sitting at the end of the bar with a good view of the tiny stage where the musicians performed. The lighting was low, and there was a gentle hum of good-humoured conversation from the small crowd.

Bars in the US that try to be British pubs are usually a disaster—chilled beer and fried food without any of the community feel. The Red Lion does a bit better, though the draft London Pride is still too cold and suffers a bit from three weeks crossing the Atlantic in the hold of a cargo ship. The bar staff are good though, and a couple have actually worked in the UK. Lara was talking to Tommy, the co-owner, and sipping a tall glass of what looked like prosecco. Tommy looked at me and started filling a pint glass of Pride while Lara slipped off her stool and gave me a hug and a warm kiss on the lips. A couple of other groups looked 'round to see who had arrived, and I felt a frisson of pride to be in the company of this lovely woman.

We bantered with Tommy and then ordered a few starters to share as our meal. The three-piece band was in great form, and the crowd broke into rowdy applause between numbers. I sent over a round of drinks when they finished their first set, and they came over and chatted with us for a while. When they left, I told Lara about the meeting the previous day.

"The thing is I really don't know how long I'll be away," I said. "It sounds like there are lots of layers to peel back, and that can be tricky."

Lara pursed her lips and looked away at nothing in particular, then back at me. "So, you're saying we might not see each other for a month or so? Are you alright with that, David?"

"Well, no. That's what I wanted to tell you; I'm not alright with it at all. I realized over the last few days that I'm more than attracted to you and, I know it's selfish, but I feel so much happier when I'm with you."

This wasn't quite what I had wanted to say. I had wanted to say that I'd never been happier with anyone in my life. I loved laughing with her, the sex was astounding, and I couldn't believe how lucky I was that she seemed to like me too. But I couldn't just say that because I was David Mallory.

Lara reached out her right hand and placed it on my cheek. "I know," she said. "I feel the same way. Come here, baby."

We slid off our barstools and moved together. She initiated a deep kiss that said what I had just failed to say. We held each other so close that we got a whoop from a table of young men on the far side of the room. Lara smiled at them as we sat back down.

"So, maybe we need to make a small commitment here," she said. "Cape Town is six hours ahead of Florida. We can chat on FaceTime or WhatsApp a couple of times a week. When you finish work, it'll be lunchtime here. It's not perfect, but it may sustain us."

"We can do that. We will do that."

I don't often do spontaneous, and some part of me was trying to prevent it, but it failed.

"Or, maybe, I don't know, do you have a lot going on right now? Could you come along with me? They're putting me up in a hotel for the whole month, and I know you'd love Cape Town."

I think I startled myself with those words, and it must have shown on my face because Lara laughed and squeezed my hand.

"Did you really just say that? It's not very David Mallory." She laughed again and ran her fingers through her hair, pushing it back from her face. "I'm really flattered that you would ask me." She looked down and then looked up and held my gaze. "We're good for each other, and I want to be with you, but maybe this is too fast."

I'm not sure if it was good or bad timing, but at that point the band kicked off their second set with John Coltrane's "Cousin Mary." It was too noisy to talk. The moment was lost. We held hands. The intimacy was there but maybe not the commitment.

I called Lara the next day and gave her the details of the flights that Emy had booked for me and the coordinates of the Cape Grace Hotel arranged for me by Pius's assistant. Despite my suggestion that modest lodgings would be fine, he'd booked me into the smartest hotel on the Cape Town waterfront.

"Why don't I run you down to the airport?" she said. "You need to be there for noon, so the traffic won't be too bad. How about I pick you up just before eleven?"

"I'd love that, Lara. Are you sure?"

"I am. See you tomorrow."

III

I started Monday with a cup of tea on the patio. The wind was off the sea, and the crashing of the modest surf provided a soothing background as I checked in with Emy who promised to visit the house each evening on her way home to make sure things were fine. I said that she should bring the children over to the beach on weekends and use the house, but she politely declined. The job was very important to Emy for several reasons, and though she was always warm and friendly, I know she felt that maintaining a professional distance was a good way to keep things straight.

At around eleven I put my bag by the front door and took a final look around. I was standing in front of Jessica's portrait with a smile on my face when I heard a car horn beep. I set the alarm, stepped outside, and locked the door behind me. The car in the driveway wasn't Lara's Volvo, and Lara was sitting in the passenger's seat, but I still didn't clue in until she jumped out of the car and kissed me. "Does the offer still stand?" she asked. "I've always wanted to visit Robben Island, and my girlfriend says the Museum of Contemporary Art is a must." She smiled. "And the hotel sounds wonderful, and you know how much I love pinotage!"

My heart stood still for a moment and then I wrapped my arms around her. "Yes, the offer still stands, and it sounds like you'll be so busy we won't have to spend too much time together! How did you do this? Are we on the same plane?"

"We're sitting together, David! I had a quiet chat with Emy yesterday evening, and she fixed everything. She's a very special young woman, that one."

"Yes, yes she is," I said slowly, feeling pleased but a little outmanoeuvered.

The Lyft driver came around the front of the car, took my bag, and put it in the trunk. Lara and I sat in the back. We made small talk for the time it took to grind down I95 to Miami International. I put my hand to the window and felt the heat through the glass as I watched the light standards and the palm trees flick past in a hypnotic stream.

This is good, I thought. For a man who favoured the safe and predictable, it was an unusual response.

"Yes, this is very good." I realized I had spoken aloud.

I looked over at Lara. She raised a quizzical eyebrow and squeezed my hand.

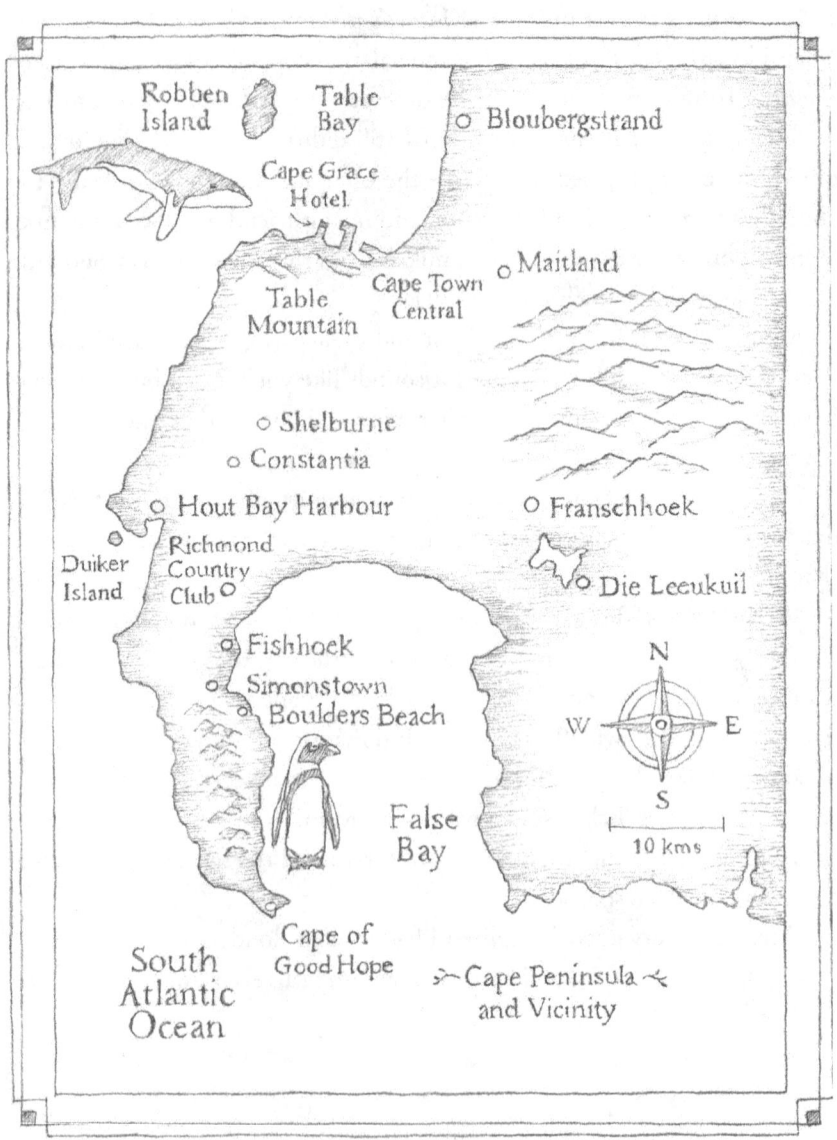

CHAPTER 4

I

The flights were particularly uncooperative. A line of thunderstorms rolled across the airport as we sat on the tarmac in Miami, and the plane was delayed two hours, just long enough to miss the connection at JFK. We were rerouted through Washington and Dakar and crawled into Cape Town at sundown on Tuesday. We squeezed into the back of a little black-and-yellow taxi that drove us the fifteen kilometres to the Victoria and Alfred Waterfront. There was still a glow in the sky, turning the cliffs of Table Mountain a warm orange as we pulled up to the entrance of the Cape Grace, which occupies its own private quay between the V&A and the yacht marina.

I've stayed in nice hotels in different parts of the world, and the difference between good and great is always the service. This hotel promised to be great. Our bags were spirited away, and we were checked in and guided to our rooms in minutes by Malcolm, the butler, who would be looking after us during our stay. The room turned out to be one of the larger suites with a bedroom, a sitting room, a small kitchen, and two bathrooms. There were floor-to-ceiling windows on two sides: on the north looking to Robben Island and on the west with views across the harbour to the ocean. Not exactly the low-maintenance three-star I had recommended to Pius, but I wasn't going to object. I figured we would likely be there for several weeks, so we might as well enjoy it.

The phone rang. It was Malcolm, who informed me that Stephen Kumalo, Dr. Croken's personal assistant, was in the Oak Bar off the lobby and would be pleased to greet us when we were ready.

I told Lara, but she was reluctant to join me.

"This is business, David. Your business. I think we should keep a distance between personal and professional."

"That's the way I've always played it, Lara, but this is a bit different. We'll be here together for some time. Pius is grateful that I've cleared my schedule for him, and he has said in so many words that he wants you to feel at home. And then there's the fact that you're clever and intuitive and could really help me on this one."

"How about beautiful, clever, and intuitive?" she said.

"Yes, that too. Come on down with me."

"OK, but I don't want to get too wrapped up in this business. I've got lots of sightseeing to do, and the pool looks rather nice as well!"

Twenty minutes later we walked into the Oak Bar, Lara holding my arm and looking splendid in a floral dress with a pleated skirt and a wide belt. I wore grey wool trousers, a white button-down shirt, a navy cashmere blazer, and glossy brown Gucci loafers with small gold buckles. The shoes cost more than the rest of the stuff put together. It was my go-to smart-casual rig, and I thought it would probably be seeing a lot of service over the next few weeks.

A tall, athletic man of perhaps forty eased himself off a barstool as the server led us toward him. His attractive face broke into a sunny smile, and his brown eyes twinkled behind horn-rimmed glasses as he reached his hand out to Lara.

"Ms. Rios." His voice was deep and his syllabication precise. "I'm Stephen Kumalo. Welcome to Cape Town. We're so glad that you were able to join Mr. Mallory. And, Mr. Mallory, Shelburne is honoured that you're able to help us with this troubling matter. Dr. Croken has asked me to ensure that you have whatever resources you require. I have sent you a text so that you have my contact information. Please call upon me at any time day or night if I can be of assistance."

"That's good of you, Stephen. Thank you. I'll try and stick to the hours of daylight if I can."

Stephen chuckled in a higher register than his speaking voice. "You don't have to worry about that, Mr. Mallory. My job description includes that wonderful last line, 'and other jobs as assigned,' and I like it that way. I never get bored!" He chuckled again. "And Grace and I have three young children under five, so I don't sleep much anyway."

The waiter drifted over, and Lara ordered a gin gimlet. Stephen asked for a Diet Coke, and I chose a Castle lager. I liked the odd cocktail, but I was raised on beer, and old habits die hard.

Stephen had reserved a table by the window where the lights of central Cape Town were beginning to twinkle in the engulfing night.

Stephen moved with particular grace. He pulled a chair out for Lara and waited until she had seated herself before lowering himself gently into his chair and placing his hands together as if in prayer. He closed his eyes for a second as if trying to compose his thoughts.

"Mr. Mallory, Ms. Rios, Dr. Croken has authorized me to speak to you about the details of the matter at hand—at least the details as far as we and the police understand them so far."

Lara looked a little uncomfortable. "Mr. Kumalo."

"Stephen, please," he said.

"Stephen." Lara smiled at him. "Are you sure that you're comfortable with me knowing the details of this case? I'm sure it's sensitive, and I would completely understand if you would rather speak to David alone."

"Ms. Rios, Dr. Croken is delighted that you're here to support Mr. Mallory, and if Mr. Mallory is comfortable with sharing the information with you, so are we. Besides," Stephen's eyes gave a little extra twinkle, "we are paying Mr. Mallory a handsome fee and putting him up in splendour, so getting two talented minds for the price of one represents excellent value." He followed this with another characteristic chuckle.

"Well," I said, smiling, "if that's the approach then I think we better use first names all around."

"I agree," Lara said, "and you do me honour by your gallant remark, Stephen."

She held his eye for a moment until he looked away.

"Let me start at the beginning," Stephen said slowly. "It was a Friday, September sixteenth, the last day of the Michaelmas quarter. We take a two-week break before the start of the Christmas quarter. The students were all in high spirits at the prospect of the holiday.

"We're lucky with our campus. It was gifted to the school by our founder, Johannes Potgieter, in 1870. We have six hundred hectares on the dip slope of Table Mountain in Constantia. Part of the property is designated as a nature reserve. A hundred years back, our forebears dammed a creek to form Plashy Pond. It's a favourite spot for our students, and it was two of our senior girls who discovered the body. They saw something in the water perhaps twenty metres out from shore but close enough for them to identify it as a corpse floating face down. They ran back to school and raised the alarm. It was just before supper, and most of the students were changing after sports. A few of them headed up to the pond before the police could seal the area. Officers from the Claremont Police Station responded with an aquatic team, and the body was retrieved and taken to the Salt River Mortuary. Dr. Croken was called to make an initial identification, and then the boy's father, Edmund Parkes, a member of our board of governors, confirmed that it was his son, Tom."

Stephen paused, passing a hand over his forehead and adjusting his glasses. "It was a terrible shock for the school. Tom was a popular boy, and his father is a leading figure in the Cape Town community. He has his detractors, but he is a successful and generous man."

I remembered that Pius had referred to Ed Parkes as an odd duck, and now here was the reserved and diplomatic Stephen Kumalo expressing cautious reservations. I made a mental note.

Stephen looked back and forth between Lara and me. "I think I have told you all that I can. Do you have any questions, or would you rather reserve them for Dr. Croken and the police?"

While I thought about it, Lara spoke. "This has been very helpful, Stephen. Thank you. But if the boy drowned while swimming in a popular spot, why are we here?"

"Indeed, Lara, indeed. I think I have come to the end of the mandate that Dr. Croken has given me. Beyond this he himself will want to explain and introduce you to those who can help you to advance your work."

Stephen stood up. "And now I will leave you to enjoy the evening. You must be exhausted. The rental car will be dropped off for you in the morning. Dr. Croken hopes you can meet him at Shelburne tomorrow at three o'clock. As I said, please call me for anything you need."

He shook hands with us and then walked gracefully from the room.

Malcolm approached a couple of minutes later and asked if we would like to eat in the dining room or if we would prefer to have dinner served in the suite. We were both beginning to flag a bit and cheerfully opted for the suite. We ordered from the impressive menu, added a bottle of Kanonkop Black Label Pinotage, and then took the elevator up to the fifth floor.

Housekeeping had been by to turn down the bed and leave us a little plate of chocolate and fruit. The waiter arrived thirty minutes later, opened the wine, carved the chateaubriand, and drifted from the room. We looked across the table at each other and nodded.

"I think I could get used to this, David. Yes, I think with a little effort I could. If this is school life, I missed my vocation."

"It's very far from normal, Lara. Shelburne is one of the few schools in the world that doesn't have to rely on tuition for its revenues. The school is so old and wealthy that it can run its annual operation from the interest on its portfolio. Shelburne's success rests on its being clearly the most distinguished and successful school in the country. People line up to donate a scholarship with their family name on it or to be the lead gift for a building dedicated to their parents. Everything has to be done with style and elegance to support that image of excellence, and we, dear Lara, are the lucky beneficiaries."

Lara popped another piece of the exquisite steak into her mouth and raised her glass in a silent toast.

III

We'd arranged for breakfast to be brought in at 9:00 a.m., but I was still asleep when Lara woke me at 9:15. She'd already been out for a run and had showered and dressed. I felt like a bit of a slug as I poured myself some coffee and forked a selection of fruit onto my plate. I had been exhausted by the flight, and I wondered if this was one of the things that would highlight the difference in our ages. I still felt that I could do anything, but occasionally my body begged to differ.

"How do you feel, David? You looked very tired last night." Was Lara's tone just a little maternal?

"Pretty good, thanks. I should have drunk more water on the plane. I'll go for a splash in the pool before dressing. Would you like me to give you the famous Mallory mini tour of Cape Town this morning? We could find something light for lunch along the way and still be at Shelburne in good time.

"That would be lovely, David, but what I don't want is for my presence here to be more work for you."

"Lara, that's the opposite of what I feel. Your being here gives me confidence, makes me happy, and as Stephen said, gives Shelburne two great minds for the price of one!" I threw my napkin at her as I headed to the wardrobe to dig out my swimming trunks. "I'll be back in ten minutes. Do you want to come down?"

"No, thanks. I'm going to check my emails. A couple of deals were about to close when I left. I want to make sure everything went smoothly with the bank. Enjoy your swim."

The rental car was sitting in the shade when we stepped out of the lobby into the Porte Cochere. It was a massive red Land Cruiser, the opposite end of the Toyota hierarchy to my little Corolla in Boca and far more than we needed. Malcolm pulled it around for us and showed us a couple of features of the GPS. Lara elbowed me elegantly out of the way and jumped in the driver's seat.

"If I'm coming along, I'm going to make myself useful. Would you like to sit in the back, and we can pretend you're more important than you are?"

I sat in the front.

We didn't have time for an extensive tour if we were to be at Shelburne on time, so we settled for a visit to the University of Cape Town and lunch at Groot Constantia, the ancient winery founded by the Dutch in 1685.

It was approaching 3:00 when Lara turned in at the Shelburne gatehouse. The uniformed security guard checked our ID, gave us security passes, and then stepped back, offering us a snappy salute and a winning smile. First impressions are important, and this was a good one. We drove along the winding driveway between century-old Yellowwood trees. The road climbed gently for a kilometre or so until the school buildings came into sight.

The central block clearly dated from the nineteenth century. It was built in a symmetrical Georgian style of pale limestone. Green ivy wound its way up the walls. The Land Cruiser's tires crunched on the gravel as we approached the main entrance, and we parked in a visitors' parking spot beside a Porsche and an Aston Martin.

By the time we were out of the car, two students in school uniforms were standing five metres away with their hands behind their backs.

"Mr. Mallory, Ms. Rios, welcome to Shelburne. We're honoured by your visit," the girl greeted us. "My name is Kristy van Kleef. I'm a prefect here, and this is my colleague, Aphiwe Tshabalala." The boy stepped forward and shook our hands, Kristy followed suit. Their grips were firm, and they maintained eye contact. "Dr. Croken has asked us to bring you to his office. Will you follow us please?"

The two young people engaged us in sophisticated small talk as we climbed the stone steps and entered the panelled entrance hall. The wooden parquet floor gleamed, and large gilt framed portraits of school worthies looked down at us with varying degrees of disdain.

"This is the original school building dating from 1870. That portrait on the far left is Dr. Potgeiter, the school's founder," Aphiwe said in a confident yet respectful tone. The portrait showed a stern white-haired man in a black serge jacket, wing-collared shirt, and a grey ascot. "Of course, Shelburne was a boy's school back then," Aphiwe continued. "Girls were admitted in 1960, and the school was racially integrated when Madiba came to power in 1994."

"I know there was a lot of fuss about both those things," Kristy offered, "but it has made us a much better school, much more relevant to the South Africa of today."

"You're certainly excellent spokespeople for the school," I said.

"Thank you, sir." Kristy smiled. "We're both guardians of Shelburne. We're elected by our peers, and it's the greatest honour bestowed at our school, but we look at ourselves more as servants than leaders. There are ten of us. Our job is to maintain the spirit and traditions of the school, and part of that job involves hosting guests on campus."

"Do you think you would be able to give us a tour of the school after we've met Dr. Croken?" Lara asked.

"That would be wonderful." I added. In fact, I had been about to ask the same thing. I've found that interactions with students are always more candid and revealing than conversations with adults.

I was sure Pius would offer us a tour, but we would learn more from these two excellent young people than we would from a paid school employee.

"But maybe you have a class you can't miss?"

Aphiwe looked modestly at the floor. "Actually, sir, one of the criteria of being a guardian is that you're in good academic standing. I have double physics this afternoon, and I wouldn't mind missing that at all." He grinned sheepishly.

"Same here," Kristy said. "I have a Chaucer seminar—which I really like, by the way—but I love showing my school to guests, so, yes, if Dr. Croken approves, we can do that."

We approached a tall oak door. Kristy knocked and then opened it. We entered a small office that led into the headmaster's study. The receptionist made a discreet call and then showed all four of us into the study.

The room was sparsely but richly furnished—floor-to-ceiling bookshelves on one side, a couple of large oil paintings of nature on one wall, and windows along a third. There was a large and beautiful old desk in front of the bookshelves. On it was nothing but a laptop and a cellphone.

Pius and Stephen sat on opposite sides of a low table in front of the windows. They rose to greet us.

"David. So good to see you again." Pius shook my hand while placing his other hand on my shoulder. Perhaps more familiar than our one previous meeting merited, but that was clearly his style.

"And, Ms. Rios, I'm really pleased that you're here with us. Welcome. Come. Sit. Aphiwe, Kristy, thank you for your kindness. You may return to class."

"Uh, Headmaster," I began, giving him his formal title in front of the students, "these two have been stellar ambassadors for Shelburne, and we wondered if you would allow them to give us the tour that you spoke of?"

The hint of a cloud passed behind Pius's eyes. Was someone questioning his authority? He smiled and nodded at the students. "Please rejoin us in ten minutes."

We sat around the table, which looked out over the playing fields. Stephen Kumalo sat back in his seat. Clearly, this was Pius's meeting.

"Stephen has briefed you. He will have done it well, for that is how he is." He nodded to Stephen, who bowed his head slightly. "But I requested that he allow me to talk to you personally about the reasons why I have asked you to work with us. The real tragedy is that a boy has died. Tom was a fine young man, highly regarded by the school community; his future was bright. That is the real tragedy."

It was clear that Pius was sincere. He took a deep breath and then exhaled slowly. "But now our efforts must be focused on healing the school community. We build a resilient school culture here through lessons from triumph and from tragedy. That is the Shelburne way. But there is a problem. You see, the pathologist has raised a concern that casts some doubt on the circumstances of Tom's death, and that has called the police verdict of accidental death into question. Until the truth is ascertained, it will be impossible to achieve community healing. While you may think me crass, as the leader of the school I have to say that the uncertainty is exceptionally harmful to the reputation of the school. Generations of former students are watching us. The country is watching us."

He paused, looking down at his hands. "The press loves the prospect of a national institution mired in scandal. David, Lara, we live or die by our reputation. We must get to the bottom of this for Tom's sake and for the school's, and we must do it in as discreet and sensitive a way as possible. That is why you're here."

Pius stood and walked over to the windows. He remained silent, looking out at the students on the cricket field for a moment before turning back to us. "Stephen has arranged initial meetings for you tomorrow with Detective Chief Inspector Olivier of the Cape Town Police Service and with Dr. Gauri Naidu, the pathologist. Tom's family supports your involvement, and the chief inspector is willing to have you engaged.

"Dr. Naidu is at the top of her field, and it is she who has doubts about details of Tom's death. She is willing to discuss the case with you. Stephen will give you the timing and contact information. Beyond that I will leave it to you to decide who you think can help you. Stephen can help you schedule meetings."

Pius resumed his seat and looked me in the eye. "You're free to go where you need to go and to ask whatever questions of whomever you choose including me. Please use Stephen as our go-between, and update me when you feel that you've made progress. This may be as straightforward as it looks, a death by misadventure. In some ways I pray that it is. But either way we need this resolved. At Shelburne we have resources. I'm putting those resources at your disposal. Do you have any questions?"

I shook my head. "Not at this moment. Thank you for your confidence in us. I will tell you everything that I think you need to know as we proceed."

There was a discreet and timely tap on the door, and Aphiwe and Kristy entered the room.

"Is this convenient, Dr. Croken?" Kristy ventured.

"Almost miraculously so, Kristy." Pius smiled at the students. "Please leave nothing out of the tour, and feel free to answer any questions that Mr. Mallory and Ms. Rios may have for you."

Hands were shaken all around and then we followed the students out of the cool shadows of the old building into the bright sunlight.

IV

Let's just say that the Shelburne campus was as impressive as any I've ever seen, and I've seen many. It combined delightful old-world charm and gravitas with a progressive philosophy. It boasted a blazingly fast fibre-optic network and a library with eighteenth-century texts. There were all-weather playing fields alongside gardens laid out by the early Dutch settlers. We gradually wound our way around the grounds, our student guides telling us the story behind everything of significance and throwing in their own personal favourites. It was clear that they were in love with the school.

Lara was in awe; this was not her world, and she peppered the students with questions. The answers were always delivered with pride but also with modesty.

After perhaps an hour, we found ourselves at Plashy Pond. The students had been instructed to leave nothing out of the tour, but I could sense that they were nervous about this final location and weren't sure if we knew about the recent tragedy, which gave me the chance to introduce the topic.

"Dr. Croken has told us about Tom's death," I began. "It must have come as a terrible shock to the school." The anxiety lifted from their faces, replaced by sorrow.

"I can't believe it happened," Aphiwe said quietly. "I'm so sad for Tom's brother and his family. It's a bad thing for Shelburne, but Dr. Croken is doing a good job of getting us through it."

"It's more personal for me," Kristy began. "Senior students like us act as mentors for the grade nines. Tom was my mentee last year, and I got to know him really well. He was a cool young guy. He was modest, but he wasn't shy, and he'd talk to me openly about things that were important to him. It almost feels like I've lost a little brother. I can't imagine what it's like for his family."

I caught Lara's eye as we both realized our good luck in having Kristy as our tour guide. Perhaps later it would be important to find out about the things that were important to Tom Parkes, but now wasn't the right moment.

Kristy and Aphiwe brought us back to the headmaster's office where we thanked them effusively. I shook hands, gave them my card, and asked them to get in touch if their education or careers brought them to North America. Lara gave them both a double kiss and said she hoped we would meet again. Lara is talented at making the right first impression, gaining trust in short order. I know it takes longer for people to break through my reserve. Her skills would be useful in the weeks ahead.

We wrapped up with Pius and Stephen and then pointed the Land Cruiser back toward the hotel where Malcolm met us in the lobby and inquired after our plans for the evening. Lara said she would like to take a walk along the waterfront. Malcolm recommended a couple of restaurants and offered to make a reservation.

We opted for Sevruga. After eating the parmesan gnocchi and pan-fried prawns, we decided we'd made the right choice. We ordered coffee and sambuca and held hands across the table. We'd shared a bottle of Chenin Blanc with dinner, and I was feeling mellow and happy.

"Do you remember on Exuma you said that we should be patient and find out more about each other before we make a commitment?" I said.

"I'm not likely to have forgotten," she said, smiling.

"So maybe this would be a good time for me to tell you a story from my murky past," I ventured.

"The darker and murkier the better. Leave nothing out." Lara gave my hand a squeeze.

"I don't want you walking out before we've finished our coffee, so I'll start with something manageable. How about I tell you how I met my ex-wife?"

"Joanne. Yes, that sounds good. Tell me how you met Joanne."

"Right. Well, let me set the scene. You have to imagine me as an eighteen-year-old arriving at the University of St. Andrew's. It's early September on the

North Sea coast of Scotland. The days are getting shorter, and there's a chill in the air . . .

V

My first year in halls was a disaster. I found it hard to make friends. I was identified and spurned as English by the burgeoning group of young Scottish nationalists at the university. I wasn't rich enough to cut it with the" Sloane Rangers," the horsey set who were attracted to St. Andrew's if Oxbridge wasn't an option. I ended up drinking in quiet pubs frequented mostly by townspeople.

I had a couple of outings with people who, like me, were finding it difficult to find a group. Henry was the son of a country vet from Dorset. He was clever and funny but talked about himself too much. There's such a fine line between interesting and odd, and Henry was definitely odd. Sarah was a ridiculously attractive girl from North Wales. She was the last person who should have lacked self-confidence, but she did. My first serious sexual encounters took place in her dorm room in Hepburn Hall. Sarah would sneak me in during the afternoon when the director, a ferocious physics professor named Dr. Aitcheson, would least expect intruders. The bed was narrow, and the heating didn't come on till evening, but Sarah was warm and kind and seemed to know a lot about giving and receiving pleasure. I was lucky to have been taught by such a skilled instructor. We enjoyed a happy month together, and I'm sure we'd have lasted longer if I hadn't contracted gonorrhea. Peeing became agony, and one of my testicles swelled up to the size of a tennis ball. I screwed up my courage and visited the university health centre where a young doctor examined the evidence, then gave me an antibiotic injection in the buttock and some carefully measured advice about how to prevent further exposure. I shared this with Sarah, who was sympathetic, but it became clear as we spoke that she had multiple current sexual partners of both genders. I had thought we were in love, and I became pompous and behaved very badly, storming out and leaving her in tears—the last thing she needed.

St. Andrew's is a small town, and I spent the next year crossing the street to avoid her. Months later, perhaps a sign of the onset of some kind of belated maturity, seeing her drinking alone in a student bar at lunchtime, I ventured over to speak to her and apologized for my behaviour. She was very nice about it, but then, Sarah was very nice. To this day I blush at the memory.

Realizing that life in halls wasn't going well, I placed an ad for an apartment in the *Courier* in the middle of the Candlemas term and a week later was interviewed by the four residents of a large farmhouse about five kilometres outside of town. I moved in at the start of the Michaelmas term the following September, and from then on, my university life became what I had hoped it would be.

I'm a bit of a conformist, and conforming at Nydie Mains Farm meant growing hair to the middle of my back, smoking a fair amount of pot, and staying up till the small hours talking music and politics in front of the fireplace, which might even have had a fire in it if anyone had any grant money left for coal.

There were three girls in the house—Sadie, Jane, and Chloe—and a boy, Martin, who was Jane's cousin. They were good, generous young people, and we enjoyed our year together. Sadie had a car, but it was a tiny two-seater Austin Healey, so we would usually all walk into town together in time for our first lecture. We'd often walk back together at night too, talking or singing to keep up our spirits against the wind and the dark. Sadie's parents were titled, had pots of money, and indulged their only child. This was very good for the rest of us too as Sadie would often bankroll food and beer supplies for the last few days of term when the rest of us had run out of funds.

The winter seemed to last forever, but by the start of April the wildflowers in the woods were beginning to push through, and lapwings were building their ramshackle nests in the field next to the house. The girls decided that a large party was in order, and so it was that on a sunny Sunday afternoon, dozens of people streamed up from the town and descended on Nydie Mains, some clutching bottles or cans, others with food offerings. We had all worked hard to get the place looking respectable. Martin and I had set up tables in the overgrown walled garden, and Jane and Chloe had made bread and prepared some salads. Sadie had bought the ingredients for jugs of Pimm's. A friend from the student union had set up a sound system, and the strident chords of Zeppelin, Black Sabbath, and the Clash were alarming the sheep two fields away.

I was wending my way through the clumps of people seated on the grass when I tripped over Oliver, Sadie's calico cat, who was snaking around soliciting treats. As I lurched forward to keep my balance, a fair portion of the Pimm's in my just-recharged glass ended up on the shirt of a young woman sitting at a table with two other girls.

"Oh, shit! You moron," were, as it turned out, the first words my wife ever spoke to me.

"Christ, what am I going to do? Is there a bathroom in this place?" Her accent was trans-Atlantic.

"Yes, of course. Come with me. I'll show you," I babbled, flustered by my clumsiness and by the anger surging from the girl.

I led her into the house and directed her to the bathroom. I found one of my more respectable T-shirts and handed it around the door to her. She appeared a few minutes later looking calmer and quite fetching in the oversized shirt.

"Are you always this clumsy, or did you just lose control when you saw me?" She almost smiled. "Idiot," she said, then threw a playful punch at my shoulder.

"It's getting a bit hot out there. Do you want to go for a walk, or do you have responsibilities here?" she said with the hint of a sneer.

"Yeah, sure. We can walk to the cliffs behind the house. There's a great view over to Dairsie," I said.

"I'm not sure the idea of you, me, and cliffs is filling me with confidence. Are you sure you won't stumble and push me to my death by accident?"

"No, probably not. I usually only have about one seizure per day," I said. "And anyway, if I was to push you over, it wouldn't be an accident!" I thought it was time to give her back a bit.

She gave me the most wonderful smile that I had seen in my young life to that point. "My name is Joanne, by the way. You should probably know that for the coroner's report!"

We walked to the cliffs and sat together on the mossy ground, then lay back. A red kite circled above us on the thermals. Bees were buzzing in the spring flowers, and the party seemed like it was miles away.

"This is nice," she said, reaching her hand across to find mine.

We kissed for a while and then made love. It was 1979, and if a young couple who'd had a few drinks and a joint or two found themselves alone in a beautiful place on a sunny day, that often happened.

By the end of the afternoon, it was clear to us both that we wanted to spend more time together, and over the next two years, we did. I moved in with her at her cottage in Dunino. By the time we graduated, Joanne in economics and me in mediaeval history and fine art, we didn't even question whether we would be together as we moved our lives forward.

Joanne was returning to Canada, and, as you already know, I found a way to follow her.

VI

Lara had listened quietly as I'd told the story. Then she nodded. "It's a sweet story, David. Thanks for sharing it with me. You must have loved each other a lot for a long time."

"Actually, thank *you*," I said. "I haven't been able to talk to anyone about it before. It's thirty years of my life that ended up in failure, and I don't much like thinking about it, but you're right; we were very much in love, and some good things came of it, including James."

We walked back to the hotel in an atmosphere of quiet intimacy. "You know, David, we can't change the past even though our memories sometimes try to do that for us, but it's important to come to terms with things as they really happened."

"You don't mind me talking about another woman?" We stopped and faced each other.

"What good would it do for me to say if I did?" Lara raised an eyebrow quizzically. "I'm happy to be with you, David, and I'm all grown up. We're good to each other. We accept each other for who we are. I like you for who you are." A soft breeze off the harbour blew a strand of hair across her face. I pushed it back behind her ear and pulled her in for a hug that lasted a while.

CHAPTER 5

I

We went straight to bed when we got back to the hotel, and we both slept soundly until the first light crept through the curtains. I got up and opened the sliding windows onto the balcony. The gulls were wheeling and crying over the fishing boats making their way back into harbour loaded with sardines and anchovies. I called Malcolm and ordered coffee, croissants, and fruit. Ten minutes later it arrived. I poured David a coffee and took it to him in bed where he was just stirring.

"Good morning," he said sleepily as he consulted the bedside clock, which showed 7:15 a.m. "Mmm . . . I could have slept for another hour. How was your night?"

"Great. I sleep better when I'm with you," I said. "That's probably a compliment."

"Well, we better not get used to it. I sense this case is going to involve long hours, but I think I'm over the jet lag now and raring to go."

"On that topic, I decided to stay here this morning while you visit the police. I want to help you, but this is your case, and it's your skills that Shelburne is paying for." I hoped David would be comfortable with my saying this.

"OK. We can do that. I'll tell you all about it when I get back, but I hope you'll come with me to the pathologist this afternoon. She's something of a celebrity, and it's her reservations about the cause of death that is at the heart of all this."

Lost and Found

I put some fruit on two plates and brought them across to the table on the balcony. David poured us more coffee and joined me. He stood by the railing gazing out to sea.

"Look at us," he said, turning to me and stretching his hands out by his side, palms up, like a priest giving a blessing. "Last week we were making love on a beach in the Bahamas, and this week we're shacked up in a luxury hotel in one of the most beautiful cities in the world doing something interesting and getting paid for it. Not bad, is it?" He made a face.

I smiled. "It's a lot better than that."

II

Detective Chief Inspector Cobus Olivier had no neck. His bullet of a head tapered outwards to join his massive shoulders. He wore a white shirt buttoned at the collar but no tie. He was a bit overweight, but lots of muscle rippled under the fat.

"My name is Cobus, and my last name is pronounced Olly-feer," he said in a voice with a strong Afrikaans timbre. "But you can call me Chief Inspector. Have a seat" He indicated the chair on the other side of the metal desk behind which he sat.

"Let me be clear about something, Mr. Mallory. I've told Dr. Croken that I will assist you in your work because my boss said I should, but never forget that this is a police matter, and if you do anything to impede or prejudice the investigation, my cooperation will cease."

"I'm very grateful to you for being willing to meet with me, Chief Inspector. I'll make sure that I operate within those parameters." I passed him a card from my wallet. "Shelburne has retained me to help determine the truth in this tragedy and to manage the public relations around the case. We're on the same side."

I didn't bother to say that sometimes managing the case with discretion meant interpreting findings in a particular way, not hiding or changing the facts but interpreting them in a way that was helpful to my client. The chief inspector was obviously unhappy with the arrangement that had been forced on him, so we'd get to the interpretation if and when necessary.

"I don't want to take up too much of your time, Chief Inspector, but it would be helpful if you could run through the events around the death as you understand them. I should say that I'm seeing Dr. Naidoo later today."

"Aha, Dr. Naidoo, another one of the great and the good and a Shelburne alumna you may be interested to know. There's a lot of them around this case." He didn't say it pleasantly.

Chief Inspector Olivier ran through the events surrounding the discovery of the body and gave me a summary of whom they had spoken with to date.

"We always look at the family first because thirty percent of murders are committed by family members. We spoke to the brother. He's a good kid, really broken up about his twin. He has a rock-solid alibi for the presumed time of death.

"The stepmother is an interesting woman, Lena Michaels. Twenty years younger than her husband and dresses like a prostitute. The Shelburne community put up with her because she's rich, but she'll never be one of them. On the day Tom died, she was at school, working with twenty other people on the one hundred and fiftieth anniversary gala, so she's clear.

"That brings us to the father, Edward Parkes, 'Honest Ed' to the South African business community, which means, of course, that they doubt his honesty. He's not a nice man, Mr. Mallory. He has battered his way to financial success, leaving a lot of blood on the tracks. He's been taken to court numerous times by the people he's screwed, but he can afford the best lawyers, and he's been Teflon coated until now. He was running some kind of business meeting at the time of his son's death, so there are a dozen witnesses to say he had no part to play in this. We haven't been able to talk to the boy's biological mother yet. She goes by her maiden name, Gillen, Sarah Gillen. She is sedated, in a bad way. The psychiatrist is worried about her. He recommended 'round-the-clock monitoring. Suicide watch, you might call it, but she wouldn't have any of it."

Chief Inspector Oliver stood up and wandered over to the water cooler in the corner of the office, filled a paper cup, drank it, then turned back to me. "The boy drowned, Mr. Mallory. Drowning is the third most common cause of accidental death in this country after motor vehicle accidents and falls. The only reason we're having this conversation is because the school is rich and influential enough to question the report of the pathologist who did the original autopsy and because Dr. Naidoo sees an opportunity for publicity. I don't like privilege, Mr. Mallory. I was raised in Lydenburg in the Transvaal. It's called Mpumalanga now, of course." He rolled his eyes. "It's a farming and mining town founded by my Voortrekker ancestors. You get ahead by hard work and honest dealing. It's what I understand." He held my gaze a while longer than necessary. "Is there anything else I can help you with?"

I stood, thanked him, and then left him to deal with the sizable chip on his muscular shoulders.

My session with the chief inspector had raised two problems. First, he was hostile to the idea of my participation in the case, and I didn't think I would get much assistance from him. I've had that in cases before, and it's not usually a deal breaker.

In a way the second problem was more intriguing. If Pius wanted discretion, the original coroner's report recording a drowning death by misadventure had given him that. Why had he requested a second examination by Dr. Naidoo? I plugged my phone into the car's hands-free system and dialled Pius's number.

"David." My name must have come up on his caller ID. "How did it go at the police station?"

"I don't think the chief inspector is going to be inviting me out to lunch anytime soon, but he filled me in on a couple of things. He also said something that puzzled me, and that's why I'm calling you."

I started the car, engaged the gear, and moved away. "If you're looking for a swift and discreet process, why did you question the original coroner? Surely you had what you wanted?"

"Ah, yes, why indeed? I can tell you that I thought long and hard before I did, and it has kept me awake ever since." He paused for several seconds. "I knew Tom well. The boy had been here for years. He was on the swimming team; he shouldn't have drowned. Also, a couple of the students came to see me and told me that they had been worried about Tom for several months. They couldn't specify, but they're good kids, and I trust their intuition.

"We talk a lot about honour at Shelburne. I believe that the soul of a school is its most sacred and valuable trust. Good times will come, and good times will go, but to endure and succeed a school has to know its identity, and its leader has to act in a way that protects that mission and nurtures that soul."

I hadn't seen the passionate side of Pius before, and I was impressed.

"I believe that in the long run it will be more harmful for Shelburne to accept a speedy and convenient verdict than it will be to put up with the scrutiny that is bound to come with our request for a second opinion. If that opinion confirms the original verdict, so much the better, but we will have been seen to act with diligence and honour. You've heard the saying, "The truth will set you free." Well, I believe that's correct, and that's why I made the call to Dr. Naidoo. My decision has led us to take the more difficult path, and that is why I need you. Can you understand that, David?"

I know that I err on the side of pragmatism, and I doubt I would have had the courage to do what Pius had done, but I admired him even more for that.

"I understand perfectly, and I commend you for your principles and for acting on them. Another question: do you know the boy's biological mother, Sarah Gillen?"

"Sarah is a good woman. She was badly hurt by the divorce and suffered from a deep depression. She still comes to events where the boys are involved, but apart from that we haven't seen much of her on campus for the last two years. I called to speak to her last week, but she didn't pick up."

"Chief Inspector Olivier told me that she was medicated and receiving professional care," I said. "I need to speak to her. If you do manage to connect, can you ask if she will see me, please?"

By the time we finished talking, I was back at the Cape Grace. I handed my keys to the valet. I walked across the lobby, Malcolm spotted me and told me that Lara was in Signal, the grill and bar on the second floor. I joined her, ordering a club soda and a grilled mahi sandwich, then filled her in on my morning.

"The Chief Inspector sounds like a charmer," she offered.

"You know, I think he's a good man at heart. He's grown up in a country that has changed around him to such an extent that he doesn't really know the place anymore. He'd probably be happier raising cattle on the lowveld, but he's made a life here now and is trying to make it work. He despises Shelburne and all he thinks it stands for. It could be useful for us to have that perspective as we get into this thing."

"I agree," Lara replied. "I always learn more from people who disagree with me than from those who hold my view. How did the chief inspector feel about the second autopsy?"

"He's not impressed. He thinks Dr. Naidoo is showboating."

"Do we know if she has found any new evidence from the body?"

"We do not, but she has let it be known that she has reservations about some aspects of the autopsy, and I'm hoping that we'll learn more this afternoon."

III

Dr. Naidoo had an office in the Rondebosch Medical Centre on Klipfontein Road off the busy Kromboom Parkway. We checked in with the receptionist, who called up to confirm our appointment, issued us with security lanyards, then directed us to the elevators.

"Do you know what line you're going to take with her?" Lara asked as the elevator doors closed.

"It's very straightforward at this point, I think," I replied. "We're only here because Dr. Naidoo has doubts about the boy's cause of death, so we need to know what those doubts are, and we need to make a judgement about whether they justify the painful delay this is causing. If we don't think they do then we'll advise Pius to wrap it up. He'd be happy, as would the police, and you've got to think the family is suffering terribly the longer this is drawn out. But if we think she's onto something, our job is to get to the truth. Let's hear from the doctor, and then you and I can talk about it this evening and make our recommendation."

Moments later the elevator doors opened at the eleventh floor, and we got out. A nurse in the outer office asked us to take a seat. Five minutes later a tall, striking woman wearing a lab coat walked across the wood-block floor and shook our hands. "Gauri Naidoo," she said. "I'd like you to call me Gauri." She had glossy dark hair and huge brown eyes.

"David and Lara," I offered in return.

She ushered us into her inner office. We sat in three overstuffed armchairs around a walnut coffee table. There was a silver tray in the centre and upon it sat a tea service.

"I always have tea at this time in the afternoon," she said. "I hope you will join me?"

"That would be lovely," Lara replied for both of us. "A slice of lemon for me and milk for David."

"You know each other well, I see," Dr. Naidoo said, smiling.

"We're getting to know each other better," Lara replied with a matching smile and one raised eyebrow as Dr. Naidoo poured. We had barely been in the room a minute, and I felt that the women had already decided that they liked each other.

"This is most hospitable of you, Gauri," I said. "I didn't expect afternoon tea at the pathologist's office."

She leaned back in the chair and crossed her legs. "I find that maintaining traditions and punctuating the day with reminders that I have a life outside of work gives me the strength to do my very best for the people I work for."

"Your colleagues?" I asked.

"No, David. I speak of the dead whose final journey on Earth it is my job to describe. They rely on me to discover the truth. It is work that I take very seriously."

I watched the doctor as she spoke. She maintained unblinking eye contact in a way that was both intimate and intimidating. She was a beautiful woman, and she knew it. Beneath her open lab coat, I saw a knitted two-piece beige suit and a single chain of pearls around her neck. She projected an elegant professionalism and the confidence of a woman at the top of her profession, but there was also warmth and humanity.

"We're so grateful that you have found some time for us today, Gauri," Lara said, taking the lead. "We're working with Shelburne to discover the truth about the death of Tom Graves, and we know you undertook a second autopsy at the school's request. It would be very helpful if you could give us a summary of your findings and highlight anything that concerns you about the initial report."

Dr. Naidoo stood up and walked to a modern steel-and-glass desk from which she picked up a black file folder. Moving back to her chair, she sat again, placing her hands on the file as she glanced back and forth between us. "I will do my best to explain to you in a comprehensible way something that has taken me two decades to master. You're educated people. Do either of you have a science background?"

"I took some courses in marine biology at university," Lara said. I looked at her, and she met my gaze with a deferential smile. Like so many other things about Lara's past, this was news to me.

"Excellent. That will be helpful and allow me to use the language of science as I describe my findings."

She shifted slightly but significantly in her seat, adjusting herself so that she was facing Lara more than me. "Drowning is one of the more complex causes of death. It is an asphyxial process, so you'd think it would be straightforward to describe, but it has effects on multiple organ systems, so it is, in fact, highly complex.

"As you will know, Lara, breathing is an involuntary process controlled by the central nervous system in response to levels of oxygen and carbon dioxide in the blood and tissues. With drowning victims there comes a point when they try to hold their breath to prevent the inhalation of fluid, in this case, water. They can do this successfully only to the point where the blood-oxygen level hits a critically low point, at which moment the autonomic nervous system overrides the victim's conscious will and triggers an automatic gasping response. Fluid is then inhaled. This fluid prevents the normal diffusion of oxygen across the alveolar-capillary interface. The worsening hypoxia results in a depletion of brain energy and a reduction in brain function. Irreversible cell injury occurs somewhere between four and six minutes after sustained oxygen deprivation. Cardio-respiratory arrest and death follows."

"You're saying that Tom's death followed a typical pattern for drowning victims?" I queried.

"In all respects, yes."

"So, why are we here if this is an open-and-shut accidental death by drowning?" I tried to conceal the level of frustration that I was feeling.

"If you will bear with me please, David, it will take me a few more minutes of explanation to establish my concern." Her tone was patient, like a mother reading a story to a child who wanted to skip the details and get to the outcome. I bowed my head.

"In this case there is no evidence of contributing phenomena. The tissue analysis showed no evidence of recent drug use. The water temperature was twenty degrees Celsius, insufficiently cold to produce arrhythmia, muscle fatigue, or hypothermia. The body was not entangled in debris, and there is no dangerous aquatic life in Plashy Pond. The boy was apparently in excellent health when he died. The police have determined that there is no evidence from the surrounding area of any incident prior to the boy entering the water that may have contributed to his death. There is no evidence of external injury, blunt force, or otherwise."

"So, it would be entirely possible for a pathologist to offer a verdict of accidental death," Lara said, narrowing her eyes.

"Yes, it would." Dr. Naidoo gave a weak smile. "But . . ."

"But what, Gauri?" Lara was totally focused.

"Even when the data points overwhelmingly in one direction, we still need to use common sense. Sometimes my colleagues criticize me for this approach, but it has brought me good results."

She paused to take a sip of her tea. "So, Tom was on the Shelburne swim team and was completely at home in the water. He was an athletic young man in excellent health. Some drownings are suicides, but Tom had no history of emotional instability or mental illness. He was one of the most popular students in the school, and there are no reports of bullying or disagreements with his peers. He seemed to be an unusual drowning victim, so I decided to investigate further."

Dr. Naidoo had our full attention. We were literally and metaphorically on the edge of our seats, hanging on her every word.

"I decided to run some more tests on the lung tissue. When water enters the lungs, anything that is in the water body, such as various forms of aquatic debris, enter with it, things like sand and silt, algae, and other aquatic vegetation. I analyzed it all, and it seemed consistent with the environment in Plashy Pond. I decided to run one last set of tests, and that's when I found it."

She paused for another sip of tea. She was enjoying this. She was like an actor with a great script, manipulating her audience. I was enjoying the performance. I looked across at Lara. I could tell that she was feeling the same.

"Lara, your study of marine ecosystems will mean you're familiar with diatoms."

Lara nodded but didn't speak.

"Because this is central to why we're here, I will digress for a moment to ensure that we understand the significance of the finding." She said, "we," but she meant me, only she was too diplomatic to say it.

"Diatoms are a major group of algae. They are found in all the world's water bodies, both marine and freshwater. They are also found in soil. They consist of microscopic boxes made of silica, and they are, in fact, very beautiful. Under the right conditions, a colony of diatoms can double in size every twenty-four hours. As they photosynthesize, they are responsible for about thirty percent of the oxygen produced on Earth every year. So, they are a very significant partner on this planet that most people know nothing about. You also need to understand that there are thousands of different species of diatoms, and each one has a particular set of environmental conditions in which it thrives."

She paused to take another sip of tea.

"When I ran the final test, I found diatoms in the lungs. Further analysis by my friends at the University of Cape Town showed them to be the species Cyclostephanos dubius. It's a pretty little thing. It looks like a microscopic wheel with thirty-six spokes."

"But if diatoms are found in all water bodies, how does that help us?" Lara queried.

"How indeed?" Dr. Naidoo smiled with the confidence of a conjuror, certain that she was about to pull the rabbit out of the hat.

"Interestingly for us, Cyclostephanos dubius is a fussy little fellow requiring a specific set of conditions to prosper. It needs calcareous, alkaline water with a high chloride concentration. Plashy Pond does not have these conditions. As you know the Shelburne campus lies on the western slope of Table Mountain. The escarpment of the mountain is made of a sandstone layer that lies on the Graafwater Formation, an ancient combination of shale and sandstone that sits on a deep bed of Cape Granite. Nothing remotely calcareous about any of that. You need a limestone bedrock like chalk to produce calcareous groundwater. Also, to achieve the target level of chloride concentration you need chloride bearing bedrocks or seepage from wastewater or runoff from agriculture. There are no chloride-bearing rocks in this part of South Africa, and the Shelburne campus borders Table Mountain National Park, so there's definitely no wastewater or farming runoff involved."

Dr. Naidoo sat back and waited for us to respond.

"So, you're saying that Tom drowned but not in Plashy Pond?" I asked.

"The ultimate cause of death was drowning. I'm not saying there wasn't a predisposing factor to that drowning, just that I haven't found it. And yes, my university friends have analyzed water samples from all parts of the pond, and they have found all sorts of beautiful diatoms but not one example of Cyclostephanos dubius."

There was silence in the room for maybe twenty seconds as Lara and I considered the implications of what we had just heard.

"Have you shared this with Dr. Croken?" I asked.

"I have. I'm an alumna of Shelburne, though before Dr. Croken's time. He's an honourable man and committed to his students. I know that he commissioned me to reconsider the autopsy as a sort of second opinion. He expected that I would confirm the assessment. He believed that the school community and indeed the country would see that he had been scrupulous in his process and that we could move on and allow the family to try to find some peace. In some ways I'm not sure my finding has been helpful to Dr. Croken, but he has engaged you to assist him, and from what I have learned from our short time together he has selected well."

"You're kind, Gauri, but we haven't done anything yet, so we'll need to suspend judgement on that. What is very clear is that you have done an extraordinary job."

"Not really, David. I'm competent in my field, and I have a sense of responsibility to my patients even though they're dead."

"Perhaps we can contact you again if we have questions as we move ahead," Lara said.

"You can." Dr. Naidoo placed her hand on Lara's elbow as we moved from the office. "In fact, if you have any free time, give me a call. We can have lunch, and I can show you some of my favourite parts of our beautiful city."

There was no suggestion that I was included in this offer.

CHAPTER 6

I

The car was parked in the shade, so we got in and sat in silence for a few moments.

"She's impressive, isn't she?" Lara began.

"Very. And she hit it off with you."

"Is that so surprising, David? I'm a very likeable person. Everyone says so." She glanced sideways at me and gave me a fake smile.

"Well, that's true, of course. I'm feeling increasingly lucky that you give me the time of day. But seriously, you're very good at this. People relax with you and probably end up saying a little more than they intend. So, what do you think? Do we have a case to investigate?"

"Yes. We certainly do, but we need to decide on next steps. Then we should check in with Pius, as we promised."

"Do you want to do that over dinner?" I asked.

"Not really. It feels like we've been eating steadily for days. Why don't we drive somewhere outside the city and go for a long walk? That'll clear our minds and help us think. Then perhaps we can order something small for the suite and spend the evening in." She gave me a lingering look. I widened my eyes and nodded approvingly.

"OK. Give me the keys, and I'll drive us over to Simonstown. There's a penguin colony there that's always interesting, and there's a trail along the coast that we can take for a hike."

We switched places and headed off.

I decided to take the M6, which runs along the western side of the Cape Peninsula through Camps Bay. After Hout Bay it becomes Chapman's Peak

Drive, which winds up and over the peninsula to Fish Hoek on the eastern side and then south to Simonstown.

There are about three thousand African penguins in the Boulders Bay colony, and it seemed as if they were all in action that afternoon. Some flopped out of the ocean onto the small white-sand beach that runs up between the huge granite boulders that give the place its name while others waddled sedately down the slope and disappeared into the cold waters of the South Atlantic. Others worked away amongst the low vegetation, moving stones and twigs to reinforce their nests and feeding the large downy chicks that continuously harassed their parents for more food.

I think Lara could have spent hours there watching them, but the sun had already dropped behind the height of land that forms the spine of the peninsula, and the temperature would be dropping soon, so I suggested that we head off on our hike. The trail climbed steeply and took us westwards until we had a spectacular view east over False Bay. The air was crisp and clear, and we could see all the way over to Somerset West, behind which the hills of the wine country around Stellenbosch formed a thin grey line in the gathering dusk.

We found a spot to sit on the low, springy vegetation and rested in silence for a few seconds enjoying the view and catching our breath after the climb.

"I'm thinking that we need to find a way to speak to Tom's mother, Sarah Gillen, and then meet with Ed Parkes with or without Lena Michaels before we check in with Pius," I said lying back. "That would complete a logical first round of interviews and give us everything available on which to base our next move. What do you think?"

"That makes sense. Sarah probably knew her son better than anybody. Depending on her condition, it might be a bit tricky getting to see her though. She may have arranged nursing help at home, or she may be in hospital. I wonder if Pius has had any luck contacting her."

"Let me call Stephen and see if he can arrange something. He seems to have Pius's complete confidence, and he's certainly highly organized."

I took out my cell phone to dial the number but saw that there was no signal where we were. "I'll do it as soon as we're back at the hotel. We should probably make a move; it'll be dark in an hour." I made to stand up, but Lara took my sleeve and pulled me back down.

"Come here," she said in that voice that was too deep for her petite frame. She rolled on top of me, and I looked up into those remarkable green eyes.

"Kiss me, David."

I did as I was told.

II

Back at the Cape Grace, I called Stephen, who said he would arrange the meetings. Lara ordered some dinner. I inspected the well-stocked bar fridge in the kitchen and opened a beer, then poured Lara a glass of pinot grigio.

"I'm going to jump in the shower," I called through to the bedroom.

I was enjoying the hot water battering my head and shoulders when I was aware of an image moving beyond the opaque glass of the shower door. A second later the door opened, and Lara stepped into the shower.

"There's a water shortage in Cape Town right now, so I thought this would be the responsible thing to do," she said.

Showering with a beautiful naked woman was not a typical David Mallory activity, but time spent with Lara over the past few weeks had led to growing confidence about quite a few new things.

"It's making me feel like doing some things that might be rather irresponsible," I said, putting my hands on her hips and pulling her close.

"Slow down, slow down." She smiled and reached for the soap. "Turn around while I wash your back. I'm hungry, and dinner will be here in ten minutes."

"I'm not sure I can wait till we've eaten." My voice was a little hoarse.

"Yes you can." She turned me around and kissed me. "Anticipation is ninety percent of the pleasure or pain in anything. Remember that," she said, giving me a knowing look.

In Greek mythology, which I had adored as a child, Hypnos was the personification of sleep. He lived in a cave next to his twin brother, Thanatos, the personification of death. No light fell upon their dwellings, but poppies and other sleep-inducing plants grew in profusion in front of the caves.

The next morning, as I struggled to come to the surface from the deepest sleep I'd experienced in ages, I thought maybe Hypnos had paid me a visit.

More likely it had been the result of the small but delicious dinner, half a bottle of old vine zinfandel, and two hours of the most profoundly exciting lovemaking of my life.

Lara had led us through a succession of intimacies, each one related to but exceeding the erotic power of the one before. Normally, I make love enthusiastically but quietly. Not that night though. When we eventually climaxed, I suspect that most of the fifth floor must have heard about it.

Turning over in bed, I found that Lara was still asleep, her arms behind her on the pillow and her lips parted. As I watched her, I felt a sensation coming over me that I hadn't felt in decades: a desire to protect and cherish, a need to be with this woman, and a desire to hold her and love her.

Lara stirred, and I leaned over and kissed her lips. She gave me a drowsy smile and put her arms around my neck.

"That was quite a show we put on last night." Her voice was still fogged with sleep. "You did really well for an old man."

She moved her hands down my body and tickled me.

"You bring out the best in me, baby," I said in a fake American accent. "Want to see if you can do it again?"

She did.

III

It was Friday morning. David was making coffee when the phone rang at around 9 a.m. I answered. Stephen was on the line. He told me that he had been able to get in touch with Sarah Gillen but that she wasn't available that day.

"Ms. Gillen is reluctant to meet with anyone at present, but Dr. Croken has vouched for you, so she will see you on Sunday morning at ten o'clock. I have sent you a text with the address. Mr. Parkes is out of town on business this weekend, and I have made an appointment through his secretary for Monday. He invites you to meet him at the Richmond Country Club for lunch. He's playing a round of golf in the morning, but he will be finished by noon. It's just this side of Fish Hoek, so you will need to give yourselves forty-five minutes to get there."

I thanked him and asked him to tell Pius that we would give him a report midweek.

Playing golf so shortly after his son's death said something about Ed Parkes, but I wasn't sure what.

It looked like we had today and Saturday clear, which was no bad thing. It would allow us to get rid of any remaining traces of jet lag and to recover from the previous night's exertions. Each time I started to make love, I never quite knew how it was going to go; sometimes I thought it was going to be fabulous, and it fell short, and sometimes the reverse happened. The night before it had kept getting better and better, and I could feel that we were crossing new thresholds of intimacy and trust.

I'd had to screw up my courage to come on this trip with David. I didn't want to endanger what we had begun to build by forcing us together too soon, but it was going really well. David was happy to let me work with him, and I think my skills complement his. He's a sweet man, clever and experienced, but he can be a bit stiff on first acquaintance. My approach is to try and establish a relationship first and get to the business second. Between us we were a good team.

I passed Stephen's message on to David while he was shaving.

"Looks like we can be tourists for a couple of days," I said. "What would you like to do?"

"Probably sleep for about twenty-four hours." David smiled at the bathroom mirror.

"Well, that's your own fault for being addicted to sex."

"No, it's your fault for being irresistible and leading me astray."

"It seemed to me like you knew the route to 'astray' like the back of your hand."

"Well, we have plenty of time, so you choose first."

"That's easy," I offered. "It has to be Robben Island."

"Great choice. Let's check the ferry times. My choice is to take the cable car up Table Mountain and walk back down the Platteklip Gorge Trail. We can do that tomorrow."

It was a five-minute walk from the hotel to the dock, and we made it onto the 10.30 a.m. boat. It was a glorious day, so we climbed the steep metal stairs to the open-top deck. There was hardly anyone on the boat, and we had several rows of seats to ourselves. When we got underway, I found the breeze off the cool South Atlantic water was a bit chilly, so I took a navy down jacket out of my backpack and pulled it on. David put his arm around me and held me close.

"Perhaps this would be a good time for me to tell you a story from my past," I offered.

David was a private person, and I was impressed that he had told me the story of how he met Joanne with such candour the other night. If we were to keep moving forward, I needed to find the same courage. With his arm around me and the sun shining down on us, it felt like the right moment.

"Yes, please. I better know what I'm getting into. Maybe you'll provide me with an excuse to throw it all over."

He was joking, but that was exactly what I was afraid of. However, we'd come a long way in the past few days, and risking the consequences of honesty felt better than living under the threat of secrecy.

"OK. Fasten your seatbelt. Here we go." I gave his hand a squeeze.

IV

David already knew I was born into a middle-class family in Usaquen, a well-to-do northern suburb of Bogota. My mother died giving birth to my brother, Enrique, when I was three. I never met Enrique, who lived only a few days, and afterwards my father fell into a depression, drinking heavily and then moving on to various drugs. He couldn't look after me, so his mother and father took me in. They were older, but they were loving and did their best. It was they who brought me up and they who I call my parents.

This was as much as I had told David, but there was more.

You have to realize that the drug wars consumed Colombia for two decades and formed the backdrop to my childhood. My biological father was killed in 1981 on my fifth birthday in what the police said was a drug-related gang shooting.

In 1985 the M19 guerillas entered the Palace of Justice and took dozens of hostages. When the army stormed the building, one hundred people were killed, including half of the members of the supreme court. This was the final straw for my parents, who sold their apartment and the small chain of clothing stores that had been in the family for four generations, and we moved to Miami. We rented a house in Miramar and the next year bought a pretty bungalow with a big garden backing onto the Riviera Golf Club in Coral Gables.

I attended a Catholic high school nearby where there were more Latinos than Caucasians and where Spanish was the language of the halls and playing fields. I had a few friends, but I only ever invited one to my home, and that happened only once. I loved my parents, but I was embarrassed that they were so much older. I felt I had to explain, and that explanation necessitated telling more than a casual friend wanted to know. I've always been disappointed with myself that I couldn't be proud of them. It felt like I was betraying their love.

I worried a lot about failure and worked really hard, with the result that I graduated toward the top of my class and was awarded a scholarship to study marine biology at the University of Miami. The campus was three blocks from our house. Looking back, I wonder if things would have turned out differently, and perhaps better, if I had moved away for college, but I had a sense of duty to my aging parents and wanted to stay close to them.

I continued to study hard, and I did really well during my first two years; my professors were already talking about graduate work.

My parents were more than comfortable, and they gave me a generous allowance, but I wanted the independence of my own money, so I worked three nights a week waiting tables at the Ritz Carlton in Coconut Grove. The hourly wage was miserable, but the tips were great. The wait staff pooled all the tips, and I walked away with $100 most evenings. After a few months I bought myself an old VW Beetle convertible with faded maroon paint, a couple of tears in the beige soft top, and quite a bit of style. I called it Lenny after Lenny Kravitz, whose music I loved and who I had a bit of a crush on.

Lenny meant that I didn't have to take the bus to work, and it made it easier for me to hang with my university friends. The Keys were a popular spot on the weekends. We would take tents and camp on the beach in John Pennekamp State Park. I'd spend the day with the others snorkelling on the reef just offshore and lying in the warm undulating ocean watching schools of blue tangs drift past my facemask. In the evening we'd gather up driftwood for a fire, beer would appear, and someone would have a few joints to pass around.

I didn't think of myself as attractive because I wasn't blond and skinny, but I got a lot of attention from the boys in the group, and my girlfriends said they were envious of my green eyes, so I concluded that I must look OK.

I dressed modestly, usually high-waisted stonewashed jeans and a crop top covered by an oversized long-sleeved shirt. I was a good Catholic girl, but I was also nineteen, and I wanted to try new things.

Perhaps it was to overcome my shyness; I'm still not sure, but I started to drink quite a lot on those outings, and considering I had little experience with alcohol, I wasn't a very skillful drunk. On one occasion a girl took my car keys away because she was scared for me. On another occasion I got into an argument with the state park police and ended the conversation by throwing up all over the officer's neatly pressed uniform.

It was on one such boozy weekend trip that my life took an important turn.

One of the boys in the group had been showing interest in me for a few weeks. His name was Marcus Crandall, and he was a third-year engineering student at the U of M. He was from Trinidad and was tall, good looking, and wore his hair in dreadlocks. Lots of the girls were keen on Marcus, and he'd featured in a couple of my dreams. I think I was attracted to him because he was different, and I felt a need to break out of my careful, conservative mode.

On this particular day, the sun had set, the bonfire was burning down, and I was sitting with a group drinking beer and talking about the recent World Trade Center bombing in New York. Marcus sat down beside me and offered me a drag from his joint. After a few minutes, the group decided to go for a night swim before retiring to the tents. Marcus and I stayed by the fire, and soon enough we were kissing. One thing led to another, and before long we had taken a blanket up to the shelter of the sea grape trees and were making love.

Of course, I made sure he was using protection; I even watched him as he put it on. The last thing I needed in the middle of my undergraduate program was to get pregnant.

However, as you've probably guessed, I did get pregnant. The very first time I had sex, I got pregnant. It wasn't supposed to be like that. After I got the test result, I called Marcus and told him that he was the father. He was very gentle on the phone, but he was obviously stunned. He asked if I was going to get an abortion, and I said I didn't know. He said it was obviously my choice but that he thought it would be for the best. I hung up, and we never spoke again.

I told my parents. The conversation was really difficult for them and for me. There was a lot of crying.

After much thinking and praying, I decided to go to term. The university was understanding and said I could defer my junior year for twelve months, but when Alejandro was born, and I held him to my breast, I knew he would always come first. When he was nine months old, my mother offered to look after him during the day, so I could go back to college. I took her up on the offer, but I just couldn't focus on my studies. Instead, I took some licensing courses and got a job as a junior broker in a real estate firm in Flamingo. I turned out to be really good at it and was soon given all the listings on Fisher Island and Key Biscayne. I didn't have to sell many houses in a year when they were going for $10 million, and I was getting 5 percent of it. I soon became the top-selling broker, and I made a lot of money.

The hours were flexible, which meant I could spend quality time with Alex. I saw other mothers with their children, and I realized my relationship with my boy was special. Even though it shattered my plans and changed my life completely, I never regretted getting pregnant. Having Alex is the best thing that I will ever do in my life.

The siren on the ferry cut into my narrative and I looked around to see that we were gliding into the small harbour on Robben Island. I exhaled loudly.

"That's probably more than you bargained for in one sitting," I said.

"It's a powerful story, and you tell it beautifully. Perhaps we can find the right time to talk more about Alejandro."

"We should. I know you know the ending, but there are things I'd like to talk through with you. There's nobody else I would tell, and you're a good listener."

David kissed my forehead. "And I didn't realize you brought a small fortune to this little relationship of ours. I could give up work and be a kept man!"

"Is that what we have, a relationship?" I asked.

"It's what we're building."

"Is love involved?"

David thought for a moment. "If love is trusting each other, wanting to be together, and sharing what's in our hearts then, yes, love is involved."

"So, say it," I said. "Say that you love me."

David turned to face me, smiled shyly, and took both my hands in his. "I love you, Lara Rios."

V

Sometimes it's possible to bring a thing into existence by saying its name. It was almost a relief to say the word "love." It had been lurking in the background for weeks, and over the last few days it had started jumping around waving its arms, desperate to be recognized. I didn't think I'd ever feel this emotion again, and it felt different than when I was a fumbling teenager at university. This time it was a more conscious commitment. We weren't starting out on life's tortuous pathway, naïve and starry eyed. We had already experienced the joy and despair of life, and we understood in a more profound way what it meant to make a commitment to another person. I was a little anxious that there were things about me—attitudes, fixations, and phobias—that could put us at risk, but if we wanted this to work as much as I thought we both did, we could overcome those things. I was a fairly old dog, but I thought I was still capable of learning some new tricks.

If I had to choose one emotion that flooded over me as we walked down the ferry's gangplank onto Robben Island, it would be liberation. Liberation from a life of self-imposed solitude, freedom to reinvent a life for both of us. The irony was not lost on me. I had been liberated on arrival at the very place where so many had been incarcerated. I had gained a sense of freedom on the island where they had lost theirs.

VI

Oh my. What had we done? I'd pushed David to say that he loved me. Only my parents and my son had ever used those words with me before. Others probably would have, but I hadn't let them.

David is a very intentional man. The fact that he said those words told me that he had already considered it and committed to it.

Was I ready to love him back? I thought so, but I worried that my broken heart wouldn't allow me to give him the partner he deserved. But I know that

I overthink everything, and I remembered what my father used to say about even the longest journey beginning with the first step.

The guides on Robben Island are all former inmates. Our guide that day was Patrick Matanjana, who'd spent twenty years in the cell next to Nelson Mandela. He spoke with no bitterness about the people who had stolen the best years of his life and who had subjected him to physical pain and degradation on a daily basis.

"Madiba always said that we must rise above our persecutors," he said. "You must hold onto your spirit, your dignity, and your humanity in the face of evil."

He took us to the lime quarry where the prisoners had laboured every day, breaking boulders into gravel.

"You see how bright it is with the sun shining off the white rock? That is what caused the snow blindness that afflicted Madiba for his whole life afterwards. But it is also here that he taught us what we needed to know to launch the liberation of our country. As we laboured, he would talk to us about philosophy and economics. We would discuss politics and plan for the day when our opportunity would come. The guards never knew, but we called this place the University of Robben Island." Patrick smiled widely, his eyes flashing in his wrinkled face.

We visited Mandela's cell, a tiny concrete box seven feet by nine with a barred window in one wall. The light was left on day and night for the eighteen years that Mandela was jailed there.

"Madiba would look out from his window. He would watch the trees and shrubs bloom and wither as season succeeded season, but he never gave up hope."

Our tour ended back at the ferry landing. We thanked Patrick effusively; his personal history with the place had moved us."

"You're good people," he replied. "I wish you a long life filled with love and grandchildren." We laughed with him. "And remember what Madiba said 'It is always impossible until it is done.'"

VII

We rose late the next morning and made it down to the lobby at around 10:00 a.m. Though the sun was shining around the city, we saw clouds covering Table Mountain.

"You should go anyway," Malcolm reassured us. "When it looks like this, the top of the mountain is usually above the clouds, and you will get some great views."

He was right. The cable car rumbled its way up through a bank of grey clouds at the halfway point but emerged into brilliant sunshine by the time we reached the top at one thousand metres.

We strolled around the deeply dissected plateau-like surface of the mountain, marvelling at the views north to the beaches of Bloubergstrand and Robben Island and south across False Bay. On the east side, the remnant clouds and mist drained away down the valleys stretching below us.

Rock hyrax, known locally as dassies, scampered around the cliffs. They looked like portly meerkats, but the pamphlet we'd been given with our cable car tickets offered us the unlikely fact that they were most closely related to elephants and manatees.

Lara had brought the binoculars and was able to confirm that they had two unusual canines protruding from their top lip—vestigial tusks, according to the pamphlet.

I got us cups of tea from the restaurant, and we found a cluster of rocks forming a kind of big armchair looking west out over the ocean. We made ourselves comfortable, and Lara put her arms around me. We watched an Agama lizard sunning itself, its head a beautiful iridescent turquoise. As I raised the tea to my lips, I felt a shiver run through my body, and I knew at once that, as had happened in my past, I was about to have a panic attack. I was sitting in one of the most beautiful places on the planet with a woman who said she loved me and with a future that looked promising, perfect conditions for my counterintuitive response.

Lara felt me tense.

"What's the matter, David?" She raised her head from my shoulder and gave me an anxious look.

I gazed into her eyes, the green irises sparkling with flecks of gold. She cared for me in a way that no one had for decades. I had made a commitment to her. I had to do better than this. If I could put this behind me by force of will, I would. *"It's always impossible till it's done."* I pursed my lips.

"Nothing's wrong, Lara. In fact, I can't imagine how things could be much better."

I felt my pulse slow, and the tingling sensation in my chest abated. I kissed her.

That evening I asked Malcolm to make reservations for us at the revolving restaurant on top of the Ritz. I also asked him to have them put a bottle of Krug on ice for 7:00 p.m. We had something to celebrate.

We took a cab to the Ritz and stopped into the lavish lobby bar where we had a cocktail and ordered our food. Lara opted for the slow-cooked citrus chicken supreme, and I went for the creamy smoked salmon linguine with basil and cherry tomatoes. Our cocktails finished, we took the elevator to the twenty-fifth floor and the maître d' showed us to our table and introduced our server. The champagne was uncorked, and Lara tried it.

"Just right. Are we celebrating something, David?" she asked coyly.

"Well, at least one thing," I said.

We raised our glasses.

"To love and the pursuit of happiness," I said.

Lara smiled. "I'll drink to that."

CHAPTER 7

I

Sarah Gillen lived in the neighbourhood of Maitland, east of the waterfront. As Lara piloted the Land Cruiser from the hotel through Woodstock, the roads got rougher, and the homes got smaller. Shopping centers gave way to strip malls, and payday loan stores took over from health food shops.

"I'd expected the former wife of 'Honest Ed' Parkes to be living in something grander than this," Lara said as we pulled up at the address Stephen had given us.

The house was a small clapboard bungalow set back from the road and surrounded by a large well-kept garden. As we pushed open the wrought-iron garden gate, its rusty hinges gave a high-pitched squeal. In response, frantic barking started from somewhere inside the house.

I rang the doorbell, which inspired the barker to redouble its efforts.

The door was opened by a woman in her forties wearing faded blue jeans and a grey T-shirt. Her hair was strawberry blond, her eyes were grey, and she wore a chain of blue lapis stones around her neck. Even though she was pale, she was very pretty.

"Can I help you?" she said in a quiet voice lacking in inflection.

"We're looking for Sarah," Lara said.

"You've found her. You're from the school?"

"I'm Lara Rios, and this is my colleague, David Mallory, and yes, Shelburne has asked us to look into Tom's death. We're so sorry for your loss."

"I told them I'm not ready to talk about any of this," Sarah said while standing aside and ushering us into her compact living room. A small white dog sniffed us suspiciously as we entered. Sarah indicated that we should sit, and the dog gave a final half-hearted yap as we did so.

"We know how difficult this must be, but we believe that the sooner we can assemble all the pieces, the sooner we can help you find some closure on this tragedy," Lara said.

"You say you know how difficult this must be," Sarah replied, "but you don't, do you? How could you? My son has died." She didn't cry, but her emotionless voice and wooden expression said more than tears ever could.

There was a long pause, which Lara ended.

"Actually, Sarah, I do."

The two women looked at each other across the small room. Sarah stood and took a step toward Lara who left her chair and met her halfway. They put their arms around each other and stood there in silence holding each other.

After perhaps a minute, Sarah pushed Lara to arm's length but still held onto her, looking unblinking into her eyes. "Two weeks ago I thought I was the only mother in the world who had ever felt this way," she said.

"I know," Lara replied softly. "I felt the same way when Alex died. As time passes you will meet many women who have lost a child. It is your sorrow for life, but if you're lucky you can come to terms with it and endure, maybe even find happiness again, although I know you can't imagine that right now."

"No, I can't." Sarah moved back to her chair.

"What do you want from me? What do you think I can tell you that the police don't already know? I have answered a thousand questions already."

Lara sat down and looked over at me.

I leaned forward in my chair, careful to keep my voice quiet and gentle. Lara had set the perfect tone for us with her genuine empathy, and I didn't want to spoil that. "Sarah, it would be helpful for us to know more about Tom. What kind of boy was he? What did he enjoy doing? What were his dreams for the future? Did he have any problems at school? The kind of things that a mother knows best."

"You're asking me to talk to you about my son? You want to get to know Tom? I wish the counsellor and the psychiatrist had given me a chance to talk about Tom rather than asking me about how I was feeling and whether I had suicidal thoughts. That's all I want to do right now. I want to think about Tom and talk about Tom every minute of every day. Poor Sam, he must be feeling neglected on top of everything else. I think he despairs of me." She smiled wistfully.

For the better part of an hour, Sarah painted a picture of a capable, well-adjusted adolescent boy who loved reading and rugby; a boy who dreamed of going to university in the US on a swimming scholarship; a boy who was kind to others and who had experienced his first crush; a boy who had his insecurities but who was growing out of them. The story was similar to those we had heard from Pius, Chief Inspector Oliver, Kristy, and others. Tom was a happy, popular young man. Sarah spoke with the love and honesty of a mother who knew her boy.

"How did Tom get along with his father?" I asked.

"Have you met Ed?" Sarah replied.

"Not yet. We have an appointment with him tomorrow."

"Ah." One syllable implying many more. "Tom and Sam are very different boys. They are . . ." She paused and bit her lip. "They *were* best friends, but they were very different. Sam takes everything at face value. Tom is . . .Tom *was* more introspective. He asked questions; he wanted to know the reasons why things happen. Sam idolizes his father. He admires his success, his brashness, his nice car, his toys. Tom was hurt by the divorce and was very attentive to me after it happened. He blamed his father for breaking up the family. I know that's a bit naïve, but it was how he was. Tom had a highly attuned sense of right and wrong. He thought his father broke too many rules."

"And did he?" Lara asked.

"He's a billionaire, Lara. I don't think you get that rich without stepping on people, without bending those rules you can bend and breaking or changing those you can't. I know that sounds cynical, but I lived with Ed for fifteen years, and I know how he is."

"You must have loved him when you married him," Lara said.

"I've thought a lot about that over the past two years," she said. "I think I was in love with the image Ed projected. He can be very charming, and he had big dreams. I don't think Ed ever loved me. I used to be quite good looking, and I think Ed wanted to be seen with me on his arm. I'm a person who likes to please others, and I know Ed saw in me someone he could manipulate. Ed is not a nice person. His ego is his moral compass. And he's a bully."

"Did he hurt you?" Lara asked. "Physically, I mean?"

Sarah stared hard at a point on the floor "Yes, he beat me more than once. It usually happened if a business deal had gone wrong or if someone was standing up to him, calling his bluff." There was a long silence. "The night that the boys were conceived . . . he raped me."

Lara glanced at me. "Did you report it to the police?"

"What would have been the point? He knows the top brass. He would have made it go away. I should have left him, but I was scared, and when the twins arrived, they provided a reason for me to stay in the marriage."

"You're still a very attractive woman, Sarah," Lara said.

Sarah gave her a sad smile but said nothing.

I had to ask. "Have you had any contact with Lena Michaels?"

"Poor Lena," Sarah replied. Not the response I had expected.

"She's from an impoverished background and I think she sees Ed as a ticket to riches. We've talked a couple of times. She's actually quite sweet. If she toned down the clothing and the image, she might have a better chance of making friends in the Shelburne community but that's not what Ed wants. He wants the world to see a young woman in a tight skirt and a tube top fawning over him. It's a bit sad and pathetic. I don't envy her."

"You've been incredibly helpful to us," Lara said, "but I think we've taken up enough of your time, and we should go now." She stood, and I followed her lead.

"No, actually, thank you both. This has been good for me."

Lara stepped in to give Sarah another hug.

"You don't ever need to talk about Tom in the past tense. He's alive every day in your memory. Keep breathing, Sarah. You can get through this. Keep breathing, and call me if you need to talk."

Sarah opened the door for us. The little white dog gave my trouser leg one last sniff as we walked away.

II

We picked up the R27 and drove for fifteen minutes to the beach at Bloubergstrand. We didn't speak much. I parked the car in a slot on the seafront overlooking the wide expanse of beach and the big Atlantic surf.

"That wasn't quite what I was expecting," I said, staring ahead through the windshield.

"She's been through a lot but she's strong," Lara replied.

A few surfers were riding the big green rollers, gulls hanging in the air overhead.

"She doesn't have much good to say about her former husband." I turned on the engine, rolled down my window, and turned it off again.

"I believed her. It wasn't to her advantage or her credit to describe what a bastard she'd spent fifteen years with, but she's ready to be honest with herself. I liked her a lot."

The salty tang of the ocean and the raucous screaming of the gulls wafted in through the open window.

"Everything she said about Tom adds to the mystery of how a well-adjusted boy who was a strong swimmer drowned in a lake he'd swum in a hundred times before. Also, it seems odd that he chose to go swimming alone, don't you think? The boy had a legion of friends."

"It's more than a bit odd," Lara said, "but I'll think better with some oxygen in my lungs, so let's take a trek down the beach and then, if you're good, I'll buy you an ice cream."

I smirked. "Thanks, Mum."

We left our shoes in the car and walked barefoot along the strand. The wind was fresh and in our faces. That and the loud crashing of the waves made conversation difficult, so we walked briskly for maybe five kilometres, turned around, and walked back at a gentler pace.

I reached for Lara's hand.

"You do realize I wouldn't have been allowed across the threshold today unless you had been with me, and even if I had made it inside, Sarah wouldn't have shared what she did in the way that she did."

"You know, I tend to doubt myself, David, but yes, I agree that my presence was important today. Sarah needed to speak to a woman. We're both women who have lost a child, and that is a powerful sisterhood. No one else can know how that feels. Tomorrow with Mr. Parkes will be different though. Perhaps it would work better if you saw him on your own."

"No, you read people better than I do, and I'd really like you to come along. Unless you would be uncomfortable meeting him after what we heard from Sarah."

"I'm fine with it. I'm really rather a strong person, David." Was there a note of rebuke in her voice?

We walked up the slope of the beach to the road, found a general store, and ordered our ice cream.

We had dinner in the suite again that evening. After dinner I called Jessica in the UK. She sounded happy with life at Cambridge. She loved living in college. The teachers were super smart, and she had made some friends. There was mention of a French boy named Stephane, and I couldn't help grimacing. She said she was hoping to come and visit me in Florida for New Year. Could she maybe bring Stephane?

"Of course," I said. I'd have to get used to the idea that she wasn't a little girl anymore. She told me she missed me. I told her the same.

After I hung up, I told Lara about the boyfriend.

"What do you want more than anything else for Jessica?" she asked.

"I want her to be happy, and I want her to be independent."

"Think back to when you were her age. If you're honest, you'll admit that the important lessons were learned when you stepped outside your comfort zone and tried something new, even if it was a disaster."

"I know all that," I said. "I spent thirty years telling parents that they needed to allow their children room to grow, but it's a bit harder when you share DNA with the person!"

"The important thing is that she's willing to talk to you and tell you the truth about what she's doing. I'll bet she tells you stuff she doesn't tell her parents."

I knew that was true, but it helped to hear Lara say it.

III

A light rain was falling when we awoke on Monday morning. The tail of a cold front moving up from Antarctica had brushed the Western Cape overnight, and there was a chill in the air, unusual for October. However, by the time we were ready to head out and meet Ed Parkes, the sun was peeking through the clouds, and the cape sparrows were drinking water from the puddles in the parking lot.

Lara drove. She was an excellent driver; confident but careful. I was enjoying the opportunity to spend more time looking at the scenery. The vehicle hugged the twisting road as we again headed for Fish Hoek, arriving at the Richmond Country Club in good time for our noon rendezvous.

We left the car with the valet and walked into the clubhouse. We announced ourselves at reception and were shown to a table at the far end of a large dining room. Antique golf clubs and sepia photos of sportsmen from another era decorated the bleached pine panelling of the walls. On the floor a vast swath of red-and-green tartan carpet ran from wall to wall.

The server brought us water and asked if we would like to order a drink; we said we were expecting someone else and that we'd wait.

From where we sat, we could see the golfers coming off the eighteenth tee, and we challenged each other to guess which one was Ed Parkes.

Just before noon a party of four men left the green with handshakes and back slaps. One of them was a tall man wearing khaki slacks and a bottle-green V-neck sweater over a pink golf shirt. Something about him made us look at each other and say, "That one," in unison.

Perhaps five minutes later, the same man strode across the tartan carpet toward us.

"You are Ms. Rios and Mr. Mallory, I think?" He stretched out a long arm and shook hands with us in turn.

A server approached and held the chair for him as he sat down.

"A bottle of the Constantia Chenin Blanc and three glasses please, Linda," he said.

"Right away, Mr. Parkes. Can I bring some starters for the table?"

"Have the chef put together a plate of the grilled scallops with 'nduja butter, and bring some sea bream ceviche. Then we'll have the roast tenderloin, medium rare. And bring a bottle of the ninety-eight Pinotage with that. We have to show my new friends here how we do things at Richmond."

Hospitable or overbearing, time would tell. With the server gone, his tone changed. "I cannot fathom why Dr. Croken is wasting your time. The first coroner made an entirely professional assessment. The boy drowned. It happens a lot in our country."

He spoke of his son as if he was just another young person who had died by misadventure. There was no warmth in his voice; neither was there regret.

"We need to bury the boy and move on. All this screwing around isn't helping anyone, and it surely won't bring him back."

Up close I could see that he'd had cosmetic surgery. Living in South Florida, I saw a lot of that and recognized the signs. The skin on his tanned face was pulled just a little too tightly across his cheekbones, causing the corners of his mouth to be lifted into an unnatural and slightly ghoulish permanent smile. He'd also had filler injected into his lips, and they looked too soft for a man of his age, almost feminine. It made for an incongruous effect.

"We're here to do the job we've been retained by Shelburne to perform, Mr. Parkes. If that allows us to confirm the original findings, we will do that," I assured him.

"And if it doesn't?" His voice was cold.

"Then our mandate is to explore other possibilities."

"Surely you must want to be fully satisfied about the cause of Tom's death, Mr. Parkes," Lara said.

"That's all we're doing here," I added, "trying to ensure that the truth is served."

The wine arrived. Parkes inspected the bottle, gave an affirmative grunt, and the sommelier opened it. He waited while Parkes sipped and approved it and then poured three glasses.

Right behind it the starters were served.

"I find that the truth can be overrated," Parkes said. "What we have now satisfies me and works for Shelburne. Why the hell would you mess with that?"

He helped himself to some scallops and pushed the plate toward me.

"I'm not sure that the boy's mother would agree with you," Lara said.

"You've met her, have you? I hope she was on her meds. It's not pretty otherwise," he sneered. "She's wacko. Has been for years. I couldn't take it anymore; that's why I kicked her out. I couldn't trust her. Have you seen where she lives? I give her a pile of alimony, and she lives in a shack in Maitland. By the way, my lawyers have lodged an appeal to cut the payments now that she only has one son to support."

He reached for the ceviche while he was still chewing the scallops. "Hey, help yourself, little lady, while there's still some left."

Lara didn't respond, but I saw the muscle in her jaw tighten. She hadn't touched her wine. But we needed to find out what we could, so we had to keep the conversation going. I served myself some ceviche and offered to put some on Lara's plate. She shook her head.

"How was your relationship with Tom?" I asked. Might as well go straight at it.

"What do you mean by that? The usual, I imagine. He was my son, so I loved him even though he inherited some of his mother's unfortunate traits."

"Such as?"

"Such as he was always thinking about people's feelings and talking about doing the right thing. I hoped both the boys would grow up to take on the business I've built, but he'd have been useless. He'd have looked for 'win-win' outcomes and met people halfway. Business doesn't work that way, Mr. Mallory."

"And how does it work?" I asked. Parkes was opening up, and I wanted to keep him going.

"Someone wins and someone loses. Croken said you're a successful man, Mallory. I'm surprised you don't know that. I do what's needed to win, and I do so consistently. Tom was too soft; he'd have been a failure. Sam, on the other hand, there's a young man who will go far."

"What is your business, Mr. Parkes?" I'd done my homework, and I knew, but I wanted him to tell us. I wanted to hear how he described it.

"You haven't heard of me, Mallory? That's not very impressive. Most people in South Africa know me. I have a finger in many pies. Petrosur, the biggest oil company in southern Africa, that's me. The Golden Horizon chain of casinos, I founded that. Fidelis Healthcare, Canova Agriculture Holdings, both hostile takeovers. Kimberley Mining, I bought that from the Brits for a song—screwed them. Armstrong Security Services; nice to have some muscle at your beck and call. I've made a few enemies, Mallory." He smiled as if that was a badge of honour. "So, you see, it's hard to live for a day in this country without buying something from one of my companies and giving me some of your money."

"Dr. Croken said you're generous with your money," Lara said, re-entering the conversation.

"It's good from a tax perspective," he replied. "If I don't give it away, the government gets it, and I don't like that." He grinned. A bit of ceviche was stuck between his front teeth.

"I understand you have been philanthropic to the school," Lara said. She even managed a smile.

"Look, I went to the school. Hated every minute of it, by the way. Couldn't wait to leave. But, hey, the boys go there. Lena, that's my wife—my new wife—she needs something to do, so I made a deal that if I coughed up some cash, they'd make sure she got some volunteer jobs around the place. They put me on the board, so that's good for my image. Shelburne is a bastion of respectability. So, yeah, you could say I'm a philanthropist." He laughed and took a big swig of his wine.

At that point an older man with a florid complexion and a large gut waddled up to the table and patted Parkes on the shoulder.

"I hear you won a bunch of money off those stiffs this morning, Ed," he slurred.

Parkes flinched at the man's touch. "Fuck off, Ernie. Can't you see I'm busy?"

"No need to be like that Ed."

"Yes there is. Now fuck off back to the bar, you old drunk."

Parkes leaned back in his chair and sighed. "Shit, this isn't going very well, is it? Look, if there's anything else you want from me, call my office." He stood up just as a small squad of servers arrived to carve and serve the roast.

He reached for his wallet, pulled out a sizable wad of notes, and threw them on the table as a tip.

"Take it away. Eat it yourselves. I don't care."

He looked across at Lara. "You're a pretty little thing, aren't you?"

He gave her a lascivious smile, his overly plump lips pulled back over his teeth, then turned and stalked off across the tartan carpet.

"Get me out of here," Lara said. "I need a shower."

IV

I drove back to town while Lara sat fuming in the passenger seat.

"What a repulsive human being. How can anyone think they're allowed to act like that? Do you think he has any idea what he sounds like? Imagine Sarah having to live with that creature for fifteen years."

I hadn't seen Lara so annoyed before. It was impressive.

"It happens a lot, especially in South Florida where the super rich congregate," I said. "Their wealth seems to make them forget they're still part of the human race. They don't need to be nice to anybody to make a living, so they choose not to be. Then they think the rules of society don't apply to them, and they construct an alternative universe that's whatever they think it is. It doesn't happen to them all though. I know some very down-to-earth billionaires who realize their wealth was, in large part, a matter of good luck, but Ed Parkes isn't one of those."

"He's just lost a child, for heaven's sake," Lara fumed. "All he could do was criticize the child and slander the mother."

"I know how cross you are, and I agree his behaviour was appalling, but we're here on a job, so we have to focus on what we have learned, not on his obnoxious personality. If we hadn't been on business, I would have asked him to step outside for what he said to you."

"You would? Oh, David that is so sweet of you, and I believe you would have. Your British sense of chivalry would have demanded it."

"Duelling pistols at twenty yards. He would have died like a dog." I smiled across at her.

"I know you're right," she said. "I need to be a professional if I'm going to be helpful to you, but it was the way he looked at me. It was like a threat.

"And, by the way, you don't need to worry about fighting duels for me. My parents made me take Tae Kwon Do classes in Bogota. Those were dangerous times, and they thought a girl should be able to defend herself at least from predators if not from the cartels. I really enjoyed it, and I've kept it up ever since. I've made it to black belt, blue collar, so, if unarmed combat is involved, you're fairly safe hanging around with me."

"You're a very surprising woman, Lara," I replied, and I wasn't joking.

"So, what did we learn?" I asked. "Did he say anything that needs further investigation?"

"I thought there were two moments when he said more than he intended. One was when he showed us his preference for Sam, and the other was when he said he didn't trust Sarah."

I nodded. "Bingo. That's what struck me too. I think we need to go back to campus and speak to Kristy van Kleef. She said she knew Tom like a brother from her role as his mentor. Perhaps she can shed some light on Tom's relationship with his parents, but before that we need to speak to Sarah again and see what this issue of trust is all about."

"She gave me her mobile number; shall I call her?"

"Do that. Perhaps we can drop in now. Tell her we won't keep her long."

Forty minutes later we pulled up in front of the clapboard bungalow again. Most of the people in Maitland are black or coloured. A vigorous game of soccer was happening in the street outside the house involving children from both communities. A porch ran the full length of the front of Sarah's house, and she was sitting in its shade watching the game and sipping a cup of what looked like herbal tea. Her little white dog sat on a cushion at her side. She beckoned us to the two other seats.

"Welcome back," she said, smiling. "I didn't think I'd see you again so soon. I was afraid I talked your ear off yesterday."

"Thanks for allowing us to drop by," I said. "We had lunch with Mr. Parkes, and there was something we wanted to ask you about."

Sarah wrinkled her nose. "How did it go?" she asked, looking at Lara.

"Well, it was interesting and helpful, I think." Lara's tone was calm and professional.

"I hope you don't mind if I'm rather direct in asking this, Sarah," I said.

"Ask away," she replied. "I spent years making excuses for Ed to myself and others, so you won't surprise me."

"At one point in our conversation, he said that one of the reasons for the divorce was that he didn't trust you anymore. What do you think he meant by that?"

Sarah stood up and walked to the porch railing. The dog followed her. She watched the children playing on the street for a few seconds before turning back to us.

"It's hard to say," she began. "Ed's business dealings got increasingly complex over the years that we were together. I wasn't any part of them, but

I was in the house when he made telephone calls, and I was at dinners that were designed to grease the wheels of business, so I had a fair idea of what he was doing and how he was doing it."

Out on the street a goal was scored, accompanied by cheering. Sarah turned and applauded, and the children waved back at her.

"I got to know that the casino business was in trouble. The government had increased the regulation on gambling, and the profit margins were lower. Ed was trying to find ways to generate more value from the properties, and that involved meeting with some pretty shady characters. I'm not sure exactly what he was up to, but I'm sure he got himself involved in something that he couldn't control, and he wasn't used to that.

"I heard him on the phone in his office one time when I was sorting through the boys' outgrown clothing in the next room. When he hung up, he left the office and was surprised to find me in the passage outside. He wasn't happy, and he started screaming at me, calling me a snoop and a spy. He really lost it. I told him I didn't hear anything, but things got a lot worse between us after that."

"Was there anything else?" I asked.

Sarah looked sad. She picked up the little dog and let it lick her face. "There was this one time when Ed invited two couples around to dinner. He said it was business. It wasn't unusual for him to bring clients around from time to time, so I didn't find it surprising. But the following week, I was watching the news, and there was a report of a fatal shooting in Polokwane. They showed a picture of a man whom they said was suspected of running drugs into South Africa from Mozambique. He was one of the men who'd sat at our table the week before."

Lara and I sat up in our chairs.

"Do you remember the man's name?" I asked.

"Only because it was memorable. Ed introduced him to me as John when he came to dinner, but the television reporter said his name was Juan 'Snake Eyes' Gonzalez, and he was involved with a Colombian cartel." Sarah let out an embarrassed chuckle. "I know it's not funny, but I sound so ridiculous standing here with a fluffy dog in my arms on this quiet street with the children playing on the road and telling you about a dead drug lord called 'Snake Eyes.'"

Lara smiled back at her. "No. I get it," she said. "You're certain it was the same man?"

"I have no doubt, unfortunately."

"Did you talk to Ed about it?" I asked.

"You won't understand this, but it really wasn't possible for me to do that. Ed would have gotten very upset, and by then I was frightened of him."

"I do understand," Lara said.

"How long after that did he start divorce proceedings?" I asked.

"Not long. The man was murdered in July, and Ed's attorney served me the papers in September. On my birthday, actually. I wouldn't be surprised if Ed chose the date on purpose."

Lara stood, and I followed suit.

"Again, Sarah, this has been incredibly helpful to us. Be assured that your comments will be held in confidence. If we feel we need to share them with anyone, we'll ask your permission first."

"I'm not worried," she said. "I really don't fear anything anymore. Do what you need to do, I'll be OK."

The women embraced, and I shook Sarah's hand. We walked back to the car. It's size and opulence were out of place in that modest street. A couple of the youngest children were running around it, jumping up and down trying to see in the windows.

"I'll drive," Lara said, and I passed her the keys.

As we drove off, out of habit, I glanced in the side mirror. Apart from the kids, the street was empty except for a small red sedan parked two houses down.

"What would you like to do for dinner tonight?" Lara asked. "I'm starving. You probably noticed that I didn't have much enthusiasm for lunch."

"Me neither. I had one scallop before I lost my appetite."

"Let's ask Malcolm what the chef recommends and have that served in the suite. Trying not to throttle Ed Parkes took a lot out of me, and I picture us being busy tomorrow."

"You called it right. That's perfect. We could go for a swim before dinner if you're up for it."

We were back at the hotel in twenty minutes. The valet took the keys from Lara. As we walked into the lobby, out of the corner of my eye I saw a small red sedan cruise through the forecourt.

V

We took a shower after our swim and then lay on the bed together. I knew Lara had been hurt by Ed Parkes, though she was determined not to show it. She rolled over and threw an arm across my chest.

"Would you really fight for me?" she asked.

I nodded. "I would."

She wriggled up the bed and kissed me. Then she straddled me.

"I would fight for you; you know that, don't you?" she asked.

"I believe you would, and I wouldn't like to be the person on the receiving end."

She frowned. "Are you mocking me?"

"No. I wouldn't dare."

"Very wise," she said, giving me a fierce look. Then she slid down beside me, and we held each other close.

Dinner arrived an hour or so after we had finished making love.

The chef had surpassed himself. We started with smoked trout with watercress and tarragon and followed that with a seafood-and-chorizo paella served with grilled broccolini. It was so good that there wasn't much conversation, just gentle sighs of appreciation. We drank most of the bottle of Pinotage that Malcolm had recommended, and it was excellent.

"We should probably check in with Pius tomorrow," Lara said as we pushed our chairs back.

"You're right, and I'll ask if it's OK for us to have a conversation with Kristy. It's only nine o'clock. Let me call Stephen now and see if he can fix it up."

I got Stephen on the third ring. I could hear domestic sounds in the background, including one child who definitely didn't want to go to bed.

"Let me look at Dr. Croken's commitments." There was a pause. "Yes, he's available after chapel. Please come by at nine thirty tomorrow morning. I'll look at Kristy's schedule and see what might work for her, but you will need Dr. Croken's permission to speak with her."

"Of course. Thank you, Stephen. See you in the morning. Goodnight."

We took our wine out onto the balcony. The water in the harbour was flat and calm. Sirius and Alpha Centauri twinkled brightly in the deep-purple canopy as the last of the daylight was drained from the western sky. I put my arm around Lara's shoulder.

"I'm pretty sure we were followed back from Sarah's place today," I said. I didn't want to alarm her, but if we were in this together, as we surely were, we needed to be clear about the risks.

"The little red car?" she said, cool as a cucumber. "I wondered about that."

CHAPTER 8

I

The Shelburne campus was looking particularly splendid when we arrived. The jacarandas were laden with purple blossoms, and pink orchid-like flowers hung from the cape chestnuts. A gang mower was cutting stripes across the formal lawn in front of the original building as we pulled into one of the visitors' parking spots. We inhaled the smell of newly mown grass as we made our way to reception, where we were greeted warmly and invited to take a seat. Pius swept through the front entrance a few minutes later. He was wearing an academic gown that billowed around him.

"Lara, David, so good to see you. Come in, come in." He ushered us into his office.

"Sit, please sit." He pointed to the table by the window as he hung up his gown and joined us. "Can I get you anything? I was going to have some rooibos tea. Will you join me?"

We said we would, and he called through to the outer office.

"So, tell me what you've been up to and what progress you've made. I'm all ears."

It took the better part of thirty minutes to run through the events of the past several days, Pius punctuating our narrative with questions. When we had finished, he leaned back in his chair.

"So, you would say that we're justified in looking at this thing more closely?"

"I'm afraid so," I said, nodding. "The police aren't very interested in pursuing it, but we believe there are several loose ends that could unravel if we pull at them."

"No, no. Don't be afraid to tell me that. We have to get to the truth. It's the only thing that will bring a proper resolution. Stephen tells me that you would like to speak to Kristy van Kleef."

"We would. She was Tom's mentor last year, and I think she has a good understanding of the boy."

"I would normally require a female employee of Shelburne to sit in with you, but I suspect that would inhibit Kristy," Pius said. "You're a former headmaster, and Lara will be with you, so I'm willing to waive that protocol. I have spoken to Kristy, and she's prepared to speak to you, but please bear in mind that she is seventeen years old and that she is in my care. She is waiting for you by the old tennis court. It's a quiet, discreet location, and I thought meeting outside might be less inhibiting. Stephen will show you the way."

We found Kristy sitting on a bench in the shade of a tall lilac bush. In contrast to the poised school ambassador of our first visit, she looked young and nervous.

"Hello, Kristy," Lara said, sitting down beside her. "Thank you so much for being willing to chat with us. I know it's not easy."

"Thank you, Ms. Rios." The girl relaxed perceptibly.

"I think it's probably better if we all use first names, so it's Lara and David."

"That's contrary to our guardian training." Kristy smiled. "But I'll try."

"Why don't you start by telling us about the Tom you got to know last year," Lara said. "We'll have some questions later, but that would be a great place to begin."

Kristy was hesitant at first but soon hit her stride, and in five minutes she had described the boy we had gotten to know through his mother.

"And you were fond of Tom?" I asked when she had finished.

She smiled. "It was hard not to like Tom. I should probably say that I think he had a crush on me at first, but by the end of the year we had become just good friends. As I told you before, he was almost like a little brother to me."

"Did he talk to you about his father, Kristy?" Lara asked.

The girl dropped her eyes and exhaled. "I was afraid you were going to ask me that." She took a deep breath. "He talked a lot about his parents. He hated his father for the way that he treated his mother. He told me that he was violent with her."

"And?" Lara prodded.

"And . . ." Kristy shifted uncomfortably. "Tom told me that his father was mixed up in some pretty bad stuff. Criminal stuff."

"Did he ever specify what kind of criminal stuff?" Lara pressed.

"Drugs," Kristy said softly. "He said his father dealt drugs through the casinos."

"Did he tell you what made him think that?" I asked.

She turned toward me. "He said his father shouted a lot and that he overheard some phone calls."

"Did he say what kind of drugs?"

"No. He didn't know."

"You have been very brave, Kristy." Lara reached out and touched her hand. A tear rolled down the girl's cheek. "What you have told us will help us to find out the truth, and that's the best thing we can do for Tom now."

"I know." Kristy sniffed. "But I miss him."

We walked her back to school and checked in with Pius, telling him that we would give him another update in a few days. He wished us well and then we walked back to the car.

"We've got some thinking to do," Lara said.

"We do," I agreed. "Let's drive over to Kirstenbosch Gardens; it's just around the corner. We can go for a walk and a talk. We're going to crack this one; I can feel it."

II

Kirstenbosch was amazing. It's one of the best botanical gardens in the world, and it was the perfect time of year to visit with so much coming into springtime bloom. It was almost incongruous to be strolling through such beauty talking about such dark topics.

We walked the trails for an hour and ended up on the boomslang, a boardwalk built high in the forest canopy.

We talked through the pattern that was emerging. Dr. Naidoo was convinced that there was something suspicious about Tom's death. Tom hated his father. His father was a sociopath. Both Sarah and Kristy had said it was possible that Parkes was involved with organized crime. We thought we had been followed from Sarah's house to the hotel. There was nothing definitive, but there was a lot of background noise.

David was leaning over the railing of the boomslang when his mobile rang. He spoke for a few seconds and then rang off.

"It looks like our next step has been decided for us. That was Dr. Naidoo."

"Don't tell me. She wants to take me shopping," I joked.

"Well, she probably does, but right now she wants to meet us at the Rondebosch Medical Centre. She thinks she may have found some new evidence."

III

"Milk in your tea, David? I've forgotten. I know Lara takes lemon."

"Yes, please." David said.

Dr. Naidoo performed her daily tea ceremony. She took a sip, then set the cup on the table, placed her hands on her thighs, and looked back and forth between us. "As you know, I'm convinced that Tom died in a location other than Plashy Pond. This necessitates that his body was moved from the place of death to the pond. I just wasn't satisfied that I had read his body fully and completely. There were no obvious signs of external trauma, but that does not rule out the possibility that a pathogen was introduced into his body. The puncture mark from a syringe, for example, would be very hard to detect."

"If he was poisoned wouldn't that show up in the blood work that was done?" I asked.

"Not necessarily, but we'll get to that. I spent the whole of yesterday morning going over the surface of his body using epiluminescence spectroscopy. I used a dermatoscope, which is a magnifying lens with an attached light source. Typically, we use it to identify melanomas in the living, but it comes in handy with the dead as well. It took me several hours, but finally I found a small puncture wound toward the top of one buttock."

"If Tom was experimenting with intravenous drugs, surely that's an unusual location to choose," David offered.

"Unusual and highly unsatisfactory, David. Intravenous implies injection into the vein. The buttocks are fatty tissue."

"Of course. I stand corrected." David looked slightly miffed.

"Could he even physically have managed to inject himself there?" I asked.

"It would not have been impossible, but it would have been difficult. Improbable. It seems much more likely that the syringe was inserted by someone else."

"To what end?" I asked.

"That would depend on what was injected, if anything. That led me to consider substances that could have been injected but would not be easily detectable in a post-mortem. There are a number of candidates, and I had my suspicions, but I try to be diligent in following the scientific method." She paused to take another sip of tea.

"I ordered both histopathological and directed toxicological analyses of the tissue around the puncture site. I also called in a few favours and had my colleagues at the university hospital run mass spectrometry on a sample of vitreous humour that I extracted."

"Vitreous humour?" I asked.

"It's a colourless jelly that we all have between the lens and the retina in our eyes. The results came in this morning, and they are as I suspected. They indicate that someone gave Tom a large dose of insulin by injection."

"Surely insulin isn't toxic," I said. "Lots of diabetics inject themselves daily."

"Indeed, it's a lifeline for millions," she said. "If your pancreas is unable to produce the correct quantity of insulin, the injection of a measured dose will allow you to live a full and active life. However, the injection of a large dose of insulin into a person who has a normally functioning pancreas will have severe consequences and is extremely hard to detect in a post-mortem."

"If you're right, how do you think Tom died?" I asked.

"I think we can say that the ultimate cause of death was drowning, Lara. As you know, water containing diagnostic diatoms was found in the boy's lungs. That suggests he was not dead when he entered the water. However, the symptoms brought on by an insulin overdose are many and unpleasant. His blood glucose level would plummet, causing sweating, anxiety, and tremors. Beyond that his central nervous system would begin to shut down. Eventually, he would experience loss of consciousness and convulsions. Death would normally follow."

"The poor boy must have suffered terribly." I couldn't bear to think of someone doing that to a child.

Dr. Naidoo nodded. "It's not pleasant. I postulate that Tom was introduced into a water body at the point that he was convulsing and semiconscious and that he drowned before he died of insulin poisoning."

"What will you do with these results?" I asked. "Surely the police will have to reopen the investigation."

"I'm duty bound to alert Chief Inspector Olivier. You have met him?"

"David has," I replied. "I haven't yet had the pleasure."

"I think he has already made up his mind on this case," Dr. Naidoo continued. "However, the analyses that we have in hand are of a quality to be admissible as evidence in a criminal prosecution, so he may choose to take a second look."

"If he does, we'll work with him," David assured her. "If he doesn't we'll move ahead anyway. Frankly, I think I'd prefer the second option. What I'd like to do right now is head back to Maitland and talk to Sarah about this new information. It will be devastating for her, but it may make her want to tell us more about whatever shady business her ex-husband was involved in. I had the sense that she knew more than she was telling us."

I shook Dr. Naidoo's hand. Lara got a hug. We headed out from the cool of the office building into the bright sunshine of the street.

IV

I called Sarah's number, but there was no reply. I thought she'd be OK with us turning up unannounced, so we set off. We were getting to know our way around town, and we arrived at Sarah's street without having to resort to the GPS.

It was around 5:00 p.m., and the shadows of the trees were lengthening across the road as we approached the house. Lara knocked. There was lots of barking, but no one answered the door. She tried again, with no result. It seemed unlikely that Sarah had decided to leave the dog unattended, so I moved around the side of the house and looked in a couple of windows. The little dog saw me and redoubled its barking, but I couldn't see any sign of Sarah.

The bungalow was surrounded on three sides by a high wooden fence. The back garden was small but attractively planted with perennials and shrubs. There was an old apple tree in the centre of the small lawn. When we saw it,

Lara and I stopped short. Hanging from one of the lower branches was Sarah Gillen's body, rotating slowly in the gentle breeze. A blue wooden stool lay on its side in the grass beside her.

Lara gasped and clutched my arm. I was just as startled. I'd seen my share of society's underbelly, but I hadn't run into many corpses.

Slowly, we advanced toward where she hung. It was obvious that she was dead. Her eyes were swollen and rolled skywards, and her tongue protruded from between her blue lips.

"Please get her down, David," Lara said.

"We can't, Lara. It's a job for the police. Stay here while I make the call. I'll wait out front."

V

I liked Sarah, and she liked me. We had shared a heartbreaking experience, and we would have become friends; I know it. But that wouldn't happen now.

I took two steps toward the body and put my arms around her waist. I held her for maybe a minute trying to give her a moment of human affection before her body was carted off and dissected at the morgue. The police would tell me that I had contaminated the crime scene, but I didn't care.

Her body felt cool. "I know how you were feeling; you know that, don't you?" I think I spoke those words, but maybe I just thought them. "We know the pain, and we know the guilt, but remember that Tom loved you. When you strip everything away, it's the only thing that endures. Without love there is nothing."

We waited for about ten minutes till a squad car and an unmarked police car pulled up at the house. A few of the neighbours were out on the street attracted by the commotion and flashing lights. Two uniformed officers got out of the patrol car, and the man whom I recognized from David's description as Chief Inspector Olivier emerged from the other.

"Mr. Mallory," he said to David, "are you involved in all the deaths in Cape Town or just the high-profile ones?"

"I think you'll find there's a connection between this one and Tom Parkes," David said. "The woman hanging from the tree is Tom's mother."

The crime scene squad arrived and began their work. The crowd outside grew larger. There were tears as they realized what had happened. Sarah hadn't lived there long, but she'd won a lot of hearts.

Olivier asked us to meet him at the station in the morning. He also asked us to surrender our passports, which didn't feel very good, but we complied.

"Just a formality," he said. "You discovered the body, so you're suspects until we can eliminate you. We'll talk about that at the station."

Usually when I'm upset about something, I want to be alone, and that was my first thought as we drove away from the house. It was quickly overtaken by the realization that what I really wanted was to be alone with David.

"Do you remember the way to Bloubergstrand?" I asked as I pulled up at a traffic light. "I'd like to take another walk on the beach with you."

"Sure thing," David said. "Turn right at the next light and then you'll recognize the road."

I parked on the seafront just as we had forty-eight hours earlier. So much had happened in that short time.

The wind off the water was cool. I took a light fleece from the trunk and pulled it on.

We walked along the beach for a few minutes, but there were too many people around for what I wanted to do, so I took David's arm and steered him toward a surfing rental shack. We sat in its shelter, our backs against a wooden wall. We were out of the wind, and the sun had made the sand pleasantly warm.

VI

Alex loved playing soccer. He played on the wing, and his coach said he had the skills and attitude to get a scholarship to college if he worked hard.

He came home from practice one Friday evening complaining of a headache and feeling nauseated. He thought he might have given himself a concussion, so I took him to see our family doctor, who prescribed rest and no contact sports for two weeks.

Things didn't improve, so he went back a few days later, and the doctor ordered an MRI. That was on a Tuesday. On Wednesday morning I received a call from the nurse saying that Dr. Mendez wanted to see me. I asked her what it was about, but she was evasive.

Juanita Mendez is Colombian like me, and she'd been Alex's family doctor for all of his fifteen years.

I remember every single detail of that visit: the chill of the AC as I entered the Medical Arts building, the whirr of the elevator, the tiny jolt it gave as it stopped at the eighth floor, and the smell of disinfectant and floor polish in the hallway leading to Dr. Mendez's office.

The nurse waved me straight in, and I sat on a plastic chair on the other side of a grey metal desk from Dr. Mendez. She avoided the usual pleasantries and spoke in a quiet but direct way.

"The MRI has revealed some irregularities in the structure of Alex's brain, and we need to perform a biopsy."

I wasn't so much upset as surprised. Alex was an athlete and the epitome of a healthy adolescent.

I looked at the picture of Dr. Mendez's children set in a silver frame beside her computer. "What sort of irregularities?"

"I don't want to speculate before we do the biopsy, but the MRI has revealed some small tumours. They may very well be benign, and fortunately, they are in a place that makes them operable if required. We need to move quickly, and I have taken the liberty of booking theatre time for Alex tomorrow at Jackson Memorial. Even though it's only a biopsy, because of the location, it constitutes major surgery. We will need to give Alex a general anaesthetic. The procedure usually takes about two hours. Because Alex is a minor, we need your consent."

"Would you do this if it was Sacha or Gracie?" I asked, nodding toward the picture on her desk.

"I would," she said, nodding.

"Very well. I'll speak to Alex tonight. He knows that something is wrong. It's the first time he's ever really been sick, and he knows he's not right. What time do you want us at the hospital?"

"The theatre's booked for ten tomorrow morning, but the prepping will take about two hours, so please arrive at seven thirty. Check with Natalie on your way out; she has the paperwork you need to sign for consent and insurance."

I sat in the car in the parking lot for maybe twenty minutes. I felt strangely calm and detached. I think I'm pretty level-headed, but I began to imagine that what Dr. Mendez had said hadn't really happened. Perhaps it was a dream, a nightmare. I pinched myself and closed my eyes, then opened them again as I had when I was a child and wanted to escape from a bad dream, but nothing was different.

Less than twenty-four hours later, we had the results of the biopsy, and it couldn't have been any worse. Alex had glioblastoma.

I picked up a handful of the warm pink sand and let it sift through my fingers.

"How are you doing?" I looked over at David, offering him a rueful smile. He nodded and urged me on with his eyes.

The neurosurgeon with whom we spoke was a New Yorker named Ari Shapiro. He was encouraging but realistic; I could tell that Alex liked him. He described the treatment that he recommended: surgery followed by radiation and then a course of chemotherapy. He showed us diagrams and models of the brain and explained that glioblastoma is a difficult cancer because it grows into the brain tissue. While surgery can remove large parts of it, it can't get it all. That's where the radiation and chemo came in.

I cried when I was alone in bed most nights, but it wasn't so much because my baby's life was in danger; it was because Alex was so brave and had such a great attitude. He went at it as if it was just another challenge like introductory calculus or playing the guitar, both of which he'd mastered the year before. He tried so hard to cheer me up even when the chemo made it hard for him to get out of bed or eat anything. His shaven head was traced with scars, and the backs of his hands were bruised from the many catheters.

This was how things were up until the point when, after three surgeries, Dr. Shapiro called me in on my own and said we had a choice to make. He could perform another surgery with the radiation and chemo as a follow-up, or we could move to palliative care.

"What are the chances of success with another surgery?" I asked.

"You never know, Lara, but Alex has not responded as well as I had hoped, and I know that his quality of life is deteriorating. Because Alex is sixteen, it's you who will need to give me direction." He looked almost embarrassed to say it. "I know it's impossible . . . look, talk to Alex about it. I've seen the relationship you two have. You'll get it right."

"How long will he live with palliative care?" I asked

"The data suggests that from this point with a glioblastoma as aggressive as this one, three months would be the average of what we could expect."

"How will it progress?"

"Typically, drowsiness, maybe difficulty swallowing, usually headaches, but if you choose to go that route, the hospice is set up to give him the best care, and they will administer drugs to mitigate the symptoms."

I stood, and we shook hands.

"Take your time with this," he said.

The next morning after I'd helped Alex to the bathroom and washed him, I brought him a smoothie, which was the only thing he could keep down.

"What did you and Ari talk about yesterday, Mum?" He said it with the shadow of a smile on his lips because he knew.

He was pale and thin, and he had to grip the cup hard to stop his hand from trembling. We talked for at least an hour. Alex had already made up his mind before I even got around to telling him the choice that Dr. Shapiro had offered us. Alex didn't want to live if living was like it had been for the past year.

How could a sixteen-year-old look death in the eye and speak so calmly? His courage gave me courage, and he absolved me from the impossibility of making the only possible decision. My heart was breaking as I reached over to take his hand. He smiled at me.

"Come on, Mum, let's make a plan. No time to waste."

That was on November 4. I buried Alex nine weeks later.

I had to stop and breathe so as not to cry, and I didn't want to cry in front of David

"For the first few months after he died, I kept a journal, but the only entries were about the real estate business. Not because my dealings with the wealthy clients were so fascinating but because focusing on what I did helped me push aside what I felt, if only for a while. Perhaps it's a bit like why teenage girls cut themselves. The pain of the wound masks the pain in their hearts." I looked up at the sky and blinked back the tears that were forming despite my efforts.

"Where is Alex buried?" David asked, breaking a silence that had lasted maybe thirty seconds.

"My parents bought a family plot in Caballero Rivero in Little Havana. It's where they're buried. He's there, and there's a space beside him for me. It gives me some comfort to think of my bones resting beside his, but I'm hoping I won't be taking up residency for a while yet."

David smiled.

"There's one last thing that I want to tell you," I said. I realized this had been a heavy story to lay at David's door, but I wanted him to know everything.

"During Alex's illness I considered trying to contact his father. I really should have; I suppose he deserved to know even though he had never made any attempt to see Alex or to support us. I called a friend who I sometimes saw at the gym and who I knew saw Marcus from time to time. He gave me a number, and when I called it was answered by a young woman who announced herself as Bethany. I asked to speak to Marcus and was surprised by the long silence that followed.

"'You don't know?' she said eventually. 'No, how could you?'

"'Don't know what?' I asked, slightly irritated by her tone.

"'Marcus passed away two months ago,' she said. 'He had an inoperable brain tumour. The doctor called it glioblastoma.'

"I was stunned; it was my turn to be silent.

"'I'm so sorry,' I said. 'Are you . . . were you in a relationship with Marcus?'

"'Yeah, we'd lived together for five years. We have a girl, Regine. She really misses her dad. The doctors told me that there is sometimes a hereditary component to that kind of cancer, so I'm scared for her. She doesn't know that, of course. Why did you want to speak to Marcus?' she asked.

"I couldn't imagine that she would want to hear the reason that I had called, so I took the coward's way out and hung up."

"I don't think that's cowardly," David said. "Sometimes it's better not to know everything."

We sat in silence for several minutes watching the waves break and listening to the gulls screaming.

"How do you deal with the death of a child?" David asked at length. "I think I have a good imagination, but I can't conceive of how you must feel. There are so many dimensions to it."

I had to think for a moment because I'd never actually tried to verbalize how I was coping with it, if I was.

"It's so complex and all-consuming. There's the guilt that somehow it must be your fault, a feeling of shame that you've failed as a mother and the black despair that the child you carried for nine months, who grew inside your body, doesn't exist anymore. I went through all that, and I'm still alive to talk about it, but I'm not sure why. There were certainly moments when I wished I could end the pain.

"What do I feel now? Well, I think Alex and I had a slightly unusual relationship; we became friends, so I just miss his friendship, but you'll never guess what the worst thing is."

"I wouldn't presume to try."

"The worst thing for me is the fear that I will forget him, that there will come a time when I can live for a day without thinking about him. That would be the ultimate betrayal, and yet I want to live. I don't want to live alone, but I can't burden a partner with the weight of my loss."

David turned and put his hands on my shoulders.

"If that partner was me, you could. Alex's life and death have shaped you and made you who you are, the woman I want to live with. Alex would always be part of that."

I couldn't think of a reply that would do justice to that beautiful sentence, so I didn't say anything, but I stood and held my hand down to David, who took it and pulled himself upright. We returned to the car and drove back to the hotel in silence.

VII

Back in our suite, I took a shower. I stayed in there much longer than usual. I think I was trying to process the tumultuous events of the day, to sort out the pain from the promise.

We had a light supper, talking through what had happened and what it meant, then went to bed early.

I often have lucid dreams, but my dream that night was particularly vivid, and in the morning I could remember every detail.

In the dream a young boy emerged from a dank cave into bright sunshine. Older men dusted him with gold and sat him on a jewelled throne. The throne was lifted onto a raft, which the men pushed out onto the dark waters of a lake. Beside him a girl knelt holding a magnificent black panther on a silver chain. As the raft neared the middle of the lake, the boy and girl looked up at the sky where a giant condor soared, balancing on the thermals.

"Now is the time," the bird said, its voice sounding like that of an old woman. The boy stood up, stepped to the side of the raft, and dove into the jet-black water with youthful grace. A tear the colour of sapphire ran down the girl's face. The big cat turned, smiled at her, then licked the tear away.

In my home country of Colombia, magical realism is a powerful force combining dream with reality and this was a dream I didn't want to end. I found the beauty and serenity of the scene comforting, but inevitably the morning light found me, and I woke to find David kneeling beside the bed kissing my forehead. He pulled back, and I saw an anxious wrinkle at the corner of his eyes. I smiled at him and pulled him closer to me.

CHAPTER 9

I

Cape Town Central Police Station is a squat, four-storey red-brick building at the intersection of Buitenkant and Albertus streets in the heart of the city. It had been the centre for detention and torture during the apartheid era, and there was a splendid irony that the District Six Apartheid Museum now lay directly opposite on the other side of Buitenkant.

Lara and I checked in at reception. A uniformed female officer took our fingerprints and a DNA sample before showing us up to DCI Olivier's office on the fourth floor.

"Don't mind his manner," I said to Lara as we emerged from the elevator. "He's probably got a heart of gold, and I'll bet his mother loves him!"

"We have nothing to fear from him," Lara replied, "but we do need to be able to get on with our work, and being prime suspects for a murder would put a bit of a crimp in that, so let's play this straight."

Olivier's office hadn't changed an iota from my last visit, but the same could not be said for Oliver, who appeared to have had a personality transplant. He stood as we entered and pulled out a chair for Lara.

"Come, come. Sit down, Ms. Rios. Can I get you something to drink? The coffee looks like they get it from a vuil stroom, but it's hot, wet, and caffeinated." He chuckled at his own joke and then returned to his side of the desk.

"No thank you, Chief Inspector Olivier," Lara said. "We're anxious to eliminate ourselves from your inquiry and get on with our work, and we know you will have lots to attend to as well."

Lost and Found

Olivier took a deep breath and exhaled. He squared the sheets of paper on his desk, looked distractedly out the window, glanced at Lara, and then turned to face me.

"Mr. Mallory, I may have given you the wrong impression the last time you were here." He was clearly struggling to say something important. "I spent the morning with Dr. Naidoo, and I'm now convinced by what she has shown me that Thomas Parkes was murdered." He picked up a pen and fiddled with it. He wasn't making eye contact, and a pink flush was rising up his wide neck toward his small ears.

"I would go so far as to say that my initial analysis was incorrect," he struggled on. "If the boy was murdered, particularly if it occurred in the way that the evidence suggests, it seems possible to us that his father's shady dealings and dangerous business associates may be involved. I have put some inquiries out on the street, and it now appears to me that we need to investigate Parkes' involvement in the Golden Dawn Casino business. My sources suggest that there's a link between these venues and the distribution of cocaine and methamphetamines in Mpumalanga and beyond. Ed Parkes may be a big shot in his own world, but if he is tied into the drug trade, he will be in over his head and dealing with some desperate characters who will balk at nothing to claim the riches on offer."

"Thank you for your candour Chief Inspector Olivier," I began.

"Look, man, you can't go on calling me that," he said. I raised my eyebrows quizzically.

"Yeah, I know what I said last time, but things have changed. My wife says I'm as stubborn as a mule, which may be true, but I'm also a realist, and trying to discern truth is the reason I do this job. I'm about to suggest that we work together on this, and you can't be calling me Chief Inspector Olivier every two minutes, so Cobus is fine. Hell no, nobody calls me Cobus, apart from my mother. I probably wouldn't even respond if you said it. Coby, OK? Call me Coby."

I was taken aback by the change in tone and the offer of teamwork. It was going to be one of those moments when I opened my mouth and hoped I would think of what to say before my tongue started wagging, but before I could utter a sound, Lara spoke.

"Coby, we would be delighted to work with you. You're the law enforcement professional here, and we could learn a lot from you."

Coby was too big a man to simper, but it was close. "Well, I—"

"It seems to me a bit of a jump to link the boy's murder to the drug trade," Lara said, cutting him off, "but you're an officer with great experience, so I'm sure the street info and your instincts will prove to be a winning combination. How do you suggest we proceed from here?"

Lara was using a friendly but professional tone that, combined with her warmly mellifluous voice and a modicum of flattery, commanded the policeman's full attention.

"Well, Ms. Rios—"

"Lara and David please, Coby," Lara said.

"Well, Lara, first, I need to inform you that Ms. Gillen's death was not suicide. We found some viable fingerprints on the blue stool that you saw lying beside the body. When we ran them through the SAPS database, we found a match: Martim Ronaldo, an unpleasant customer with a long record sheet. He broke out of Ebongweni super-maximum-security prison in KwaZulu-Natal last month. It was an inside job, and those usually require a load of cash, drug money perhaps. He was serving a life sentence for the rape and murder of a teenager in Pretoria.

"There is no evidence of robbery at the house, and the clumsy attempt at staging a suicide raises more questions than it answers, but it looks as if Ms. Gillen died because someone thought she knew too much.

"As for you two, well, we have your prints and DNA and the evidence of the neighbours who saw you arrive two minutes before you called the police, so we can eliminate you from the inquiry. We now have two active murder cases, and I think it's safe to assume they're connected. This also provides us with more reason to think the boy's death was not accidental, over and above the forensic evidence."

Lara was visibly upset by this news, but she held it together. I knew she had empathized with Sarah, and the thought of her being executed in such a brutal way was painful.

"From where I sit it looks as if we now all have the same objective. You need to find Tom Parkes' killer, so Shelburne can heal, and I need to find

Tom and Sarah's killer, so we can put him behind bars. Same job, different motivations, don't you agree?"

Lara looked at me and then back at Coby. "We agree, and together we will be more than the sum of our parts. How should we proceed?"

Coby blew out his cheeks and exhaled. "I've been thinking about that all morning. My street sources are only so much use. We need to see if we can make a connection between the casinos and the drug trade. I propose that we travel together to visit one of the Golden Dawn Casinos. My face is well known to the criminal element, but yours are not. I suggest that we visit the Golden Dawn Casino Resort in Polokwane with you two in the guise of tourists, possibly tourists with a drug habit, if you'd be up for that."

Lara and I exchanged a look.

The big question that needed asking was why would we choose to walk into potentially deadly danger in disguise posing as addicts, but that seemed a bit difficult to approach head on.

"Why Polokwane?" I asked. "Surely there are Golden Dawn casinos much closer than that."

"So, here's the story." Coby looked a bit relieved that we hadn't rejected his plan out of hand. "We know that most of the street drugs that enter South Africa originate in South America or Southeast Asia and enter the continent through Mozambique, usually hidden in cargo ships unloading at Maputo. The border between Mozambique and South Africa runs down the middle of two national parks, Kruger in this country and Parque Nacional de Limpopo in Mozambique. There are only three or four viable roads through these wilderness areas, and they are heavily patrolled by game wardens looking out for poachers, so a direct route across the border at that point is not attractive. The preferred route for the traffickers is north from Maputo into the southeast corner of Zimbabwe and then into Botswana on one of the many bush roads, usually through the Tuli Block. Few of them have border posts. From there the drugs can either be driven into South Africa over the bed of the Limpopo in the dry winter season or paddled across in canoes in summer. Polokwane is the nearest casino to the Botswana border, so I figure it's the right place to start." Coby pushed his chair back and looked back and forth between us.

"It's possible that our identities may be known to those involved in Sarah's death," I said. "We were followed from her house to our hotel by two men in a small red sedan."

"Did you get the make or licence plate?" Coby asked, leaning forward with his elbows on the desk.

"No. But I don't think we can guarantee that we're anonymous."

Lara decided not to skirt around the elephant in the room. "Coby, of course we want to get to the bottom of this case, but it's obvious that there's a level of risk. Actually, let's call it what it is, *danger* in what you're proposing. What can be done to mitigate that?"

"You're right, of course." Coby almost seemed pleased that the question had been asked. "I've thought a lot about that, and I know I'm asking a lot. I have arranged with the Polokwane SAPS department to have two of their best officers as back-up. They will be in plain clothes and wearing wires, as will you. We will be able to stay in touch with you at all times. David, I assume you know how to operate a pistol?"

In fact, I had no experience with small arms.

"My father owned a beautiful pair of matched Purdey shotguns. He would take me shooting for sandgrouse in Argentina when we lived there, but that was a long time ago. I could use a lesson."

"That can be arranged, David," Coby said. "We have a shooting range in the basement of this building. Perhaps you would like to try your hand as well, Lara." Coby smiled at her.

"Actually, Coby, I have a concealed-carry permit in Florida, and I'm a licenced small-arms instructor at the Delray Beach Gun Club," she said calmly.

I turned to look at her, and she met my gaze. Yet another talent that I knew nothing about.

"Superb." Coby did a reasonable job of disguising his surprise.

"You won't have brought your weapon with you from Florida though, so we can look through what's on offer downstairs. I'm sure you won't need to use them, but I'd be more comfortable if you had guns."

We trailed Coby by a few yards as we made our way to the elevator.

"What do you carry? A pearl-handled derringer concealed in your clutch purse?" I asked quietly.

"A Beretta nine millimetre in a shoulder holster if I'm wearing a skirt and jacket or an ankle holster if I'm wearing pants," she replied.

I smirked. "You're full of surprises."

"Yes, I am," she replied as the elevator doors closed, and we headed down to the street.

II

We tried a new restaurant for dinner that night. Malcolm had recommended the Test Kitchen, and he wasn't wrong. We both had the coconut langoustines and split a bottle of Graham Beck Brut Zero. We talked about what we were heading into, but neither of us questioned that it was the right thing to do. It certainly wasn't what I'd expected when I'd agreed to come on this trip with David, but I wanted to help get justice for Sarah Gillen and her son, and I had come to the realization that David needed me to help him get through this even if he hadn't realized it yet himself.

It was 10:00 p.m. when we got back to the suite but only 4:00 p.m. in Miami, so I checked in with the office. A waterfront home on Key Biscayne had finally sold after months of litigation over the state of the boat dock. I'd put a lot of work into that sale, so it was a relief to get it closed and a pleasure to check my current account at SunTrust and see the commission payment sitting there. I moved it into my investment account and then poured myself a small cognac and curled up on the sofa.

David called Pius and left a message giving a brief outline of what we had done and where we were heading. He called Stephen as well and gave him more details, asking him to pass them along to the headmaster. I heard an infant wailing in the background.

I fell asleep as soon as my head hit the silk pillowcase, and I didn't dream or move a muscle until David woke me shortly after 6:00 a.m. We showered together, which had become our norm, and we had a more substantial breakfast than usual because we knew we'd be travelling most of the day.

We took an Uber out to Matroosfontein and met Coby at the Mango Airlines check-in counter. Our flight to Polokwane connected at Oliver Tambo International in Johannesburg. The first flight was on time and uneventful.

I like a window seat. I spend the majority of any daylight flight looking out the window and imagining what it would be like to live in the towns and countryside that we pass over. If we are over the ocean, I look out for cargo ships and try to guess where they have come from and what they're carrying. Even at night I'll check every so often to see if the darkness is punctuated by the sparkle of a small town or the glow of a city.

We had a two-hour layover in Johannesburg, so I suggested a coffee. We found a Mugg and Bean opposite the gate for our second flight. Out of the office and the strictures of the city, Coby really opened up. He told us about his wife, Hanna, their three young daughters, his flat-coated retriever, Muddy, and his love of hunting in the Lowveld and the Bushveld. He also turned out to be a bit of a comedian and made us laugh with his hunting stories. The tension that I had thought would characterize our time together had completely evaporated, and I looked forward to getting to know Coby better. It was also reassuring to be on a team with someone who looked as if he had been hewn from a large block of granite.

III

We landed in Polokwane late in the afternoon. The airport lies north of the city, and the casino is situated on a low bluff on the south side of a creek called the Sandrivier. We collected our bags and picked up the rental vehicle that Coby had organized. It was a Toyota Hilux double cab in a questionable shade of khaki. I knew from the part of my youth that I had spent in Pretoria that such vehicles were known locally as bakkies and were the preferred form of transport in that part of the country. It reminded me of a cut-down North American pickup truck with a bit more style.

Lara and I threw our bags in the back while Coby placed his on the ground and pulled out two handguns and shoulder holsters.

"These are for you," he said, offering us the Glock 9 mm's that we had practiced with back at Central. Lara and I looked at each other. Lara raised her eyebrows. The guns were a confirmation that we were heading into danger.

Coby drove with Lara up front and me in back. He had a forceful driving style. It wasn't aggressive, but he ran through the gears making sure he took every opening and mumbling to himself a couple of times as other vehicles wandered from their lanes.

We pulled up to security at the main gates of the casino complex, gave our names, and were waved through. The driveway wound uphill between

Lost and Found

jacaranda trees. There, as at Shelburne, they were dripping with purple blossom, their natural beauty a stark contrast to the gaudy monstrosity that soon appeared in front of us.

Neon lights flashed around a sign that announced, "Golden Dawn – Everyone's A Winner, Baby." A young black woman jumped out from behind a valet desk and opened Lara's door.

"Welcome, ma'am. Welcome, everybody." She was dressed in a gold sequined jacket and form-fitting shorts. "My name is Lucky, and before you leave you're all going to get lucky." She laughed at her tired line and, gesturing at a boy who scooped up our bags, led us inside.

Entering the lobby, we were assaulted by a wall of sound produced by a four-piece band dressed in gold and blue who were belting out Neil Diamond's back catalogue. I couldn't hear anything the front desk person said to us, but Lara nodded and smiled, so I assumed that she'd understood it all. We headed to the elevators accompanied by the boy with our bags. He couldn't have been more than fourteen.

"I'm in 311, right across the hall from you two," Coby said. "I hope you're not planning to party all night. I'm looking forward to catching up on some sleep. I love my girls more than life itself, but Hanna's been working nights at the hospital the past three months, and I'm lucky if I get four or five hours between the glasses of water and bad dreams."

"You're safe with us, Coby," Lara replied. "David snores a bit, but I'll give him a dig in the ribs if he starts up."

"That is a complete fabrication," I began rather indignantly until I saw both Lara and Coby smiling at me.

"Let's meet in the bar at eight, and we'll have a scout around, get the lay of the land," Coby said.

"See you there," I replied.

IV

Whoever did the interior design for the casino must have been going for a very special look. Tacky meets vulgar possibly or perhaps a Disneyworld-influenced Turkish brothel. Our room featured a canopied four-poster bed with mirror tiles in the canopy. A gilt rococo table sat in front of the French windows leading to the balcony. On the table was a huge vase of plastic flowers covered with dust. An enormous TV dominated the wall opposite the bed. It was currently turned on and advertising the adult channels. David stared in horror at the offerings.

"Well, that's us all sorted for later," I said. "What do you fancy? 'You've got Male,' 'Riding Miss Daisy,' or perhaps 'Boobyguard'?"

I reached for the remote and turned the TV off.

"Thank God for that." David sat down on the end of the bed and looked around. "This place is like a bordello."

"You're speaking from experience, I assume," I said, batting my eyelashes at him.

"Don't be ridiculous," he replied, looking a bit cross. "I know we were spoiled at the Cape Grace, but this is horrible. I'm almost embarrassed that you have to stay here." David usually had a philosophical attitude to the more lurid aspects of contemporary culture, but that evening he sounded his age. "I mean, what if a family with children walked into their room, and this was the first thing the children saw?"

"It's just a job, David," I said, sitting down beside him.

"Back in Cape Town, you reminded me that we had to look at this whole thing professionally and not get distracted by some of the more colourful details. Well, we have to do the same here. It's sweet of you to worry about me, but you don't have to." I leaned over and kissed his cheek. "Now, let's get changed and meet Coby downstairs. If this is what the guest rooms look like, I can't wait to see the décor in the bar."

V

I had to remind David that we were supposed to carry our weapons and then help him to adjust his shoulder holster so that his jacket hung naturally. We left the room and took the elevator down to the bar.

The Royal Flush featured subdued lighting and smelled of stale beer and cigarette smoke. A polished oak bar stretched the length of one wall, and a dozen customers were dotted around the room seated on dark leather armchairs and sofas, their eyes all turned toward the corner of the room where a young woman wearing a micro bikini was gyrating around a shiny metal pole. She was doing her best to look as if she was feeling amorous, but her eyes were tired. One of the customers, a large white man in a Hawaiian-print shirt, waddled up to the small stage and tucked a R100 note in the elastic of the girl's thong. She blew him a kiss.

Coby was sitting at the bar sipping a Castle lager from the bottle and chatting to the server, a tall older black woman with bright red lipstick. She wore gold bangles from wrist to elbow on her right arm. She laughed loudly at something Coby said.

"Hi, guys," Coby said, standing as we approached. "Do you want to sit at the bar, or shall we get a table?"

"The bar's fine with me," I said, pulling out a stool.

I ordered a glass of pinot grigio from the server, whose name was Gloria, and David joined Coby with a lager, asking for a glass when he wasn't given one.

"Gesondheid!" Coby said, clinking his bottle on our glasses.

Gloria was at the other end of the bar serving a young couple, so I thought it was safe to ask Coby about the details of our police support.

"The couple at the table in front of the stage are with the police service in Nelspruit," he said. "The local station chief thought it would be better not to use his people as they'd be easily recognized."

I swivelled around slowly, surveying the room

"The man in the Hawaiian shirt?" I probably sounded surprised.

"Hendrick Malan," Coby said. "And his partner is Lilitha Nondela."

A beautiful young woman sat across the table sipping Pepsi from a bottle.

"He just tipped the dancer," I said.

"They are operating under cover," Coby replied. "Trying to be authentic." He touched the front of his shirt. "Hey, Hendrick, keep your eyes open, and look at something other than that girl's ass occasionally."

He winked at me, then grimaced at the reply he received. I realized then that he was wearing a wire.

We ordered fried shrimp and rice and had another drink. By the time we'd finished, the dancer had left the stage and had been replaced by a middle-aged female patron who was doing a karaoke version of Bette Midler. She was clearly quite pleased with herself and hooted and applauded as she made her way back to her table where she high-fived her companions.

I was just about to offer a comment when Coby stood up.

"In the interests of authenticity, let me offer you my version of an Elvis classic." He grinned and made his way to the man operating the sound system.

"Good Lord." David looked horrified. "Surely he's not going to sing."

But sing he did and rather well in a pleasant light tenor. The audience, which had now grown to about fifty people, clearly hadn't expected this and broke into loud applause.

"Thank you. Thank you very much," he improvised in a southern drawl when he finished.

I slipped off my barstool. "In the further service of authenticity, I'm going to sing a duet with him," I said to David, then walked away before he had a chance to protest, which I knew he would.

We spoke to the sound man and then Coby took my hand as we launched into "Can't Help Falling in Love."

I have to say that we were really quite good. The audience even stood and demanded an encore, but while authenticity might have helped our cause, notoriety certainly would not, so we stepped down from the stage and headed back to the bar.

"That was quite something," David said, smiling at us, but I could tell he wasn't pleased. "Did you ever see 'The Singing Detective'?" he asked Coby. "If the producers had heard you, Michael Gambon would never have gotten the part."

"I love to sing," Coby said, refusing to pick up on the cool tone of David's compliment. "I sang solos in the church choir in Lydenburg before my voice broke, but I never get a chance now apart from in the shower." He gave his characteristic disarming chuckle. "Lara, you were wonderful. If policing doesn't work out, I think the pair of us could take this on the road." Another chortle.

"Just to drag us back to why we are here," David offered with a hint of sarcasm in his voice that didn't suit him, "I don't think we've found out much this evening other than that you two could be the next Sonny and Cher." David looked quite pleased with this, but Coby and I gave each other a blank look, not catching the reference.

"We've found out more than that, David." Coby was no longer the lager-sipping crooner; he was back in his detective persona. "You may not have noticed, but there are cameras everywhere. I'm asking myself why."

Lost and Found

I glanced around. "I didn't see any."

"They're embedded in the crown mouldings that run along the top of the walls. They're also in the public bathrooms, which is illegal, of course. It's the sort of thing that you'd expect to find in a penitentiary or a high-security military installation, not in a casino. Even in public areas, if you're going to put people under surveillance, you must have signage telling them so."

"So, what do you think it means?" I asked.

"Well, two things come to mind. It's possible that management is trying to supplement the casino's gambling income with a bit of blackmail. The Golden Dawn does a brisk trade in illicit relationships—one-night stands. If those are caught on camera, people will pay a fair sum to prevent a spouse or an employer from finding out."

"Do you think there are cameras in the guest rooms too?" David asked. He was leaning forward, more focused now.

"I wouldn't be surprised, maybe hidden behind the mirrors in the bed canopy," Coby replied.

That was an unsettling thought.

"But I don't think that's the real reason. Installing those cameras, the monitoring equipment, and the personnel is a very expensive proposition. I think it's a security issue; however, security for the core casino business is normally handled by a team of bouncers. You don't need all this high-tech equipment. So, what would justify the investment?" Coby searched our eyes for an answer.

"I think the management is playing in a much higher-stakes environment than poker and blackjack," he continued. "If this place is the conduit for large quantities of drugs coming into the country, and that's our hypothesis, they're going to be dealing with some really unpleasant customers. They can use the threat of evidence from the cameras as leverage to keep everyone playing nicely."

"But the video evidence would also be a liability if it was discovered by the police or a rival gang of dealers," I pointed out.

Coby nodded. "It would indeed. The monitoring equipment must be protected very securely, and it needn't even be here in the casino. In fact, it could be anywhere."

"So, are we any further ahead by being here?" David queried.

"We don't know that yet, but we may be." He fixed his eyes on David. "I love birds, David. I love to study them in the wild and take their pictures. If you're on the trail of a rare and secretive bird, you need limitless patience. You may have to sit in a blind for days before you get a glimpse and days more before you get a chance to use your camera. But if you're patient enough, you will be rewarded. That's how I look at this. We don't know what we don't know, but chances are that by being here we'll pick up some clues that may lead somewhere. I know it seems like a long shot, but that's how it works."

"We've had a tiring day," I offered. "How about we get some sleep and meet up again for breakfast. Would eight o'clock work?"

"Sounds good, Lara," Coby replied. "Look, I know this is all a bit different for you both, but it's great to have three pairs of eyes and to have you both to bounce things off. I think we're in the right place."

Back in the room, we were soon in bed, but the prospect of distant watchers beyond the mirrored canopy extinguished any affectionate behavior. After exchanging chaste kisses, we lay in the darkness. I could tell that David was asleep within minutes, but it took me a little longer. I'd caught a glimpse of something in his behaviour that night. Perhaps jealousy was too strong a word, but there was something.

A few years before that, I had gone on a couple of dates with another older man. He was kind and gentle, but in conversation his attitude to people my age, though not me in particular, seemed condescending. David hadn't liked me singing with Coby, and he'd let us know it. I wasn't sure what it meant, but it didn't make me happy.

VI

I surfaced before daylight and lay there dozing. I felt anxious about something, but I couldn't quite place it. My thoughts cohered as the first grey light of dawn peeked between the heavy curtains. I realized I had acted badly toward Lara the previous evening. Who did I think I was, her father? Her husband? The juxtaposition of those identities was troubling in itself. She was a grown, successful woman, and our relationship was premised on us being two independent adults who spent time together because it was more rewarding than living alone. It's hard to change attitudes at my age, but I could at least modify a couple of my behaviours. I needed to apologize to Lara for sulking when I saw her enjoying herself with someone other than me. I'd ask her to go for a walk after breakfast, and I'd tell her then.

Showered and dressed, we headed down to the restaurant. Breakfast at the Golden Dawn took the form of a buffet. We picked up some fruit and croissants, and I added some smoked salmon to mine. Then we steered through the tables to where Coby was sitting behind a plate heaped with sausage, bacon, and scrambled eggs. He was buttering a bagel and looking very happy.

"What a great way to start the day," he said, beaming. "Breakfast is my favourite meal of the day, and when it's free and someone else has cooked it, it's even better." He grinned broadly and took a sip of his coffee.

"Sleep well?" Lara asked.

"I always do. It's one of my special talents," he replied, chuckling.

"Mind you, it took me a while to realize I couldn't go to sleep on my back, like usual. Every time I opened my eyes, I saw this ugly overweight old white guy lying in my bed. It was horrible." This observation resulted in a full-fledged laugh, and it was genuine enough that we couldn't help joining in.

"Here's the plan for today," Coby began, but the thought was interrupted by some loud popping noises from the direction of the car park. I had some smoked salmon on the way to my mouth when Lara grabbed my arm and pulled me to the floor. Coby was on his feet and moving in a crouching run toward the lobby, his pistol held in both hands in front of him.

"What's going on?" I asked, realizing Lara had her gun out and was scanning the dining room.

"I don't know, but that was gunfire from the parking lot."

I hadn't recognized it. It didn't sound like the ferocious discharge from my father's shotguns.

"Do you have your gun with you?" Lara asked.

"No, I left it in the room," I replied sheepishly.

"It's probably a good idea to carry it at all times if this is how it's going to be," she said.

"Let's go and see what's happening," I said.

"Let me go first. Follow me, and keep your head down."

We moved between the tables, which were empty of gamblers at that early hour, passed through the lobby, and crept out into the parking lot where

Coby and Lilitha Nondela were crouched on either side of the rather large body of Sergeant Hendrick Malan.

It was obvious that he was dead. His eyes were rolled back, and a dark red stain was expanding slowly from the hole on the front of his yellow T-shirt. Another puddle of blood crept out onto the ground from beneath his massive shoulders.

The young policewoman was looking in vain for a pulse on Hendrick's neck, and Coby had his phone out calling the emergency services.

Lara holstered her gun, then stepped a few feet away from the scene and beckoned to me. She was pale, and her lips were trembling slightly.

"Coby and the other officer will be occupied here for a while. We should take a look around the grounds. Why don't you go and get your weapon, and I'll meet you back here?"

When I returned maybe three minutes later, Lara had her arms around Lilitha, who was obviously upset. Her partner was being loaded into an ambulance, but nobody was in a hurry anymore. Lara disengaged and walked over to me.

"Lilitha says that Malan was having a cigarette in the parking lot when he was shot from a passing car. Whoever it was fired at her too, but she managed to duck behind a truck. She's pretty shaken up. She says it was a black Mercedes sedan with two men in it. It must have checked in and out at the entrance gate. Let's head down there."

It took us ten minutes to walk down the hill to the gate. It was a beautiful morning. The beauty of the robin's-egg-blue sky and the caress of the gentle zephyr contrasted starkly with the roar of the ambulance as it passed us en route to the morgue.

Before we got to the gatehouse, we saw that the barrier was raised. That wasn't right. Our suspicions were confirmed when we arrived and pushed open the door to the little building. The body of a uniformed security guard lay slumped over the desk, his uniform torn with several bullet holes. The intruders must have killed him on their way in and left the barrier open for their escape. The ambulance driver would have had no reason to suspect anything was wrong.

I called Coby and told him what we'd found. He and Lilitha raced down the hill in her unmarked police car and were with us within a minute.

Lost and Found

"The poor man has been shot with an automatic weapon," Lilitha said. "It will be the same gun they used to kill Hendrick."

"These guys are professionals," Coby observed as he pulled on latex gloves and began to examine the body and the little office. "We're up against some bad people here. I think it's time for you two to head back to Cape Town and leave this mess to Lilitha and me." He sounded sombre.

"Lara and I discussed this two nights ago, before we left," I said. "I've been hired to get answers. Lara wants justice for Sarah Gillen and her son. We're in this together until we get to the truth. So, we appreciate your concern, Coby, we really do, but we're here to stay."

Lara nodded her assent, and Coby shrugged, "Don't say I didn't warn you."

VII

With the security guard dead, it looked like there would be no way to identify the car by way of its licence plate, but then I remembered what Coby had said about the surveillance cameras. Leaving the detectives to assess and secure the gatehouse crime scene, Lara and I walked back up the driveway. We spoke to the young man on the reception desk and asked to see the manager on duty. He dialled an extension and spoke in a hushed voice to the person on the other end.

"Please follow me," he said, coming out from behind the desk and leading us down a carpeted corridor to an office with "Duty Manager" etched on the glass.

The duty manager was a middle-aged man with very dark skin and tufts of grey hair on his head. He was obviously alarmed at the morning's dramatic activity and was happy to let us see the security videos. Leaving his office, he led us a little farther down the corridor to a room where a young woman sat in front of a bank of monitors and what looked like a large mixing board. It was an elaborate system, as Coby had speculated it would be. The young woman had been on duty when all the excitement took place, so she knew which cameras had captured the action. The gentle hum of the air conditioning and the occasional clack of her keystrokes were the only sounds in the room for the few minutes it took her to isolate the footage and then play it for us.

The car appeared on three different screens. It was a late-model Mercedes 500 SEL sedan. What looked like two people could vaguely be seen through the darkly tinted windows. The rear licence plate was clearly visible on one of the screens. The black letters stood out against the reflective yellow plate: B962BPC.

We watched as the car circled the car park and slowed down by the two officers. The passenger window rolled down, and a burst of semi-automatic gunfire hit Hendrick Malan in the chest and neck. There was no audio, but the video evidence was dramatic. Small dark circles appeared on Malan's shirt as he sank to his knees, reaching for his gun, but he was dead before he could clear it. We saw Lilitha spring behind a Ford truck and fire at the retreating car as it accelerated from the parking lot, leaving dark rubber marks on the asphalt.

Lara made a note of the licence plate as I thanked the technician and the manager. We left the room and walked along the corridor toward the lobby. I think we had both been running on nervous energy for the past hour, but now as I thought about what we had just witnessed and what that implied for the nature of our investigation, my legs just about gave way under me. I looked over at Lara, and I could tell from her ashen face that the shock was becoming real for her too.

We sat beside each other on a love seat in a corner of the lobby. I took her hand. "This is a little more than we bargained for," I said. "I know we discussed this in Cape Town, but things have escalated. You bought into an African vacation, and it's turned out to be a deadly proposition. I'm getting paid for this and I guess I have a professional responsibility to keep going but you don't have to put yourself through this."

She squeezed my hand and closed her eyes for a moment before she replied. "Since Alex died, I've had a different relationship with life and a different outlook on death. I don't fear death anymore. I mean, sure, I'd rather live a happy life to a ripe old age, but I don't fear the fact of death. I don't worry about not existing or about the details of dying like I did before. It's almost as if I've died already, and this time now is all a bonus. I know it sounds strange, but it's like a gift that Alex has given me." She was silent for a moment, but I didn't want to reply. "So, the risks that we might face here don't worry me. I don't have anyone for whom I'm responsible, and my affairs are all in order. I really like being with you, and what's more, I suspect you can't shoot straight."

She smiled at me, and I saw that the colour had returned to her cheeks.

VIII

We met Coby and Lilitha in Ace's High, the restaurant where we had been having breakfast before the mayhem started. Neither David nor I had an appetite, but we had coffees while Lilitha toyed with a Caesar salad and Coby munched his way through a cheeseburger and sweet potato fries.

We gave the licence plate number to Lilitha, who took one look at it and then raised her eyebrows. "This isn't a South African plate."

We looked at her in surprise as she continued. "It's a Botswana registration. Each area of the country has its own set of three letters. I'll check but I think BPC is reserved for the area known as the Tuli Block. It's not far from here, about three hundred klicks due north just across the Limpopo. The river forms the boundary between the two countries. It's the route that we think most of the drug traffickers use to bring their goods into South Africa from Mozambique."

"That's what I told them," Coby said.

"So, this fits in pretty well. Run the plates will you, Lilitha, and confirm the ownership of the Mercedes. It's possible the plates were stolen but it's worth a try."

Lilitha fixed Coby with an expressionless stare as if he had asked her to run along and get him a cup of coffee, but she stood and left the table to make the call, returning a couple of minutes later.

"A vehicle of that description is registered to Shashe Safari Camp," she said. "It's the most expensive camp East of the Okavango Delta. They charge up to one thousand dollars US a night, so most of the clients are from overseas. I happen to know the camp because last year an American tourist was killed up there. He was on a tour organized by a South African operator, so I was assigned to straighten out the paperwork and repatriate the body."

"A death on safari is incredibly rare," Coby remarked. "What happened?"

"It was mostly his own fault. He decided to jump out of the safari vehicle to get a better angle for a photo and was trampled to death by a young bull elephant. The tragedy is that the guide had to shoot the elephant."

"Whereabouts is the camp?" David asked.

"The main camp is a hundred kilometres north of the Botswana border, so about four hundred kilometres from here," Lilitha said. "It's on the south bank of the Shashe River where it meets the Tuli. The northern bank is Zimbabwe."

"So, it could be a perfect location to tranship drugs destined for the South African market." David sounded quite excited.

"Maybe," Lilitha offered. "It's really remote up there, but it's right on the route that we know the traffickers favour. And it has its own airstrip, so it can fly international guests in directly from Jo'burg. I suppose that could be an advantage for drug runners and—"

"Slow down, slow down," Coby interrupted. "We're getting way ahead of ourselves here. What we know is that Hendrick Malan was killed because someone identified him as a police officer and made the reasonable assumption that he was at the casino to interfere with whatever operation they're running. They must have thought he knew more than he did. Because the car is registered to Shashe, we need to have a look at the place. It's a good lead, but we have to be careful. Now that they've killed one policeman, there's no greater jeopardy for them in killing a couple more."

"I should go," Lilitha said curtly. She didn't like being interrupted. "I know the place."

"You can't," Coby replied. "Hendrick's killers will have identified you as well as me. That rules us out."

"But we can," I said. "There's no evidence that whoever is behind this knows who we are or what we're doing. What you need is a couple of high-end tourists. And I know where you can find them." I looked across at David, who nodded.

"I'm not sure I can let you do that." Coby sounded genuinely concerned.

"I'm not sure you can stop us," I said, offering Coby one of my wider smiles. "And I've always wanted to see a leopard in the wild."

CHAPTER 10

I

Twenty-four hours later we were heading north on R521 out of Polokwane, the giant bulk of the Blouberg massif looming to the west and the sun beating down on the dark strip of pavement. Lara was driving the khaki Hilux, and there was very little traffic on the road. She looked across at me a few times. We were getting to know each other well enough that there was an unspoken language between us.

"Are you sure you're OK with this?" I felt her asking.

We both knew that what we were involved in now was nothing like what we had expected when we arrived in South Africa. The unhurried comfort of the Cape Grace and the reassuring gravitas of Shelburne had been exchanged for what was literally a drive into the unknown.

We did not have to do this. No one would question our decision if we called it off and headed home for the sanctuary of South Florida where there would be other jobs more in line with my skill set and where Lara could focus on making pots of money in real estate.

But Lara's quiet determination gave me confidence, and while doubts may have existed in our unspoken thoughts, the idea of giving up and going home had never passed our lips.

The night before, I'd called Stephen Kumalo to bring him up to date on what we were doing and to ask him to authorize the considerable expense we were going to incur for the Shashe visit. His voice was as calm and affable as always. The sound of his lively children in the background didn't seem to faze him at all. He asked several questions about the details of our plan and expressed concern that we should exercise every care.

There was availability at Shashe, and we'd booked in for four nights. Game drives occurred in the early morning and late afternoon, so there was plenty of downtime during the hottest part of the day. That would give us sufficient time to scout around.

The road was straight and empty, and after a couple of hours of driving through an increasingly arid landscape, we arrived at Alldays, a dusty intersection with a petrol station, a diner, and little else. We topped up with diesel, drank some tepid coffee, and then I took my turn behind the wheel.

Beyond Alldays the road deteriorated rapidly. It was still paved, but the construction company must have skimmed a lot of money because it was pitted with some of the deepest potholes I had ever seen. I failed to spot a couple until too late, and the truck shuddered and skidded sideways before correcting itself; not a road I would want to drive in the dark.

It was only seventy kilometres from Allays to the border, but it took us more than two hours of carefully skirting craters to reach the little community of Pont Drift, so it was the middle of the afternoon when we pulled in. Most tourists leave their cars on the South African side of the border and transfer to vehicles owned by the safari lodges they are heading to on the Botswana side. In the case of Shashe, which is more remote, they would be shuttled by light plane from the Limpopo Valley Airport. We, however, intended to drive up to Shashe ourselves.

It was almost the end of the dry season, and it had been a particularly severe one, so there was no water in the Limpopo. I let a little air out of the tires to help them better grip the loose sand, engaged the low gear, and pointed the bakkie at the dry riverbed. We bumped across to the Botswana side and pulled into the border post.

It closed at four, but we arrived with twenty minutes to spare. We showed our passports, driver's licences, and the letter of permission to cross the border given to us by the car rental company.

Inside the small wooden building, posters warning against child trafficking and domestic violence and urging the use of contraception as a way of limiting the transmission of STDs papered the walls, but notwithstanding the grim messages all around, the staff behind the counter were an absolute delight and seemed genuinely pleased to welcome us to their country.

"There's a lesson here for US border services," Lara said as we walked over the soggy mat intended to disinfect our shoes and strolled back across the parking lot.

She jumped into the driver's seat, and we rumbled off along the dirt road, leaving a cloud of fine white dust in our wake.

II

We started off on the transit road that links some of the safari lodges in the southern part of the Tuli region. About thirty minutes later, a sign indicated a right turn toward Shashe Game Lodge. From there on the road became very rough, and I began to wonder if we wouldn't have been smarter to go by plane after all.

We crossed a number of dry streambeds, bouncing down the side in low gear and grinding up the opposite bank. Driving slowly around a sharp bend in the track, we came across a giraffe standing in the road, delicately picking the few remaining dry leaves off an acacia tree. It stopped eating and slowly turned its head to look at us. Its beautiful brown eyes were moist and framed by impossibly long lashes. We stopped, and I turned off the engine as we watched it continue to browse. I reached for David's hand.

"Lots of firsts on this trip for me, David," I joked.

He nodded and smiled. "We should start to see quite a bit of game now that we're away from the main camps."

David knew southern Africa quite well. His family had lived in Pretoria for a number of years when his father was first secretary at the British embassy. He had gone to a boarding school, Southland College, and hated it. He told me that when he was running his own schools and had a decision to make, he often thought of what they would have done at Southland and then did the opposite.

The giraffe finished eating and moved elegantly away from the road. I started the Hilux, and we drove on.

The next hour was like being in our own wildlife documentary. Impalas and zebras grazed on sparse, dry grass, water buffalo stood in the shade of mopane trees, and we even saw a pride of young lions lazing in the sand of a dry river bottom. They yawned at us as we passed within twenty metres.

The sun was getting low in the sky when David touched my arm and asked me to stop. He pointed to a big marula tree. There on a lower branch lay a leopard licking a dead gemsbok that it had hauled up into the tree.

"They drag their prey up the tree to prevent it from being stolen by hyenas," David explained.

"Surely a leopard is stronger than a hyena," I replied.

"Leopards travel and hunt alone. Hyenas operate in packs. The bite from a hyena's jaws could cripple a leopard. Even lions are wary of them."

We watched for a few minutes, but the sun was almost on the western horizon, so we pressed on and soon came to a sign announcing the Shashe Reserve. The big wooden map beside the entrance gates showed that we had another ten kilometres to go to reach the main lodge, but the track was in better repair now, and we rolled up to the main building just as dusk fell.

We were greeted by smiling uniformed porters who took our bags and showed us to reception, where an elegant middle-aged woman copied our passports and beckoned to a girl to whom she gave the number of our accommodation.

"Elspeth will show you to your tent," she said.

I turned to David. "Tent? We're camping?"

"Don't worry," he replied. "One thousand dollars a night buys you a really nice tent."

We followed Elspeth out of the main building and down a sloping path to the edge of a large waterhole. The path continued around the water's edge for maybe a hundred metres and ended in front of a canvas structure that would have been fit for the Great Khan himself. The entrance was lit by two flaming torches supported by cast iron brackets. Elspeth held back the tent flaps, and we entered.

The interior was enormous and sumptuous. The canvas walls were hung with colourful silk batiks, and deep woollen rugs lay on the floor. Large burgundy leather couches surrounded a low glass table on one side of the space while a dining table and chairs were arranged on the other. The interior was lit by occasional lamps that cast a warm, subdued glow. Behind a tapestry screen lay a king-size bed covered by a gold duvet and dark blue cushions. Elspeth showed us the bathroom, which had a flush toilet and a bucket shower.

"Just call us when you want a shower, and the men will come and fill up the bucket with hot water," she said. "We hope that you will join us for cocktails on the veranda in the main building at eight o'clock. Dinner is served at nine. We recommend an early night because the morning safari starts at five o'clock. Rusks and a pot of tea will be brought to your tent at four thirty. Will there be anything else?"

"I'd love a shower before dinner," I said. "Can that be arranged?"

"Of course, madam." She took the radio from her belt and spoke a few words. "It will be ready for you in five minutes." Elspeth gave the smallest of curtseys and then left us.

"Will this suit you?" David asked.

"I believe it will," I said, surveying the splendour.

I took my clothes off, hung them up, and slipped on the cotton dressing gown that was folded on the bottom of the bed. Sure enough, within five minutes I heard the low murmur of voices through the thin canvas wall of the tent as two men hoisted buckets of hot water into the shower cistern.

"Mind if I join you?" David asked.

"Of course," I replied. "You can wash my back."

Halfway through our shower I began to feel a pleasant sensation between my legs. It reminded me that we hadn't made love for several days.

"Maybe you'd like to wash my front as well," I offered.

David turned me to face him, put his hands on my buttocks and drew me toward him. I could feel that he was having similar emotions. He kissed me gently, pulling on my lower lip with his teeth in a way that I found erotic. I reached down and took hold of his erect penis.

"Let's take this to bed, shall we?"

After we dried each other, I lay across the bed, my arms above my head. More often than not I take the lead when we make love, but that night I wanted to lie back and be seduced. David approached the bed and knelt between my thighs. He leaned forward and ran his tongue over my nipples then down the plane of my stomach. He kissed me on the pubic bone and then slipped a finger inside me. I let out a groan and propped myself up on my elbows to watch as his tongue circled my most sensitive spot. I put a hand on the top of his head and pushed him down a little deeper.

"Is this right?" he asked.

"You know it is," I whispered.

After several blissful minutes, he raised himself up on his arms and entered me. I wrapped myself around him, and we held each other's gaze as we worked each other to a beautiful climax.

Afterwards we lay together enjoying the warmth of each other's bodies. I stroked David's hair and kissed his ear. Each day together we were learning new things about each other. There was unexpected intimacy in healing each other's wounds.

III

I know I should give up questioning myself, but I'm always amazed that Lara enjoys our lovemaking as much as she seems to.

For the months immediately after Joanne and I first met, we would make love morning and night without fail. On weekends I would get up and make coffee and bring it back to bed. There were times when we didn't get up again until dark. We would talk and play music and enjoy each other's bodies in such an honest and carefree way that it almost removed the sexual energy from the act itself.

But then a distance developed between us. Even after we were married I had the sense that Joanne was judging me and that I never quite measured up.

Maybe she was right, but it wasn't a recipe for a successful relationship. It meant I was always trying to please her and earn at least her acceptance, if not her approval. After a while I just got tired of trying. After James was born, and our lives got a bit busier, there were more reasons not to have sex, and without the physical intimacy it turned out there wasn't much left.

Joanne complained that I had no self-confidence, but I realize now that I had let her take it from me. With Lara, the intimacy was built around our growing understanding and acceptance of each other.

We were a little late for cocktails and I'm guessing that we still exuded a languorous post-coital glow as we crossed the veranda and ordered two vodka martinis from the smartly dressed waiter.

There was a firepit on the far side of the veranda where flames leapt crackling from the resin-rich wood, sending showers of sparks into the night sky. We walked over, glasses in hand, to meet the other guests.

Lost and Found

It turned out that only two other couples were staying at the camp. Henry and Edith Goldberg were from Pittsburgh. Henry had been an orthodontist, and Edith had run the office. They had just retired, and this safari was their retirement present to each other. Henry wasn't into dialogue, and he finished almost every pronouncement with "You betcha," as if to dispel any possibility of comment or disagreement. Edith nodded supportively by his side. Both Henry and Edith were wearing purple track suits and red baseball caps.

The other couple were in their twenties, and they looked relieved to see us approach and relieve them of Henry's undivided attention. Damian de Jager, a tall, athletic young man, was a wildlife photographer. The girl, Lark Coombes, freckled and very pretty, was a freelance writer and filmmaker. They were both from Durban and had met working together on a couple of indie projects, had grown to like each other, and were just starting a serious relationship. They were at Shashe to work on an article for a South African wildlife magazine. They held hands rather defensively and, having confessed their new relationship to us, looked slightly bashful about the whole thing.

Edith said she thought it was the sweetest thing she'd ever heard.

"You betcha," Henry added.

The waiter came by to offer us a refill. Henry was drinking bourbon, Edith favoured rum and Coke, and Lark and Damian each ordered another beer. Lara asked the waiter if they could make her a margarita.

"Of course, madam. On the rocks with salt?" Lara inclined her head in affirmation. "And for you, sir?"

"Make it two margaritas," I said.

While the waiter fetched our drinks, Henry gave us his opinion of Mexico, Mexicans, Mexican drinks, and Mexican food. None of them were flattering.

"Have you been to Mexico, Henry?" Lara asked, favouring him with a beatific smile.

"Nope. And I wouldn't want to. This is our first time travelling abroad. We've never wanted to leave the good old USA, have we, Edith? The greatest country in the world. You betcha."

Edith nodded in agreement.

Lara gave me the faintest of eye rolls and then turned to the young couple. "Have you two travelled much?"

"Actually, we met on assignment in Colombia last year, and we've been to Peru and Argentina together," Lark replied.

"Habla Espanol?" Lara asked.

"Si, pero me gustaria hablarlo mejor," Lark replied.

"Me encanto su acento," I offered.

"Es muy amable." She blushed and turned to her partner.

"I'm teaching Damian, but he's a slow learner." She laughed.

"That's really not fair," he said. "My teacher's not properly qualified."

We laughed with them, and the atmosphere lightened.

The appearance of a language other than English had confirmed Henry's worst suspicions. He and Edith stomped off to their table in the dining area where Henry was soon complaining to the waiter about the number of ice cubes in his bourbon.

"You're a native speaker," Lark said to Lara, which introduced a line of conversation that was still going strong when the waiter summoned us for dinner.

"Would you like to sit with us?" I offered.

They looked at each other. "Sure, that would be great," Damian said.

Two tables were pushed together, cutlery, flatware, and glasses rearranged, and we sat down to a wonderful dinner. Between courses I was pretty sure that Damian and Lark were holding hands under the table. They looked really good together, and I hoped it would work out for them.

"I think the old folks better get some sleep," Lara said finally. "Early start tomorrow."

Damian stood and pulled out Lark's chair, which I thought was a nice touch. I looked across at them, their eyes sparkling, smiles on their faces.

"We're going to have a look at the stars before we turn in," he said.

Lark blushed and put a hand on his shoulder. "What's Spanish for star?" she asked him.

He hesitated a moment before replying. "Estrella."

She smiled. "See? I'm a great teacher."

IV

I fell asleep almost at once, and I didn't move until the server came with our tea and rusks. I dressed for the early morning game drive: cotton pants,

Lost and Found

khaki shirt, hiking boots, and a down gilet, a soft-brimmed hat to ward off the strong sun when it rose. David was still in the bathroom when I stepped outside the tent. The sky was a silky black tinged with purple on the eastern horizon. The moon had set, the brightest stars were still visible, and the air was chill.

Some birds were starting to fuss around the edge of the waterhole, and cheerful voices were coming from the direction of the main camp buildings. David appeared through the tent flap with the backpack we had agreed to share. It held our water bottles, sunscreen, insect repellent, extra sweaters, and one pair of binoculars that would be good for spotting distant wildlife and perhaps handy for discovering other things as well.

We'd be back from the drive around 11:00 a.m. Our plan was to have lunch and a short siesta and then take a covert look around the camp at the hottest point of the afternoon when most people would be asleep.

As we approached the compound, we saw two open-topped Land Cruisers ready for us with their diesel engines clattering. Henry and Edith, dressed in matching blue track suits and green baseball hats, were sitting in one, Damian and Lark in the other. One of the guides, who introduced himself as Daudi, said we could choose either vehicle. We jumped in behind the young couple. The rear bench seat was elevated, and we had great visibility. I waved cheerfully at Henry and Edith, who seemed a bit dazed by the early start.

I realized we were there to conduct a murder investigation, but I couldn't help but pinch myself as we pulled out of camp and headed across the undulating semi-desert, the beauty of the African wilderness unfolding before my eyes. Only a couple of weeks ago, I'd been going about my relatively routine life in South Florida—calming nervous house sellers and putting on a show for prospective buyers, going to the gym, shopping at Publix. And now this. I realized that as dangerous and difficult as the investigation had become, I was loving every minute of it. I had never done anything like this in my life. I was operating well outside my comfort zone, and I wouldn't have swapped it for anything.

Daudi and our driver, Mack, were sorcerers. They knew exactly where to look for the different animals. Daudi pointed, and Mack steered the truck in the direction indicated, bumping over the rutted terrain. Then herds of impalas materialized from the scrubby golden grass. Daudi offered a couple of words, Mack would change direction, and we'd find an eagle perched on a craggy tree branch. Another word, another route, and we'd find zebras bucking and kicking and chasing each other in dusty circles.

Occasionally, Damian would ask Mack if he could adjust the position of the vehicle slightly so he could get a better shot. It was on one of those stops while Damian was focusing on a gorgeous bird that we heard a terrified squeal, and a huge warthog came tearing out of the scrub onto the open area of the vlei where we were sitting.

"Hold tight, everybody. Damian, get your camera ready." Even Daudi seemed excited.

A second later, two young lions flew out of the grass at a dead run, gaining on the pig. The terrified animal jinked right and left and seemed to have gained some distance when two other lions appeared from the grass right in front of it. The warthog went down in a cloud of dust, throaty primal growls overwhelming the doomed animal's screams.

The lions began to gorge on the creature while its hind legs still kicked. It was a powerful sight. We sat there mesmerized, the click of Damian's shutter punctuating the animal sounds while the four young lions, bloody to their necks, devoured their prey.

This went on for perhaps fifteen minutes with Mack repositioning the Land Cruiser to give us different views. Suddenly, all four lions raised their heads as one, all focused in the same direction. One stood and sniffed the air. Slowly, from the other side of the vlei, a group of hyenas emerged. The lions, unwilling to mix it up with the dangerous intruders, sauntered away, leaving the substantial scraps to the hyenas and the growing crowd of marabou storks gathering in the trees.

Lark turned around to us and mouthed "Wow."

We sat there for a couple of minutes more watching the hyenas crunching bones with their massive jaws while the vultures hopped around, ugly feathered hags waiting their turn with ill-concealed bad grace.

"Shit, wasn't that something," Henry exclaimed from the other car. "You won't see that in Pittsburgh, eh, Edith? That was something, you betcha."

The rest of the drive continued its magical unfolding. As the sun rose well above the rim of the horizon, the big predators looked for shade in which to rest up for the day, leaving the field to the antelopes, jackals, mongooses, wild dogs, wildebeest, giraffe, elephants, and all the other animals that we encountered that morning.

It was after 11:00 a.m. when we pulled into the camp. The six of us sat together around a table in the shade of an awning and ate a substantial early lunch. Damian was very pleased with some of the shots he had taken and showed us several on the LED display on the back of his chunky Nikon. Lark had made live notes on an iPad and told us some of the ideas she had for the article she was writing. Henry went on about the way the lions had hunted as a team, comparing them favourably to the run defense of the Pittsburgh Steelers. Edith said she felt a bit sorry for the warthog.

The sun was almost vertical, and the thermometer on the veranda indicated 38°C as David and I walked back to our tent.

"Let's rest up for a couple of hours," David said. "It's hotter than Hades right now. The sun will be down a bit by midafternoon. If we head out at three for a look around, we'll still be back in plenty of time for the evening drive."

I yawned. "I better set the alarm on my watch, or we'll never wake up. Early start, big lunch, and all that excitement; I'm sleepy."

"All that excitement meaning the lion kill?" David offered.

"Well, yes, that and other things," I said coyly, tipping his hat over his eyes.

V

We lay on our backs enjoying the breeze from the huge fan that rotated slowly from the peak of the tent. Lara fell asleep in a few minutes, and I turned onto my side so I could watch the rise and fall of her chest and the way that strands of her thick dark hair moved in the draft from above. I don't think it's voyeurism if you watch someone you love.

Thirty years ago, when I worked in Australia, we lived in a rambling old Victorian villa in the leafy Melbourne suburb of Fitzroy. We strung a hammock between two gum trees in the back garden, and on weekends when I wasn't involved with school duties, I'd take a novel into the hammock and read and doze. James, who must have been four or five, at that time would find me, climb in beside me, and fall asleep in my arms. I'd put my book aside and watch him as he lay there. His limbs would twitch occasionally as a dream swept over him. I'd brush a wind-blown flower petal from his corn-blond hair. I'd hold him and marvel at him till he woke. How could I have helped create something so perfect? My love for him was too big for me to bear.

I looked across at Lara, and my heart clenched with a similar emotion. I knew her loss and marvelled at her courage. Wanting to tell her how I felt, I reached to touch her arm but then pulled back, not wanting to wake her.

My eyes closed, and I joined her in sleep.

VI

We slipped on our dusty morning clothes, I swung on the backpack, and we stepped out into the heat. We had been told that we could go off on our own as long as we stuck to the trails in the immediate area of the camp. We'd also been given a whistle to blow in the event that we ran into any difficulties.

The hippos were the most likely problem for guests. They came out of the water in the cool of night to snuffle around between the buildings looking for greenery, but in the heat of day, they were submerged in the waterhole protecting their sensitive hides from the blazing sun, so they posed no threat.

We started by walking around the perimeter of the waterhole and then took a trail that ran around behind the main camp. There were half a dozen outbuildings. We saw people preparing food in one, servicing safari vehicles in another, and doing laundry in a third. We came across one windowless corrugated metal building with a sliding metal door that was secured with a hefty padlock. The word "Danger" was written in red on the door alongside a "hazardous materials" sign. Another building was simply four posts and a wooden roof providing shade for two petrol pumps. Nothing unusual or suspicious so far.

The trail took us beside the airstrip. As we drew near, we heard the whine of an engine. A moment later a small twin-engine turboprop bounced down onto the dirt strip in a cloud of dust. We watched from behind a row of scrubby bushes as the plane taxied to the end of the strip nearest the camp. The aircraft door was pushed open, and a middle-aged couple emerged, squinting into the sunlight. Their clothes identified them as tourists. Maybe this was the shuttle that ran from Johannesburg. We watched as the luggage and supplies were unloaded from the cargo bay: four suitcases, a pallet covered with cases of beer, and a yellow portable generator. The new arrivals were led away by the young woman who had shown us to our tent the previous evening.

Lost and Found

"If we don't find anything to help us in the investigation, can we stay here for the full four days anyway?" Lara joked.

"It's all prepaid, so I think it would be a waste not to," I replied. "Let's see how the next twenty-four hours unfold."

We turned to retrace our steps back to camp. The evening drive was set to leave in twenty minutes. Now that Daudi and Mack had gotten to know us a bit, I was hoping I could get some information from them without seeming overly inquisitive.

We hadn't gone ten metres when Lara grasped my arm.

"Wait, look over there." She was staring intently at a small group of trees about two hundred metres from where we stood. I slipped the binoculars from the backpack and focused them on the spot she was pointing to.

"What do you think you saw?" I asked. "An animal?"

"I'm not sure. Maybe. I'm sure I saw something."

I scanned left and right without picking up anything. I was about to take the glasses from my eyes when I caught the slightest movement in the trees. I focused more closely, and there it was. A few metres in from the edge of the trees, all but hidden in the flickering shadows, sat a half-ton truck painted in camouflage stripes. I saw two men in the cab, and in the truck bed was a large gun mounted on a tripod.

"Take a look at this, Lara." I unslung the binoculars from behind my neck and passed them to her.

She refocused the glasses. I'd become a little short sighted; her eyesight was 20:20.

"Oh my," she said. "Why would a game reserve need a heavy machine gun?"

I took back the glasses and looked at the gun again. It was about five feet long with a big sight placed on top of the barrel above the trigger.

"You're the gun expert. What kind do you think it is?"

"We don't have heavy machine guns at the Delray Shooting Club," she said with the slightest hint of sarcasm, "but the most widely used heavy machine gun in the world is still an old Russian-made model called the DShK. That would be my bet."

"What are its capabilities?" I asked as I continued to look at the weapon. "It looks rather old and evil."

"It wouldn't be much good against anything with armour plating, but for anything else it would be very effective. You could even use it to disable or bring down a plane if you had the right people operating it."

"Maybe they're expecting the camp to be attacked by a herd of enraged rhinos," I said, hoping a note of levity would ward off the uneasy feeling developing in the pit of my stomach.

"If it's a DShK, it fires 108 millimetre ammunition, so it would basically blow up a rhinoceros," she said, sounding unreasonably cool. "The Russians supplied lots of them to the FRELIMO side in the Mozambique civil war. When the war ended in 1992, most of the weaponry was never accounted for; it all just disappeared into the bush, only to turn up again in the hands of poachers and drug gangs all over the world."

"How do you know this stuff?" It wasn't a very good time to ask, but Lara kept revealing layer upon layer of talents and knowledge that I hadn't the foggiest notion about.

"I pay attention, and I read a lot." She smiled at me. "Come on. Let's not miss the evening drive. I'm not leaving here till I've seen a cheetah."

VII

After a half hour or so of driving, I did see my cheetah, but not where I had expected. It was sitting on the roof of the vehicle inside of which Henry and Edith were cowering. Edith was desperately trying to get the guide to shoo it away, and Henry suggested shooting it, but the guide gave a big belly laugh and told them not to worry.

"Isn't that a bit unusual?" I asked Daudi.

"Actually, no. The land around here is pretty flat, and there's lots of tall grass to obscure the cheetah's prey, so they look for anything high, like a termite mound, to sit on and survey their surroundings. The animals here are habituated to our presence and have no reason to fear us, so a Land Cruiser works just as well as a termite mound."

Damian and Lark were ecstatic and asked Mack to move the car into different positions where Damian got some amazing close-ups of the animal. I used the camera on my phone but was still really pleased with the results.

Lost and Found

Eventually, the cheetah climbed down onto the hood and then in one languid lollop regained the ground. It bared its fangs at Henry and Edith before strolling away.

Mack drove up to the top of a kopje, pulled on the parking brake, and killed the engine. The location gave an amazing view of the valley below. We spotted herds of impalas, wildebeest, elephants, and giraffes as the sun sank toward the horizon. Mack and Daudi invited us to jump down and, to my disbelief, pulled out a table and camp chairs from the vehicle's trunk. This was followed by an ice bucket, a bottle of gin, a case of tonic water, and some fresh limes.

"Sundowners," Daudi proclaimed.

We sat around the table and chatted about the drive and what we'd seen. After a while David and I wandered off a few paces to get a different angle on the view, and Daudi joined us.

"Everything you can see as far as the horizon is Shashe territory," he said. "The company leases it from the government."

"That's a huge tract of land," David said. "Do you know how big it is?"

"A little more than fifty thousand hectares," he replied. "We have another camp, a bush camp, over in the western part. We call it Rooi Kamp. It's pretty basic, nothing like the main camp."

"Which is absolutely amazing, by the way," I said.

"Thank you." Daudi smiled. "We aim to be the very best reserve in Botswana."

"What's the other camp used for?" I asked.

"I've never been there, but from time to time some VIP appears, and the boss flies them over there. Apparently, there's a waterhole there that attracts a great variety of animals, and I hear that you can occasionally see pangolins and aardvarks. That would be very special. Even I have only ever seen one pangolin."

"Who's the boss?" David asked. "Have we met him already?"

"I don't know his full name, but we call him Mr. Joca. They say he spends most of his time between Jo'burg and Polokwane. He hasn't been at camp for a couple of weeks, but you'll recognize him when you see him."

"Why's that?" I asked.

"Before he got involved managing Shashe, he lost an arm and an eye in the Mozambique war, and half his body is burned pretty bad. Doesn't seem to slow him down though. When he's in camp, everybody better jump!"

"Is there a road over to the Rooi Kamp?" I asked.

"There's a track. It's not used much. Rough going when the rains come."

I knew that David had been pumping Daudi for information, and I think Daudi put it down to the natural curiosity of a tourist, but we didn't want to push our luck, so I suggested we rejoin the others.

We were back at camp an hour later. It was dark, and as we walked the path back to our tent, we noticed that the runway lights had been turned on. David suggested we sneak over and have a look.

As we approached, we heard the drone of an aircraft engine. By the time we took up position behind our favourite bush, the plane had landed and was being unloaded. No tourists this time, just two pallets covered with cardboard boxes. I trained the binoculars on the boxes. Apart from identifying the words written on them as Portuguese, I couldn't make out anything else.

We were about to move away when the two men doing the unloading jumped to attention and presented a smart salute. Out of the shadows on the far side of the plane, a small man emerged. He returned the salute with his left hand; his right arm was missing.

"Looks like Mr. Joca's back in town," I said.

CHAPTER 11

I

We watched for a couple of minutes without learning anything more and then returned to the tent to shower and change for dinner. Lara had brought a couple of dresses along with her, and she wanted to wear one that night. She chose a flowing knee-length silk dress in a shade of yellow that brought out the gold flecks in her extraordinary green eyes. She wore a wide black belt that narrowed her waist even further and gold pendant earrings.

I didn't think I'd get away with jeans, so I shook a couple of wrinkles out of my blue blazer and chose a sky-blue Canali tie over the maroon Zegna. Yes, I had brought two ties to a safari camp, which probably speaks volumes about my personality. The grey Canali trousers and the inevitable Gucci loafers completed my efforts.

I wondered what role Joca would play now that he was at the main camp, but I didn't have to wonder for long because as we stepped up onto the veranda, there he was, holding court at the bar. He'd exchanged his khaki fatigues for a blue suit and open-necked white shirt and was accomplishing the remarkable feat of making Henry listen to him without interruption.

"Ah, this must be Lara and David," he said in an attractive baritone, his English overlain with the slightest of accents but one so enigmatic that I couldn't place it. He advanced a couple of steps toward us and took Lara's hand. "Ms. Rios, you grace our rudimentary camp with your beauty and elegance." He bent over and kissed it. Then he stretched his arm out to me and rotated his left hand at the last moment to grasp my right. "Welcome to you both."

His hand was perfectly manicured and surprisingly soft. He wore an onyx signet ring. His glasses had thin gold wire frames. Close up, I saw that his face had tiny pockmarks, the kind caused either by childhood illness, smallpox, or being too close to a blast. He wore a black patch over his damaged eye, and the shiny, wrinkled pink skin of a burn showed just above his collar.

Lara smiled. "We're so pleased to be here Mr. . . ."

"Please call me Joca," he said.

"We're delighted to be here, Joca, and I wouldn't call the camp rudimentary. It's simply fabulous, and the staff are the best." Lara was laying it on thick, but she was a wealthy tourist from America, and she was moving into character.

"I'm impressed that you know our names," I said.

"David, as I'm sure you know, the key to any successful business is the relationship you create with your customers, and at Shashe we are dedicated to creating the best and most enduring relationship with each and every one of our guests. People forget what you did for them, but they remember how you made them feel. Isn't that what they say?" He could have been reading from a motivational business book, but he wasn't wrong.

"Now, I'm talking too much and monopolizing you. Please come." He waved us over to the bar and turned to speak to Damian and Lark, who were perched on stools, sipping cocktails, and looking very much in love.

Joca didn't join us for dinner, but as dessert was being served, he approached and asked if he could sit with us. He pulled a chair up to our table and motioned for the waiter to bring us coffee.

We exchanged pleasantries, and I asked a few leading questions but learned very little.

"As I said earlier, it is our greatest desire that you should have the perfect visit to Shashe," he said, "so I'm wondering if there is anything that we can arrange that would help to create that perfection."

"I think our experience thus far comes pretty close to perfection," Lara purred.

"Well, darling," I said, "remember how Daudi was telling us about the Rooi Kamp?"

"Ooh, yes," she said, feigning surprise.

Lost and Found

I turned back to Joca. "I wondered if there's any chance of us visiting. Lara is desperate to see an aardvark, and Daudi said that you can sometimes spot them there."

"Daudi told you about the Rooi Kamp, did he?" For a moment a shadow passed behind Joca's eyes. "Well, I think that Ms. Rios gets what Ms. Rios wants," he said, recovering his over-the-top charm. "I'm afraid I cannot fly you there, as the plane is leaving in the morning to pick up guests from Jo'burg, but I'm told you have a vehicle, and you would be most welcome to drive over there tomorrow. It will take you about an hour. I will alert the staff at camp that you're to be shown every possible courtesy and that they are not to send you back until they have found you an aardvark." He smiled.

"That would be such a treat. Thank you so much, Mr. Joca," Lara gushed.

His smile widened. "Just Joca, please. Just Joca."

II

And so it was that the next morning we found ourselves driving slowly along the track that led out of the main camp heading west. It was pretty rough, and several times I left the track to skirt through the bush, looking for a smoother route. I was glad we had the bakkie; a car wouldn't have stood a chance.

I had put on a performance for Joca, and we had got what we wanted, an opportunity to investigate the remote bush camp. Perhaps it would lead to nothing, but there was something about Joca, his manner, his bearing, and his precise and almost oily smoothness that made me think we were onto something. I felt that, like me, he was acting. He behaved like someone in the hospitality industry. He complimented and cosseted, but beneath that, maybe well hidden but still just visible, was the persona of a warrior, a man comfortable giving orders and ensuring they were carried out to the letter. His skin was soft and his grey hair well groomed, but there was something fearful about him, a quiet menace that was more alarming than a show of violence would have been. Maybe I was overthinking things, but I was pretty sure we'd only seen one side of Joca.

Our drive was without doubt the most extraordinary of my life. Even with my uneasy mind, I was enchanted by all that we encountered. On one of my excursions off the track, we rounded a rocky outcrop and almost drove into a small herd of elephants. I stopped and turned off the engine. The matriarch took a few steps toward us and flapped her ears in mock aggression. A baby moved under the shelter and shade of its mother's stomach. A young male in *must* and dripping testosterone waved his trunk around to show us who was in charge. We sat there for twenty minutes until they lost interest in us and moved off, following the line of withered brown trees that was their only source of food at the end of a brutal dry season.

Another time we crested a rise and saw a pack of hunting dogs loping along in front of us. They stopped as one and turned their heads to face us, their noses high in the air to pick up our scent and their enormous bat-like ears swiveling. I imagined their look was one of contempt. This was their land. They roamed for miles every day and knew every inch of it, and here we were in our noisy little machine crawling along a thread of track.

After driving for perhaps an hour, we figured we must be pretty close to the bush camp, so we pulled off the track again, and I engaged the low gear and headed up to the top of a kopje to get a look at the lay of the land. David got the binoculars out of the backpack and spent a few minutes looking around.

"I think I can see Rooi Kamp," he said, passing the glasses to me and indicating the direction.

Sure enough, I could make out a few small buildings surrounded by vegetation just a shade more verdant than the surrounding scrub. Beyond the buildings I saw a small runway that had been cut out of the bush, but no planes were in view. I swiveled around in the direction that we had come and hesitated when I saw what looked like a distant plume of smoke.

"Have a look at this David," I said, handing the binoculars to him.

"I'm pretty sure that's dust, not smoke," he said a moment later.

"I think there's a vehicle following us."

"But Joca said nobody was heading this way today."

"Maybe he changed his mind."

I don't know what it was about that plume of dust, but I could feel the fateful pendulum swing, and in that moment the atmosphere between us transformed subtly but unmistakably. What had begun to feel like a luxurious vacation in an exotic wilderness had changed back into an adventure fraught with danger, and I think we both began to realize that we didn't have the skills or the experience for it.

"It's not too late to change our minds," David said, voicing our unspoken thought. "We can say I got sick, and we need to head back to Polokwane. We can be there by nightfall if we go right now. We can leave this to the professionals."

"Thank you for saying that, David, but nothing's really changed."

In a way I wished it had. I wished there was an easy out for us, a way back to the snowy linen and crystal stemware of the Cape Grace and a deepening relationship with this good man and maybe a life together, but no matter how I contorted the facts, I couldn't make them give us that escape.

"What we're doing needs to be done, and right now we're the people best placed to do it," I said. "I do feel scared, but I also know that we need to do this because it's right. It's what gives us purpose and gives meaning to our relationship. It's the mirror that lets us see ourselves as we really are."

David set the binoculars to one side and felt inside the backpack, pulling out our guns and laying them on the dashboard. We each loaded a six-round clip. I pulled up the left leg of my jeans and adjusted the ankle holster before slipping the gun in and securing it.

David put his pistol back in the pack. He wasn't comfortable with the weapon, and I wasn't sure how much use he would be if things turned nasty. I knew a lot about guns, but I'd never fired one in anger or self-defence. I wondered in that moment what it took to kill another person and whether I'd have that ability.

I reached for the binoculars to get a better look at the car that was now visible on the track about a kilometre from us.

As it jumped into focus, I realized it was one of the vehicles used on the game drives. The driver was one of the men whom we had seen unloading the plane the night before. As we had surmised, Joca was sitting in the back. He was wearing loose khaki battle dress and reflective aviator sunglasses. Beside him sat a boy who looked to be in his mid-teens. He was delicate and handsome. As I watched, Joca reached out and laid his hand on the boy's thigh.

"We better get down there before they wonder what we're up to," David said.

I started the engine and bumped down the rocky slope to regain the trail just behind Joca's vehicle. I gave a friendly honk on the horn and waved enthusiastically, slipping back into character as Joca and the boy turned to look at us.

We drove the final hundred metres into camp in convoy. I pulled in beside the Shashe Land Cruiser and jumped out, the perfect perky tourist.

"Ms. Rios," Joca said, smiling, "I'm so glad you made it here safely. I was worried for you." He looked across at the boy, and they both laughed. I couldn't read what it meant.

"Come, have some refreshments. I have a friend in camp, and I know he's anxious to meet you."

III

Joca led, walking beside Lara, his hand touching her elbow and ushering her forward. The boy was next, half a pace in front of me. The driver was behind me. It felt like a procession.

I had a chance to look more closely at the boy. He was dark and elegant, and he swung along with an athletic stride. He wore a faded navy cotton shirt, dusty brown shorts, and old flip-flops. His face was marked with ritual scarring. Three ridges ran outwards from the corners of his mouth like cat's whiskers, and sweeping scars led from the bridge of his nose across his cheeks toward his ears. He looked ferocious but also strangely beautiful. I wondered about the nature of his attachment to Joca.

On closer inspection I saw that Daudi's assessment of the camp as "pretty basic" was accurate. I counted six small buildings with walls made of plaited reeds and thatch roofs. They formed a circle around the open area across which we were walking. As we approached one of the huts, a door opened, and a man in fatigues came out and sprang to attention, holding the door open for us. Joca nodded to him.

After the glare of the noonday sun, it took several seconds for my eyes to adjust to the darkness of the hut. I heard Lara make a small sound, and I looked over at her. Her mouth was slightly open, and she was staring straight ahead.

"I expect you will be surprised to see me here, Ms. Rios." Stephen Kumalo rose to his feet and smiled at us both.

I suppose in the last couple of weeks, I had run different scenarios through my mind, but this was one that had never materialized.

"What are you doing here, Stephen?" It was all I could think of to say. I think I was in shock.

"Hmm . . ." He rubbed his chin. "Well, I suppose you could say I'm keeping an eye on you and Ms. Rios." He exchanged glances with Joca, and they chuckled together.

"Sit down, won't you?" Joca said.

One other person was in the room, a girl, maybe a year younger than the boy and, like him, very dark skinned. She wore a yellow sleeveless T-shirt and blue jeans. She also had some ritual scarring, though in her case it was on her upper arms. She was a pretty girl, but I could see just behind her eyes that there was something profoundly sad about her. She stood and walked across to Joca, kissing him on the cheek.

"Welcome home, Father," she said in a small voice.

With Stephen sitting there, it was hard to know what to say. We couldn't continue pretending to be tourists, and it seemed pretty clear that everyone in the room knew exactly who we were and what we were doing there.

Joca put his arm around the girl and pulled her close. "You have been too successful for your own good," he said to us, almost as though he regretted it. "It seems to Stephen and me that you have learned too much. What to do with you has been the subject of our discussions since you arrived, and we are not yet in agreement."

"You knew who we were when we arrived at Shashe?" Lara asked, astonished.

"Oh, yes. In fact considerably before that. Stephen has, as usual, been meticulous in keeping me informed about all matters relating to this unfortunate business. Stephen feels that it would be best to dispose of you now, but I wonder if there is some other way."

I glanced over at Lara, but her face revealed nothing.

"You will be surprised when I say this, but I hate killing. I have seen so much death, and yet I'm sickened and diminished each time I have to take a life." He looked genuinely distressed. The girl moved her arm and put it around his waist. "You're intelligent and capable people, and I believe you deserve to understand why you're here and why you may die here."

Things had moved so fast that I was scrambling to make any sense of them, but anything that gave us a little more time had to be a good thing.

"Let us sit together, and I will tell you a story," he said. The girl pulled out a chair for Joca, and he sat opposite us. She stood to one side of him, a hand on his shoulder. The boy took a chair on the other side. A deadly tableau.

"Merced, get us some tea, will you?" he called loudly to someone moving in the rear portion of the hut. "And bring some biltong and rusks if Mamadou hasn't eaten everything," he added with a laugh.

He spoke quietly to the girl in a different language for a few moments while Merced brought in a tray and placed it on the table.

"I have been very rude," Joca said. "I have not introduced you to my children. This lovely young woman is Diba." The girl nodded to us and moved her mouth in an attempt at a smile.

"My boy is Archange. He's a fine young man, but he cannot speak; he has no tongue." The boy looked at us with dead eyes.

"The children are a good place for us to start this story because they, like me, are not from here." He looked at the children as if asking their permission, then grunted and continued his story.

"We're from what is now, ironically, called the Democratic Republic of the Congo; however, it is neither democratic nor a republic.

"You're educated people, so you will know something of the tortured past of our country. Throughout its history, its riches have acted like a magnet, attracting exploitation.

"The Belgian King Leopold held it as his personal fiefdom and enslaved the people. Mobuto preferred to call it Zaire, but that was all that changed. For thirty years he stole from the people and salted away billions. The Kabilas, father and son, have used our country's minerals to line their pockets. We're one of the richest countries in the world, but our people are among the poorest."

He took a sip of his tea. "The DR Congo is a tribal country. Tribal loyalties run deep and tribal hatreds even deeper. My children and I, we are Banyamulenge, a Tutsi people, and we live in South Kivu Province in the eastern part of the country. For years we have been hunted and killed by the Congolese government and by the Hutu tribes who want our land, for it is rich in minerals. There is gold and tantalum, which is more precious than gold. Your cell phones would be useless without tantalum."

He rubbed his eyes in a gesture that gave him the look of a tired older man. "Ah, yes, that reminds me that we have not yet searched you. Archange, please check Mr. Mallory. Diba, do the same for Ms. Rios."

The children led us over to the far wall where they indicated that we should spread our arms and legs. They frisked us professionally and came away with our phones and the gun on Lara's ankle."

"Ms. Rios, you shock me," Joca mocked. "Though they say the female of the species is deadlier than the male." He laughed. "Check the backpack please, Diba."

She pulled out my gun and the binoculars and laid them on the table.

"Well, well. Quite a little arsenal you two carry with you." He raised his cup to his lips, narrowed his eyes, and looked up thoughtfully. "Tout savoir, c'est tout pardonner. Do you know that expression, Ms. Rios? To know all is to forgive all, one of the many things that the sisters taught me at the mission school in Bukavu. That's why I want to tell you the whole story, so you can understand why I do what I do. I am not looking for your forgiveness, nor do I need it, but I would like you to understand."

IV

He sat back and crossed his legs like my father used to do when he was about to read me a bedtime story. However, I suspected that the content of this story would not generate sweet dreams.

"In the last decade, the government and the Hutus have pushed us off our lands. The money from the minerals that before bought us the guns and ammunition with which we could defend ourselves has dried up. We cannot protect ourselves.

"The Hutu militias come to our villages and take our children as child soldiers, but first they make them execute their parents. Can you imagine, Mr. Mallory? A ten-year-old child forced to shoot her mother in the head. If you need help picturing it, Diba can tell you how it was for her."

He paused and looked at each of us.

"The children were carried off by the militia and given rudimentary survival training. Diba became renowned as a frontline fighter, but she was also used by the men. She has killed many times, but in some important ways there are parts of her that have died too. I hope one day to have the time and opportunity to help her heal.

"Archange had his tongue cut out when he hesitated over an order to use his machete on a baby. They would have killed him, but he was a strong fighter, and they could not afford to lose him."

I looked at Archange, who shuffled awkwardly upon hearing his name. He was probably sixteen, the age Alex was when he died. I was reminded that there are worse things than death.

"I had given up any hope of seeing my children again, but fate was generous for once, and I rescued them from a Hutu patrol that we ambushed last year. As Juliet says, Ms. Rios, 'My only love sprung from my only hate.'"

Joca was showing himself to be a complex mixture of bush fighter and philosopher

"I rescued them but not before I had ordered their execution. I was blinded by blood, and it was only when Diba, my pistol pressing into her temple, called me 'father' that I saw who she was. I was like Abraham, only God spoke through my daughter's lips.

"They are damaged but not beyond repair. I'm determined to teach them to trust again, maybe even to love again. But perhaps the teacher too is damaged. It will be hard."

He looked up, a half-smile incongruously bringing a ray of warmth to his chilling tale. "Go on then. I invite you. Ask me the question that is at the front of your minds."

I looked over at David before speaking. "Kivu is far away. Why are you here? What's the connection?"

"You do not disappoint, Ms. Rios." he smiled again. "The Banyamulenge must have the means to buy arms to defend themselves. With our mineral wealth removed, I was charged with finding what you might call an alternative revenue stream. The Russians and the Israelis are falling over themselves to sell us what we need, but they do not sell on credit."

"So, you're using the profits from importing and selling drugs to finance a brutal war?" David's tone was harsh.

"Have you not been listening, Mr. Mallory?" His smile disappeared, and the ice returned to his voice. "We're using the funds to save our people from genocide. And I do not need your judgement or your approval. You with your white man's privilege, you have no idea what it's like to fight for your life and the lives of those you love. Before the Hutu militia made my daughter kill my wife in front of me, they took my right arm with a single machete blow. I will cease my struggle when my revenge is complete." He was almost shouting by the time he finished.

"How will you know when that time comes?" I was caught up in his emotion, and he could see that my question was genuine.

"I will know it in my heart, and I will see it in the eyes of my children."

He stood. "But I think that chapter of our story is now concluded. There is another chapter, but for that we need a different narrator. Archange, take our guests to their accommodation, and see that they have what they need. Stephen, come. We have much to discuss."

V

The children led us to a small hut on the opposite side of the compound. Inside it was divided into two rooms, each with a locking door. Archange led David into the room on the right, and Diba guided me to the left. The space was perhaps eight feet by ten. There was a mattress on the earth floor and a bucket in the corner.

"It is not very nice. Not what you're used to," she said. Her English was excellent, her accent neutral and perfectly inflected.

"Don't worry about me, Diba. I'm quite a strong old woman." I tried a smile.

She didn't leave immediately, which gave me a chance to take a closer look at her. She was probably about fourteen and tall for her age. Her hair was braided in cornrows above her broad forehead. There was still a sparkle in her eye that the horrors of her childhood hadn't quite managed to extinguish.

"You're not very old," she said. "You must be about the age of my mother when I killed her."

I couldn't reply.

"Merced will bring you food. Try to sleep. I think tomorrow will be difficult for you."

She had managed to cram more misery into fourteen years than anyone would experience in many lifetimes. Even the sorrows of my life and our present predicament paled by comparison.

"Thank you, Diba." I reached out to touch her arm, but she shrank back, frowning.

"I'm sorry," I said.

She gave the slightest bob of her head and then left me alone.

Diba was right. The following morning was likely to be tough. Whatever was involved in Joca's "next chapter" wasn't going to save us.

The walls of the hut were made of reeds, and the cool night air seeped into the room. The divide between my room and David's was made of the same stuff, so we could talk to each other without even raising our voices.

Our conversation that night focused, as one might expect, on our fate.

"Joca seems to want to justify his actions to us," David spoke quietly "Don't you find that strange?"

"It's unusual, but I think he's a moral man who finds himself in an impossible situation."

"He can't let us go, can he? He's right; we know far too much."

"It doesn't look good, does it?" I said. "Stephen knows everything about us, and he wants us dead, but I get the sense that Joca holds the power, so as long as he hasn't made up his mind, we have a chance. I'd like to know what he meant about the next chapter needing a new narrator."

"We should probably try and get some sleep," David said. "We'll need our wits about us tomorrow. In the morning let's see if we can find any possible way out of here. If it becomes clear that they're going to kill us, we'll have nothing to lose by a high-risk escape attempt."

I didn't think I'd be able to sleep, but I did. I dreamed about my mother, which hardly ever happened, probably because I had had so little chance to get to know her before she died. That night I slept curled up beside her and remembered her softness and the smell of her hair.

VI

I lay still on the dusty earthen floor of the cell. I'd chosen it over the mattress, which was stained with different fluids, one of which was certainly blood. I could just make out the skittering movement of rats in the shadowed corners and hear the occasional rumble of voices from the other side of the compound.

I was close to despair, filled with thoughts of the possibility of the violent death awaiting us in the morning and the guilt I felt for putting Lara in this position. After several hours of sleepless anxiety, by one of those blessed quirks of the human mind, I found myself sinking into the comfort of memory.

It was five years ago, and I was reliving a trip I'd taken to Peru with Jessica. She was in grade twelve and was taking an elective philosophy course. She had an assignment on the Stoic philosophers, and she asked me questions about them as we drove south from Lima on the road to Chincha, the cold ocean on our right and the dry brown hills to our left.

I told her about Seneca, whose beautiful prose style I had always enjoyed. He said the happy life was not found in pleasures or possessions but in the pursuit of virtue; in finding the right thing to do and then doing it no matter what others thought or did. We may be healthy or sick, rich or poor, live to a ripe old age, or die young, but these are matters of luck, and they are beyond our control. We control only our own thoughts and actions, how we conduct ourselves, and how we treat others. I told her that people sometimes mistake Stoicism for a surrender to helplessness, but I thought it was really the opposite, a challenge to individual responsibility. Perhaps I found comfort in this idea and the sweet memories of time with Jessica, or perhaps it was the unrelenting strain of the previous twenty-four hours, but eventually, I drifted away into sleep.

I was woken after what seemed like a few minutes but was probably several hours by the shafts of pale sunlight filtering through the gaps in the walls. I forced myself to remain still for a few minutes, trying to see if Hypnos had brought me any fresh ideas. He hadn't, and I was lying there wondering about Stephen's involvement when I heard the faint hum of a distant engine. It rapidly became louder, and I made my way over to a crack in the wall in time to see a single-engine plane bump down onto the runway. It disappeared from my field of view, and I backed away from the wall just as the door to my cell opened, and Merced appeared with some flatbread and black coffee. Archange loomed behind her and locked the door again as she moved on to Lara's cell. The thought of Lara made my heart race, and I realized I was desperate to see her.

I didn't have to wait long. Diba came to get us mid-morning, and we followed her across the compound to the building we'd been in the day before. Lara reached out and took my hand as we walked. She raised her eyebrows at me and smiled as if we were going for a morning stroll along the beach in Boca. I was struggling to keep it together, but Lara seemed to have realized that so much was out of her control that a degree of acceptance might work best. Seneca would have been proud.

Joca was in the far corner of the building looking over a map with Stephen. They laughed at something, and Joca patted Stephen on the back as they walked over to us.

"Good morning. I hope you managed to get some sleep?" Joca enquired. "Stephen has a proposal that he wants to put to you. It may provide you with a way out of the difficult situation you find yourselves in. I'll let him describe the offer; he can be quite persuasive when he puts his mind to it."

Stephen, as always, looked as if he'd just stepped out of the shower. His white shirt was ironed and his brown brogues polished. He brought his palms together in front of him and rested his chin on the points of his fingers, narrowing his eyes and looking at us.

"Where to begin?" he said.

"The beginning usually works well," I replied.

"Very well, David. The beginning it is. Before I start let me say how awkward I find our present situation. I confess that I got to like you both in Cape Town, and it was my hope that you would enjoy Shelburne's hospitality, rubber stamp our findings, and fly back home. Alas, it was not to be. 'Curiosity killed the cat,' is that the saying?"

"And you want us dead." Lara made the bald statement.

"I do. But my comrade, Joca, has convinced me that it might be better to see if your love for life and, if I'm not being impertinent, your love for each other can advance our cause, and I have learned to trust his judgement."

"What's in this for you, Stephen?" Lara asked.

"Oh, dear Lara." He pushed himself back in his chair and laughed. "Always looking at the psychology of the individual. Well, you'll be disappointed in me. Money. Nothing more, nothing less. A chance to give my children some of the advantages that the Shelburne children enjoy. A chance for my wife to hold her head high. A chance to level the playing field. But you have distracted me, and I'm talking about myself, a cardinal sin in polite conversation." He smiled at us both.

"Now, to the point. We need the investigation into Tom Parkes' death to go away. It threatens to shed unwelcome light on our mission. As Joca has explained, the lives of his people hang in the balance. Don't get me wrong. Joca's fight is not my fight. I'm a mercenary here. My job is to help the drugs flow, to bring producers and consumers together, and I'm paid very well to make that happen.

"The boy is dead—which, by the way, I deeply regret. The original report ruled it an accidental death. We need that verdict confirmed. It seems to us that you're in the perfect position to bring that about. You have the credibility that your reputation brings, and Dr. Croken trusts you implicitly. There will be some tidying up to do, but we believe you can deliver us this outcome. What do you say?"

"I see one small problem beyond the moral difficulties," I said. "If you release us to do as you ask, what's to stop us going straight to the police and telling them everything we've discovered?"

"David, you're using plurals when you should be thinking singular. We would release you, but Ms. Rios would remain as our guest here until you have succeeded to our satisfaction."

"By 'guest' you mean 'hostage,'" Lara said.

Stephen shrugged. "I prefer 'guest,' but the point is moot. If you refuse, you die now. If you accept, you roll the dice and give yourselves a chance."

VII

So, there it was. Our fate was becoming clearer, but we didn't have long to think about it because at that moment we heard a squall of discordant voices from outside. Seconds later a tall figure pushed through the door. He was silhouetted against the light, and I didn't recognize him until he moved into the room. Ed Parkes threw his hat on the table and slumped into a chair. He must have flown in on the plane I had heard land a few minutes ago.

"For fuck's sake, Joca. The boy tells me that the last delivery was short. What are you playing at?" His tone was as hostile and derisive as it had been the last time we had seen him. "And in the name of all that's holy, what are these two jokers doing still alive? Are you planning to marry the girl?" He laughed at his own joke and looked at me with eyes that did nothing to conceal his lust. "If not, I'd like to get to know her better." His plump lips parted in a lascivious grin. I wrinkled my nose and looked away.

"Let us focus on business, Mr. Parkes." Joca's voice was cool, and he was clearly unhappy with the direction the conversation had taken.

"Our last shipment was short by ten kilos, but we know that's because one of the trucks had a problem on the road. Our information is that it will be here within the day. We have a strong relationship with our supplier; there is no cause for concern."

"There better not be. I've got customers for everything we can move, and they're not nice people. I'm putting my neck on the line so you can arm your brothers and sisters in the Congo. There better bloody well not be a problem."

"I think you know very well that you're being handsomely compensated for your part in our business. I think it is I who should be asking you about problems, Mr. Parkes."

"What the fuck are you talking about?" Parkes was loud, but there was a note of concern in his voice.

"Our operation works best if it attracts minimal attention. We organize the shipment from Maputo to this camp via Zimbabwe. We tranship and move the cargo across the Limpopo into South Africa. We cut and resize it and deliver it to your casinos in pretty little packages for your customers. We offer you a substantial discount, and you make a killing. Ah, but listen to me, Mr. Parkes, a killing, a Freudian slip perhaps." Joca raised an eyebrow at Parkes.

"The problem I have is that you have been killing people and making too much noise. Not good for business, Mr. Parkes. Not good at all. We have many people on our payroll all the way from the docks to the doors of your establishments, and you're putting them all at risk." He fixed Parkes with a steely gaze that clearly disconcerted him.

"You know Tom's death was a mistake." Parkes paused and bit his lip.

"I do not call it a mistake when you ask an associate to make sure the boy doesn't cause any trouble," Joca replied.

Parkes sprang to his feet and advanced toward Joca, then froze when he saw the pistol that Diba had levelled at him. I hadn't even seen her draw it. She had some special skills for a fourteen-year-old.

Joca put his hand on the girl's arm, and she lowered the gun. Parkes returned to the chair and rubbed his hands across his face. "You don't imagine I will ever forgive myself?" He said softly, clearly from the heart.

"Let us leave the boy aside." Joca wasn't interested in Parkes's remorse. "We also have the body of his mother. The police will connect the two and end up with you. Even they could not miss this. But wait, what else could you do that would stir the authorities up like a stick poked into a hornet's nest? You could kill a police officer, and you did. Stupid, Mr. Parkes. You're becoming a risk to us, and we always like to minimize risk."

There was no disguising the threat in this statement, and Parkes sat bolt upright.

"Do you have any explanation to offer"

Parkes scratched his head and glanced around the room. He looked like the school bully whose victim had called his bluff. "Sarah couldn't be trusted. She had nothing to lose after Tom died. The meds loosened her tongue, and she could tie me to the dealers. Then these two meddlers turned up. She had to be silenced." He cast a scornful look at David and me.

My heart clenched. Would Sarah still be alive if we hadn't been to see her?

"The cop was getting too close to the Polokwane operation. He was working with these two and a fat detective from the Cape."

"I think you're forgetting Constable Nondela," Joca said. He was frighteningly well informed. Parkes's expression showed that he was surprised by this news. Joca looked unimpressed.

"Well, Mr. Parkes we can't go crying over spilled blood, but I warn you to be more delicate in the future."

Parkes nodded. It was obvious that the dynamic in the relationship was changing. I doubted that Parkes had much practice at being subordinate, but Joca was clearly the boss.

"Fortunately, we have a plan that allows us to take advantage of the presence of our honoured guests." Joca indicated us with a gesture. "We're hopeful that we can undo much of the damage that you have caused. We have offered David and Lara the opportunity to earn their freedom by presenting evidence that will put the matter of your son's death to rest and point the authorities away from Shashe. They have yet to confirm the arrangement, but we feel that the case is compelling, and we hope to receive their approval."

"You're going to let them go?" Parkes's voice was high and incredulous. "You have to be fucking kidding. They know everything. They've been hanging around Shelburne, talking to the pathologist and the police. They can never leave here alive."

"Well, Mr. Parkes, I thank you for your advice, but we are confident that the arrangement that we are proposing to Lara and David offers us an almost watertight guarantee that our guests will pose no threat to us."

He stood, indicating that this portion of the business was at an end. "Now, if you will come with me, we need to discuss how we're going to respond to the increased security at the docks in Maputo. I'm considering the possibility of moving the port of entry up the coast to Beira, but there are a number of logistical issues that will bear on your end of the operation, so we must talk."

The two men left the building, Diba walking just behind them, a young and dangerous shadow. Archange inclined his head and gestured to the door. He took us back to our cells.

The afternoon dragged by. I slept on and off. Merced brought us some food in the midafternoon, and Diba brought us fresh water as the sun sank and the shadows in the courtyard lengthened.

She spent a long time with Lara. I could hear them talking through the wall. Their voices were subdued, and I couldn't make out what they were saying, but after a while I heard the key turn in the lock on my door, and Lara walked in.

"Diba says we can be together tonight," she said.

In two strides I was across the room and took her in my arms

"Did she say why?" I asked after a while.

"No, but she knows we have a decision to make; maybe that's why. And she spoke to me about the past. She loves her father, but she needs a mother. She has been through so much, but she can still put everything in perspective. She's really a remarkable young woman."

"Maybe, but she's also remarkably deadly. Did you see the speed with which she pulled the gun on Parkes?"

"Yes, but she still has dreams, and if she was taken away from all this and given the chance, I believe she could make a life for herself."

I found it almost moving that Lara could think of anybody else at a time like this. She was a better person than I was.

Lost and Found

We sat down together on the fetid mattress.

"What are you thinking?" she asked.

"I'm thinking we're not really being offered any kind of choice. I'm not willing to leave you here with them."

Lara turned to face me. "Look, David, Joca needs us, and he thinks he can read our relationship. He needs us to sort out the problems that Parkes has caused, and he thinks he can control you by keeping me here. He believes you will have to come back for me, but you know in your heart that if you do that, he has to kill us both."

I knew she was right. It was all I had been thinking about. "So, we have to try and escape even if the odds are stacked against us?"

"I think we do." She sounded so matter-of-fact that we could have been talking about the need to run down to the store for milk.

"I don't think the walls of this place would be too difficult to break through, but they don't need to be because then what would we do?" I said. "We're in the middle of a wilderness, unarmed and opposed by armed killers. I suppose we could try and take one of the vehicles, but there are others, and they would track us down in short order."

There was a look in Lara's eye that I had seen before, a narrowing and a focus that meant she had an intuition, an idea that she wanted us to explore.

"You told me once that you had your pilot's licence," she said. "There's a plane outside. Can you fly it?"

I chuckled. "If you want to die quickly. I don't even know what type it is or whether it's been fuelled. It would be suicide. And in any case, planes have keys, just like a car. You don't leave the keys in the plane."

"You might if you were in the middle of nowhere," she offered, unwilling to back down. "And we don't need much fuel because we don't have to fly very far. Polokwane can't be more than about three hundred kilometres from here, and I reckon it's due south."

"There's another plane over at Shashe main camp," I replied. "They could catch up with us in no time."

"David, you said yesterday that if we were convinced that they were going to kill us, we might as well attempt a high-stakes escape. They are going to kill us now or a little bit later, so we need to try this." She didn't blink as she held my eye.

"I'd need to have a look at the plane," I submitted in the face of her determination. "The one I saw land this morning was a single-engine plane. That's what I learned on, but I only glimpsed it for a second, so I can't tell you the make or model, and that makes a difference. The basic controls are the same on all light planes, but manufacturers set them up in different ways. I learned on a Cessna. If this is a Piper it will be more difficult."

I paused. I realized I was just making excuses for my potential failure, which was absurd. We might well try and fail. We might die in the attempt, but if we didn't try, we'd most assuredly be executed. We couldn't change Joca or Parkes; the only things we had charge of were our own thoughts and actions.

"When should we make the attempt?" I asked, suspecting she had been thinking about this for a while.

"Can you fly it in the dark?"

"Absolutely not. Or at least, I can't take off in the dark without finding how to turn on the runway lights."

"The moon is full," she said.

"No. We're going to try this, but I'm telling you, we have to do it in daylight."

"Then first light tomorrow," she said.

"OK, but it would be helpful to get a look at the aircraft tonight."

"Joca's waiting for an answer from you. We could ask to go and see him. You can see the landing strip from the main building."

And that's what we did. I lied to Joca, who was delighted with my decision. While he talked about the plans for getting me out of camp the following day, I was looking past him through the window at the little red-and-white Piper Cherokee parked by the refuelling tanks.

CHAPTER 12

I

That was one strike against our chances. It wasn't a Cessna, as David had hoped, but he wasn't giving up and we'd had one piece of good luck.

When she'd come to me that afternoon, Diba had told me that it was the birthday of one of the drivers, and there would be quite a bit of music and drinking that night. She and her brother and father would not be part of it, but she said that it would probably get a bit rowdy. She was apologetic, as though she was worried it would keep me awake.

There would be one or two sore heads in the morning, I thought, and maybe that would give us a small advantage.

By the end of our conversation, Diba had opened up about a lot of things that I hadn't shared with David yet, as they seemed so private. I'm sure she hadn't spoken to anyone like that for years. She told me that before she was captured, she had dreamed of training to be a midwife, but the sister in charge of the mission school had told her to aim higher and had talked to her about getting a scholarship to study medicine in Kinshasa. Her eyes sparkled when she spoke about it.

I asked if this was still a dream for her. She shook her head. Her loyalty was to her father and brother. She couldn't look beyond that while the struggle continued. The sparkle had gone, replaced by steel, but before we left the room, she stepped toward me and hugged me. The hug lasted for several seconds, and through the warmth of her breath on my neck I recognized the longing of a child for the things that a child should expect but which had been denied to her in the most brutal way.

But Diba was part of the problem, and I couldn't be sentimental about her.

Now that we had committed to it, David had become determined and thoughtful about our plan. Locked into the room once again, we lay awake talking through the details.

"The Piper only has one door on the right-hand side, so I'll get in first, and you follow," David said. "I think it's the four-seat version, but it's still pretty cramped. It's parked over by the tanks, but there's no way of knowing if it's been fuelled until we're underway. The strip looks clear, and it's easily long enough for a plane like the Piper. Unless things change, there isn't much wind.

"Obviously, I won't have time for a walkaround before takeoff, but the pilot probably left it ready for the next flight, so we should be OK. The takeoff speed will be about sixty knots, and we should be able to achieve that in about twenty seconds from when I take the brakes off, so perhaps there will be a minute between starting the engine, letting it warm up for a few seconds, taxiing onto the strip, and lifting off. That should be enough to get us airborne before Joca's men can react."

David was talking through it aloud, but the intended audience was himself; he was visualizing the whole thing in detail.

"So, there are just two things to think about," I said. "How we get out of this room and whether the key will be in the plane."

"Actually, there's only one thing to think about," he replied. "The key is out of our control. It's just luck, so we have to let that go."

"OK," I said, impressed with this new attitude from a man whom I know worries about the details.

"So, let's have a look at the walls and see which would be the easiest way out."

It was as we had thought earlier; the walls were not strong. They were made of reeds bundled together and tied off. These were packed together in rough wooden frames about eight feet by four and held in place by some flimsy lathes. We managed to take half of one section apart in just a few minutes. It would be big enough to fit through in the morning. We replaced the reed bundles in case anyone came around on patrol, but the sounds from the far side of the compound suggested that the birthday party was well underway, and it seemed unlikely that anyone would bother with us, particularly as they now thought that David was part of the operation.

Lost and Found

That night we lay together in each other's arms. We didn't talk much, but what we did say mattered. We talked about our future life together and what we wanted to achieve. I said I would soon be in a position to give up the real estate, David said that he was thinking about retiring from his line of work as well, and we both laughed like adolescents at that. We never mentioned the possibility that our lives might end tomorrow, though we both knew it was possible. I turned over, David moved close to me, his arms around my waist, and I fell into a sleep in which I dreamed of an eagle on whose back we flew to freedom.

II

I got up when my watch read 4:30 a.m.. The sun rose at around 5:30 at that point in the year, and it would be light enough to take off shortly after 5:00 a.m. I began to remove the reeds from the wall, and a few minutes later Lara joined me.

"Coffee would be nice," she said.

"If this goes well, we can be in Polokwane for breakfast," I replied.

If the key was in the plane, if there was any fuel in it, and if I could figure out how to operate the Piper, we really could be in Polokwane for breakfast.

We pulled all the rushes into the room, and by 5:00 a.m. we again had a space big enough for us to squeeze through.

"Remember, the door is on the right-hand side," I reminded Lara. "We need to step onto the wing, and then when the door is open, I get in first. If the door is unlocked, chances are the key is in the plane. When you're seated, get the seat belt on as quickly as you can. If the door is locked, we'll climb down, come back here, and come up with a new plan."

I moved through the hole in the wall and waited in the cool morning air till Lara was through. I took her hand, and we strolled across the intervening fifty yards as if we hadn't a care in the world.

I stepped up onto the wing, and it was then, with my hand on the door handle, that I hesitated. All or nothing. I applied pressure to the handle, and for a heart-stopping moment I felt resistance, but then it clicked, and the door opened. I stepped inside, shuffled across to the left-hand seat. Lara moved into the other seat, and I pointed at the key on a red leather fob hanging from the ignition. She grinned. Then she pulled the door closed as quietly as she could, and we both looked around. No sign of anyone stirring.

I sat there trying to keep calm as I studied the instruments. Unlike the Cessna, the Piper had a yolk control stick, but that wasn't a problem. They both served the same function. The throttle was by my right hand and the trim just behind that. I felt around with my feet and came across the rudder pedals with the brakes just above them. So far, so good.

I turned on the fuel pump and set the fuel selector to both tanks. The gauge showed that they were full. Luck was on our side. I set the mixture to "full rich" and turned the carb heater to "off."

Now the moment that would wake everyone in the camp and most of the diurnal animals within a mile. I turned the key in the ignition, and the magnetos started to rotate the engine, but it didn't fire. I tried again, and this time it caught. The noise in the cabin of a small plane is deafening, so I pointed to the headsets that were hooked above the windshield. We put them on. I set the engine to 1,000 rpm and checked the oil pressure. It was rising into the normal zone.

Lara touched my arm and pointed out my window. Two of Joca's men were running across the compound toward us. They were still a hundred yards away, but one had a pistol in his hand. As I released the brakes and increased the revs, I heard and felt a bullet hit some part of the aircraft.

The walk to the plane had shown me that the runway was sandy and soft, so I set the flaps at twenty-five degrees and pulled back on the yoke as the plane started to move down the strip. I had to counteract the nose wheel's desire to stick into the sandy surface, so I gave it more power than I normally would.

As we bounced along gaining speed, I felt another shot hit the plane at the same moment that the yolk came alive in my hands. I pulled back gently, and the plane's nose lifted toward the brightening sky.

After that we banked, and I adjusted the trim till the plane told me it was happy. Keeping the rising sun to our left, we headed south at one hundred knots. At that rate I estimated it would take us less than an hour to reach South African airspace and another hour to reach Polokwane. I'd have to break radio silence to talk to the tower there, but by then we'd be pretty well safe.

"Nice work, Ace," Lara said over the headphones.

"We've been lucky, but we're not out of the woods yet," I replied. "Joca will have called up the main camp, and we know they have a plane there. The one we saw is a twin-engine Beechcraft, and it's a lot faster than this one. I'm going to go up to five thousand feet to give us some manoeuvring room."

I pulled back on the yoke and increased the revs, and the plane responded nicely. After perhaps ten minutes, my white-knuckled hands relaxed a bit on the yoke, and I was just thinking what a sweet plane it was to fly when my eye caught sight of the fuel gauges. Instead of indicating full, they now showed almost empty. I'd just levelled out at the new cruising altitude when the engine started to sputter. Within seconds the prop had stopped turning, and the only sound we could hear was the rush of wind over the fuselage.

"What's happening?" Lara sounded tense.

"I'm not sure. It looks like we're out of fuel. Perhaps those shots hit the tanks."

I went through the restart procedure, but it was in vain. The nose was dropping, and I had to let it go to gain speed before trying to haul it back up again. I looked at the ground below. We were over the eastern edge of the Kalahari, so there wasn't much vegetation, and the ground seemed fairly flat.

"There's a line of greenish scrub just to the west," Lara said, pointing out her window and down. "It might give us some cover, and maybe there's water. We're going to need water."

I banked the plane to see what she was looking at and caught the silver flash of water. Sure enough, it looked quite promising.

I set the airplane in a thirty-degree descent, trying to remember all I'd been told about landing with a power-off glide. Thank God we had some altitude to play with. I lined the plane up with a bare brown patch of desert, and at about one hundred feet I hauled back on the control yoke. The nose came up enough that the two main wheels touched down first and slowed us a bit before the nose wheel dug into the surface. We were pressed forward against our seat belts and then thrown back into the seats again, but the plane came to a stop in a cloud of dust and sand.

We were down safely, but we were in a lot of trouble.

Duncan Roy

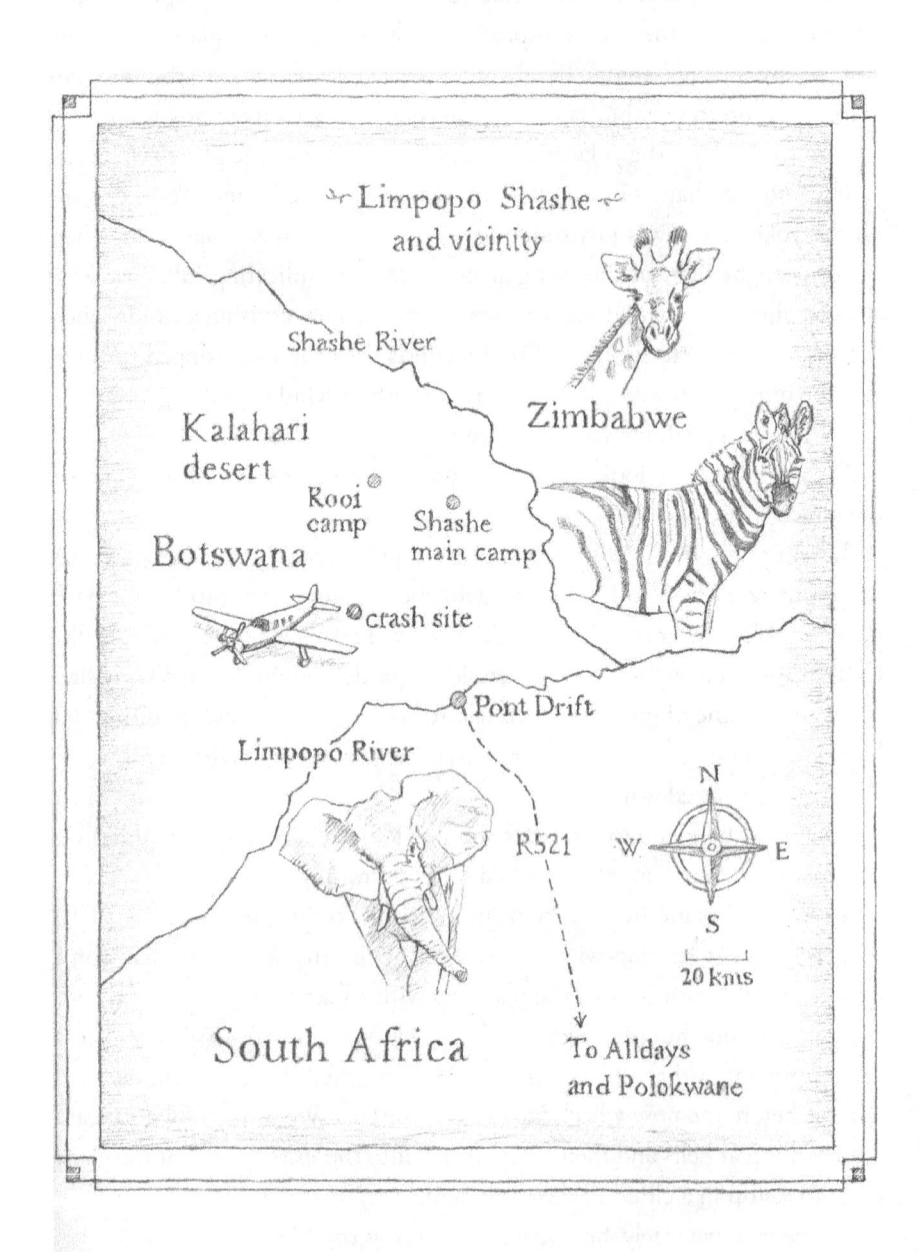

Limpopo Shashe and vicinity

- Shashe River
- Kalahari desert
- Zimbabwe
- Rooi camp
- Shashe main camp
- Botswana
- crash site
- Pont Drift
- Limpopo River
- R521
- South Africa
- To Alldays and Polokwane

20 kms

Lost and Found

III

I released the clasp on my seat belt, shrugged off the shoulder straps, and pushed open the door. The day hadn't warmed up yet, but the sun was now well above the horizon, and it wouldn't be long before we needed some shelter.

I heard David call out from inside the cabin. Seconds later he appeared on the wing carrying an enormous rifle, a leather bandolier, and a small grey metal ammunition box.

"Look what I found," he said, smiling. "This thing could stop a charging elephant."

He jumped to the ground and showed me the gun. I'd never seen that model before, but it was a part of gun club lore: a Holland & Holland side-by-side double rifle.

I gestured for David to pass the box. Inside lay fifty .700 magnum express cartridges.

"You were right," I said. "This thing is, in fact, designed to take down a charging elephant."

"I assume the safari guides carry them in case of emergency," David said. "It was in a big lockbox at the rear of the cabin. There's also a first-aid kit."

David walked around the plane and showed me the bullet holes that had pierced the fuel tanks. A few remnant drips plopped onto the dry ground. Apart from that, the plane appeared to be undamaged by our hard landing.

"I tried calling the tower at Polokwane," David said, "but the battery must have discharged. The radio is dead."

"Let's head over to the trees," I said, pointing. "We need to find some shade."

A few tired-looking acacia trees were grouped around a patch of dark mud with a pool of water at its centre. The mud was heavily indented with the hoof and paw prints of animals. A small flock of birds took off at our approach and retreated to a nearby bush where they chattered crossly. We sat down, leaning against the trunks of adjacent trees and considered our situation, which didn't look too good.

"Do you think we can walk out?" I asked.

"We may have no choice, but it would be risky. It must be sixty or seventy miles to the border, we have no supplies or water, and we're not dressed for it. And then there are the predators to think of. We've seen lions and leopards, and I think hyenas would also present a threat. The country is so open here that we could probably see and avoid elephants, but it would be risky. We've got the big gun, of course, and you know how to use it, so perhaps that's not as much of a worry."

The idea of shooting our way to safety through a cross section of Botswanan big game caused me to snort in amusement. "Let's hope it doesn't come to that," I said, seeing that David had been wrongfooted by my reaction. "How far do you think we are from the camp?"

He looked at his watch. "We'd been airborne for about twenty minutes averaging about one hundred miles an hour, so do the math. Probably too far for a ground chase from the remote camp, but the Beechcraft from the main camp could be on us in an hour, even adding in a stop to pick up Joca. He's the sort of man who will want to oversee this personally, I think, especially since we've betrayed him and caused him to lose face with Parkes."

"I'm not feeling very good about just sitting here, waiting for them," I said.

"What's the alternative? At least with the plane and the trees we have some cover. If we run now, they'll be able to track us, and they'll be properly equipped, so they'll be able to move faster than we can."

We sat in silence for a few moments thinking about the possibilities.

"If we set up here in the trees, we can hold them off till our ammunition runs out, and with your shooting skills, you can probably take a few of them out," David said.

It was a plan, but it played to their strengths, not ours, and didn't get us any further forward. The only asset we had was the rifle, and they wouldn't know whether we had found it or not. We had to think of a way of using it to maximum advantage.

I'd never held, let alone fired, a gun that size, so it seemed like a good idea to try it out before we had to use it in self-defence.

"Let me try a couple of shots," I said, opening the ammunition box. I opened the breech and slipped in two of the finger-width bullets. Then I walked a few paces away from David, raised the gun to my shoulder, and took aim at one of the Acacias on the far side of the mudhole. I knew the kickback would be fierce, so I angled myself sideways a little more than normal, but I was completely unprepared for what happened when I pulled the first trigger.

A deafening crash occurred at the same time as I was thrown over backwards with a nasty pain in my shoulder. David helped to pull me upright.

"Holy God," I said, wincing at the pain. "That thing is a monster. Did I hit anything?"

David inclined his head to a point across the mud. A stump was sticking three feet out of the ground. Above that the tree had exploded into fragments, some of which were still falling to the ground.

"Wow." I was stunned. "So, here's the good news, I think we can use this cannon as an antiaircraft gun. It will have absolutely no problem piercing aluminium and going on to do a great deal of damage."

"What's the bad news?" David asked.

"I'll have to find a way to fire it without falling on my ass."

IV

She filled the bandolier with bullets and then slung it over her shoulder. She had dirt marks on her face, her clothes were dusty, and wearing the bandolier and brandishing the large rifle, she looked unlike anything I had ever seen before: a beautiful, small-boned desperado with magical green eyes.

I took off the cotton jacket I was wearing, folded it into a pad, and tied it to her shoulder to help with the recoil.

She still had a bullet in the chamber.

"OK. Let's give this another try," she said.

She pulled the gun's stock tightly into her shoulder and then moved her shoulder back against the gun, so it was in front of its natural position.

"This is what my gun club trainers say to do, but most of them are large men, and they weren't firing a bazooka when they showed me."

She sighted on another tree and squeezed the rear trigger. Again, there was a terrific bang, and the target exploded, but this time Lara was still standing.

"It's not comfortable, but I think that technique will work," she said. "What part of the airplane should I aim for?"

I had to think about that. The answer depended on what we were hoping to achieve. Up till then I think we both felt that the best we could do would be to kill or hold off our pursuers, but that wouldn't get us away from there.

There didn't appear to be much wrong with the Piper apart from the three bullet holes in the tanks and a dead battery. We could probably use the tape in the emergency kit to patch the leaks, at least for a while.

If we could get the Beechcraft down to the ground without too much damage and somehow immobilize the occupants, we could either use it or siphon its fuel into the Piper. There were a lot of chances of things going wrong, but if we focused on what we could control, we at least had hope.

I shared my thoughts with Lara.

"I don't think we can wait until it has landed," I said. "You can fit six people in the Beechcraft, and it would be difficult for us if they landed and spread out, so if you can wait until the plane is at about one hundred feet and aim at the cockpit, we'll have the best chance of bringing it down without it exploding."

"We're assuming that they'll choose to land right here," she said. "What if they land a mile away and approach on foot?"

"It's possible, but this looked to us like the best spot to land, so it probably will to them too. The Piper will act like a magnet, and they don't know for sure about the rifle."

"Will they be killed if the plane crashes from that height?" she asked.

"I don't know. It depends what kind of damage you do to it. I'm hoping it will cause a very hard landing that will disable at least some of them but leave the plane mostly intact."

Lara looked away.

V

We sat together in the dappled shade scanning the sky to the north for what felt like eons but was probably only an hour.

We saw it before we heard it. The plane was visible from a long way away in the empty sky. As it crept across the sky toward us, I positioned myself behind a screen of tall bushes and held the rifle loosely in my arms. The pilot decided to make one pass over the Piper before circling and lining up to come in on the same strip of flat ground that we had chosen.

I raised the gun to my shoulder and pulled it tight against the pad that David had fashioned. I had bullets in both chambers, but I'd only have those two chances; there would be no time to reload.

"I'm going to sight on the plane now," I said. "It's hard for me to judge the altitude as well as aim, so tell me when to fire. I'll start with the right barrel and then readjust and fire the left."

David nodded in agreement.

Then, in that desperate moment, my brain cleared, and a sense of peace descended. Calm conquered despair as a thought took shape.

"This may not be the best time to tell you, but there may never be another. I love you, David, and if we get out of here, I want to spend the rest of my life with you." He leaned across to me, took my face between his hands and kissed me hard on the lips.

After that I gave all my concentration to breathing smoothly, which was hard because the gun was heavy.

As the plane got closer, I could see the shapes of the people in the front seats. I hadn't signed up for this trip to execute people, but there we were.

"Five seconds," David said from behind me.

"Three, two, one."

A split second after I fired, I saw the windshield explode in a shower of crystal shards. I followed the plane with the rifle and sent the second shot into the cabin just behind the first. The plane juddered, and the nose dropped. It hit the ground hard and fast and at an angle that caused the front wheel to break off before the fuselage hit the sand. We heard a hellish noise of tearing metal as the propellers bent and broke as they cut up the ground. As fragments pierced the sides of the skidding plane, I imagined the scene inside the fuselage. The plane gave a final twist sideways and then came to a stop in a plume of sand and smoke that obscured it from view.

We broke cover and ran toward the wreck, following the next stop in our plan. At the very least, the passengers would be in shock, which would give us an advantage. But as we neared the plane, I heard a moan of pain and realized from the state of the wreck that we had done a lot of damage.

David reached the plane first, and he pulled open the passenger door for me. I pointed the gun's barrel inside. It was like a scene from hell. Blood and bits of flesh were sprayed all over the cabin.

"I can count five people, David," I said, "and I don't see a threat."

I pushed into the narrow aisle. To my left Archange was strapped into his seat, his head hanging at an unnatural angle. To my right Parkes was moaning softly, blood running freely from a head wound. Joca was slumped forward, not moving, while Diba was holding her shoulder and rocking gently to and fro. The pilot was certainly dead; there wasn't much left of his head. The first shot must have hit him. That's where all the gore had come from.

"I think there are two and maybe three survivors, David. We should try and get them out of here."

Easier said than done. Parkes could almost manage on his own, but Joca was a dead weight, and even though he was not a big man, it took us five minutes to get him out and under the shade of the wing. Diba was in a lot of pain, but with my arm around her waist she made it down the three steps to the ground.

David went back into the cabin to check on Archange and then returned, shaking his head.

"Check them all for weapons, David," I said while I helped Diba sit down, propped against a wheel stanchion. Her arm wasn't hanging right. It was either broken high on the humerus, or her shoulder was dislocated. "And check in the plane for a first-aid kit," I said, knowing the one from the Piper wouldn't do the job. "We've got some work to do here."

I tried to do some amateur triage. Parkes whined and moaned as David removed the handgun from the holster at his waist, so I figured he could wait. I felt for a pulse on Joca's neck. At first I thought he was dead, but after a few seconds I sensed the faintest murmur beneath my finger, like the trembling wings of a butterfly. I couldn't see any obvious signs of trauma on his body, but just as I lifted an eyelid, a trickle of blood flowed from his ear and down onto the warm sand.

I felt behind his head and came across a large bump and then a soft spot in his skull where no soft spot should have been. My fingers came away with a trace of blood on them, but it looked as if he had suffered a bad head injury.

I heard a scuffling sound behind me and turned to find Diba crawling over to her father. I stepped aside. If Joca had a traumatic brain injury there wasn't anything we'd be able to do for him.

She sat beside him and leaned over him, making a soft keening sound. After a few seconds, I was surprised to see his eyes open. He whispered something to her in a language I didn't know. She said something in return. Summoning all his energy, he grasped her wrist and spoke forcefully to her before slumping back to the ground, his eyes rolling back in his head. This time when I felt for a pulse, there was none. Diba lay down beside the body and put her good arm protectively over her stricken father.

I knelt beside her and slipped the knife from the sheath on her ankle. "I'm sorry," I said. She didn't respond.

David appeared from the cabin again holding a larger first-aid kit than the one we had found in the Piper and also toting a good-sized plastic jug.

"Clean water," he said, holding it up. "Enough for a couple of days at least."

"Did you have a look at Parkes's injury?" I asked.

"He's got a cut on his forehead, and he's complaining about his ribs, but I think he's done better than the rest of them."

"I think we should restrain him and bandage his head; he's got everything to lose if we escape from here, so he'll be desperate, and we really need him in police custody if this mess is to mean anything."

"OK, I'll look after that," he said. "What's up with Joca?"

"He's dead."

He shook his head slowly, and a soft whistle escaped his lips. "And the girl?"

"I'll need to look more closely, but she's in a lot of pain."

While David attended to Parkes, I moved back to Diba. When I put my hand on her leg, she sat up, trying to hide a grimace as she moved.

"I need to look at your arm," I said.

She nodded. There were tear marks running through the dust and blood on her face.

I felt gently up and down her injured arm. It didn't appear to be broken.

"Can you move it at all?" I asked. I lifted it an inch, and she screamed. "Sorry, sorry. I didn't mean to hurt you."

I'd taken first-aid and CPR courses when I was younger. My parents were older, and I wanted to be able to help if they needed me. Also, I volunteered on the sidelines with Alex's soccer team, and on two occasions I'd watched as paramedics restored the dislocated shoulder of a young player. They hadn't used a local anaesthetic, but it looked like I'd need one if Diba was going to let me near her again.

I opened the Beechcraft's first-aid kit and rummaged through sponges, tape, swabs, and pill bottles till I found what I needed: syringes, needles, and two vials of Lidocaine, a local anesthetic. I took them back over to Diba.

"I think you've dislocated your shoulder, Diba. I can put it back, but I need to give you this painkiller first. I'm going to inject it into the muscle near your shoulder. Is that OK with you?"

She blinked and gave the slightest nod. She was a tough kid, but the pain was getting to her.

I screwed the needle onto the syringe and then drew the Lidocaine carefully from the small glass vial. I held the needle upright and squirted out just enough to make sure I wouldn't inject any air into her. As I cut away the shoulder of her T-shirt, I saw that her arm was fully dislocated. I used a sterile swab to clean the skin and then aimed the needle at a muscular part of her neck just above her shoulder. She was an adolescent girl, but she had the defined hard muscles of an adult.

"Come and help me," I called to David. He had tied Parkes's hands behind his back with some bungee cord and was finishing securing him to one of the trees.

When he arrived, I asked him to put both his hands on Diba's shoulder and be ready to apply pressure to guide the ball back into the socket. Diba shrank from his touch, but the Lidocaine had done its job, and when she realized that the pain had been reduced, she didn't resist any further, although she looked unhappy at a man's touch.

I tried to visualize what I had seen the paramedics doing beside the soccer pitch in Florida in what now seemed like another lifetime. In essence, one paramedic had applied traction to the arm while the other persuaded the ball back into the socket. I sat beside Diba and took her hand in both my hands. Then I placed the ball of my foot on her ribcage and began pulling her arm gently toward me. She looked alarmed but not pained.

"Good, good," I reassured her. "Here it comes."

"Push down now David," I said, and with a slight grating sensation, her shoulder was restored. I folded her arm up to her chest.

"Hold it with your other arm until I get a sling," I said, searching through the first-aid box again. I found a sling and folded the material just as I had been taught all those years ago.

"You must rest the arm for several days," I told her in a firm motherly tone.

"Yes, ma'am. Thank you," she said softly.

"You can call me Lara if you want," I offered, but she didn't respond.

The irony was not lost on me. Here I was ministering to someone who had been part of a team intent on ending my life. I was responsible for the deaths of her father and brother, and she had every reason to hate me. But she was still a child, and my urge to care for her outweighed my sense of self-preservation.

VI

Lara looked very tired. Her skin had a grey pallor that I'd never seen before. It was hardly surprising considering what she'd been through over the past hour. She hadn't had time to consider it yet, but I knew she would need time to process what had happened after she fired at the plane. The outcome was everything we had hoped for, but our actions—in particular, her actions; she had pulled the trigger—had led to the deaths of three people. If it had been the other way around, I don't imagine Joca and his henchmen would have lost much sleep over our deaths, but she had never killed anyone before, and there would be an emotional price to pay.

Lara led Diba to the treed area and helped her sit down. She poured some water into a cup that I'd found with the jug and held it to Diba's lips while she drank.

"How is she?" I asked.

"Ask her," Lara replied.

I turned to the girl. "How are you feeling, Diba?"

"Better. Thank you," she replied, her eyes never leaving the ground.

"Lara, I'm going to go and see how best to transfer fuel between the planes. I'll also need to move the Beechcraft's battery into the Piper. Why don't you try and get a little rest? You've done everything so far. I'll call you if I need help."

Lara turned to Diba. "Do I need to tie you up?" The girl gave the smallest shake of her head. "OK, I'll lie here beside her for ten minutes and try to pull myself together," Lara said.

In the Beechcraft's small cargo hold, I found an empty fuel can. The engine cowlings had been ripped off their mountings by the crash, and it didn't take me long to find the fuel line leading from the tanks in the wings to the port engine. I prised the clip off the line and pushed it into the fuel can. I heard a steady flow. When the can was nearly full, I pinched the clip back on the fuel line and carried the can over to the Piper.

There had been a roll of duct tape in the Beechcraft, which I used to patch the bullet holes. That done, I jumped up onto the Piper's engine faring and found the two fuel tank caps located on the upper surface of the wings about five feet out from the cabin. I crawled out along the wing and emptied the can into the starboard tank. I repeated this task five more times until I calculated that we had about twenty gallons on board. I estimated that would be enough for three hours of cruising at 60 percent power, and we couldn't be more than two hours from Polokwane.

I walked over to Lara to tell her about our progress, but as I drew near, I saw that she and Diba were asleep. I left them in peace.

After a few attempts, I got the twenty-four-volt battery unhooked from the Beechcraft. It was heavy, and I struggled to carry it to the Piper. It was all I could do to lift it up to the engine compartment. The Piper battery sat in the back-left corner of the engine bay just in front of the firewall and was easy to remove. The new battery was slightly bigger, but I managed to get it situated and hooked up. I turned the radio on, and it crackled—a good sign—but I didn't dare call out yet as it could be picked up back at both camps. I turned it off again, and the green power light faded

I needed to see if I could fire up the engine, but I didn't want to do that without warning Lara, so I walked back to the trees and sat down in a patch of shade. I'd been there for a few minutes taking mental stock of all that had happened that day and beginning to feel my age when Parkes shouted at me.

"Can I get some water over here?" his tone was whiny and defeated.

His voice woke Lara. After I'd taken him a cup of water and held it while he drank, I returned and knelt beside her.

"How do you feel?" I asked.

"Like I've been run over by a bus." She gave me a wry smile. "I think I'll sleep for a week when we get out of here."

"On that topic," I said, "I'm ready to try and start the Piper. You stay over here because there will be a lot of dust—at least I hope there'll be a lot of dust."

It took three attempts to get the engine to fire, but when it did it ran strongly, and the gauge indicated that we had half a tank of fuel. I taxied a hundred yards, turned around, and came back. I killed the engine, jumped down, and did an external inspection of the plane. A tiny trickle of fuel was seeping out from one of the tape-covered holes, but it wasn't too bad. I double taped it, but I didn't think it would be a problem.

We looked to be in good shape, but the hectic activities of the day had telescoped time, and the sun was sinking quickly toward the western horizon. I looked at my watch. It was 6:00. It would be fully dark in an hour, and I didn't want to try a landing in Polokwane in the dark. I shared my concern with Lara.

"But what if Joca's men come after us tonight?" she said.

"They won't," Diba said softly. "They won't come tonight." She looked back and forth between us and then held my eye. "There is only Mr. Kumalo and one other at the bush camp. They won't be concerned about us till sundown, and by then it will be too late to look for us in the dark even if they could summon the courage, which I doubt."

"OK, well, let's get ourselves set up here for tonight then," I said. "We'll need to get a fire going to keep the wildlife away. I saw some matches in the emergency kit. Also, we'll need to get Joca's body back into the Beechcraft. Animals won't trouble it in there."

"Let us look after Joca," Lara said, "When we've done that, we'll round up firewood."

I went over to Parkes. As I approached, I heard him muttering to himself. The confrontation with Joca at camp and the events of the last few hours seemed to have knocked all the bluster out of him. He turned his gaunt eyes my way.

"We aren't leaving until first light," I told him.

He grunted.

"I can't untie your hands, but I'll release you from the tree, so you can lie down."

"If you had any charity, you'd put a bullet in my head right now." His voice was a monotone.

"We need to hand you over to the police," I said. "From what we heard at camp, I'd say you can shed a lot of light on the deaths of your wife and son, and that's before we begin to talk about dealing drugs."

"Are you really as smug as you sound, Mallory, or is it just an act?" He curled his top lip as he spoke. "Have you never found yourself in a position where all the options lead somewhere you don't want to go? Have you never found yourself in a corner where the only way out is to fight tooth and nail to save something of who you are, what you have?"

I didn't respond; he was defeated and lashing out. In this state, I thought he might fill in some of the blanks, and he did.

"I don't think so. You've spent your life playing God to a bunch of children. You like hanging out with successful people, but you don't want to know how half of them made their money so long as they pay their fees and contribute to the annual fund.

"Christ! Croken put me on the Shelburne Board. Sounds like a 'fox in the henhouse' thing to you, doesn't it? No, my friend, we were a pack of foxes. The treasurer has a taste for underage girls that he indulges up at his country home in Paarl. The vice-chair launders Russian money through his bank. *Vice* chair. That's good, isn't it?" Parkes dissolved into hysterical laughter that transitioned into sobbing.

"Nothing is as it seems, Mallory. It's all a charade." He inhaled deeply and began rocking to and fro. "We've built our glistening treasure houses from dirty money. Our limousines are fuelled by the sweat of the poor. I learned to play that game better than anyone else."

He squinted as another quite different thought crossed his mind. "In the beginning I loved Sarah more than anything, and all I wanted was to lay out my creations at her feet, but she wouldn't have it. She turned out to be like you, Mallory, a sanctimonious prig. Right and wrong, good and evil, that's what she wanted to talk about while every day I went out and busted my ass to keep her in style."

"Did she want that?" Perhaps a provocation would keep him going. He didn't erupt. In fact, he looked thoughtful before replying.

"You know, I don't think she did. But what she wanted I couldn't possibly give her, and it didn't take long before we both realized that. I did love her at the start, you know, Mallory. I really did."

"But you raped her the night the boys were conceived." Was I pushing him too hard?

"She told you that? She was my wife. I wanted to have sex with her. How is that rape? In any case, the boys made her happy."

Talking of the children produced another moment of melancholy. I looked at him, steadily inviting him to continue.

"It was all a mistake," he said, his voice so quiet that I had to strain to hear him. "The boys were with me for the weekend at my place outside Franschhoek. I'd invited some of the casino managers and suppliers for dinner; even Joca was there. People got drunk and careless. Tom overheard two of them laughing about the easy money from the drug business, and he confronted me in front of my guests. He was just like Sarah; all about right and wrong, no grey areas for young Tom." Frustration mingled with affection in his voice.

"I couldn't lose face in front of those people. They live by the rules of the jungle. If I'd let it pass, they'd never have done business with me again. I had millions in loans secured against my properties, loans that were coming due. I needed the drug money to stay afloat. I knocked Tom to the ground, but he laughed at me as he lay there. I shouted at one of my men to take the boy away and deal with him. He must have assumed that invoking my rage was a death sentence. He injected the boy with insulin, and when he passed out, he dumped him in the water.

"I was walking the dogs by the lake in front of the house the next morning. They ran ahead and started making a fuss about something washed up on the beach. When I caught up with them, I found him. I should have died right there, Mallory. My fucking life should have ended right there. The fish had already eaten his eyes."

"How did the body get to the lake at school?" I asked.

"The body couldn't be found at the house. It would have created too much attention. Plashy Pond was my idea."

I found it hard to empathize with him, but I couldn't doubt that his sorrow was genuine.

"If Tom's death was a mistake, why kill Sarah?"

"I told you before. She'd figured out what I was up to. She suspected I was involved in Tom's death, and she hated me."

"You set it up as a suicide."

He chuckled. "Not my call, Mallory. That was something Stephen organized."

"Is Dr. Croken in on this? Does he know about Stephen?" For a horrible moment I thought that perhaps we had been hired to help Pius in an elaborate cover-up.

"Get serious, Mallory. Croken is as straightlaced as he looks. He believes there's good in everybody. He thinks it's his mission to help reveal it. He makes me puke."

There was a wild deranged look about Parkes now that made me worry what would happen if I released him for the night, but he would need to relieve himself, so I pulled out the gun I'd taken from him and indicated he should stand. I went around behind him and untied his wrists. He limped to the edge of the water and urinated for a long time.

When he came back, I went to secure him again.

"Hey, you said I could lie down to sleep," he griped.

"I changed my mind," I said, then gave the rope another yank, tightening his bonds. He seemed resigned and sat muttering to himself as I walked away.

We made a fire and fed it until there were good coals that would last several hours. Then we sat there, the three of us, in the flickering firelight. Not much was said, perhaps in part because no one knew where to start.

Lara and I leaned against each other, and Diba spent a lot of the time staring across at where Parkes was slumped against his tree. After a time we lay down, but Diba said she'd stay up and keep the fire going. I wasn't completely convinced that we could trust her, but Lara was better at reading people than I was, and she seemed to have formed a bond with the girl.

As I drifted in and out of sleep, I was aware of the sounds of the African bush that I had come to know from my childhood. I heard the rasping, sawing call of a leopard in the distance and the eerie call of a nightjar. After midnight I picked up the sinister whooping call of a pack of spotted hyenas. Later, their voices transitioned into the high-pitched human-like cackle that meant they had killed. They never kill their prey directly but chase it to exhaustion and then rip it apart when it is defenseless.

The stars shone with a brilliant intensity in the cold night air, and in one of those strange seemingly unconnected cognitive leaps, "St. Francis in the

Lost and Found

Desert" appeared in my mind. His desert was less savage than this one but equally beautiful. As I descended into sleep, he stepped out of the painting and walked past me into the trees.

What woke me finally was not the pale purple dawn infusing the eastern sky but the whirr of a thousand wings as a flock of red-billed quelea descended from their roosts to the water's edge below. I sat up and looked around. Diba was sitting in the same place staring at the flames that still crackled from the fire she had tended throughout the night. I looked over to check on Parkes; he wasn't there.

"Where's he gone, Diba? You must have seen him!" I said sharply.

Diba didn't reply, but she inclined her head to indicate the desert to the north.

Lara was stirring as I hurried over to the spot where Parkes had been tied up. Surely, I couldn't have done such a bad job restraining him that he'd been able to untie himself and escape. He was our star witness; losing him would be a major blow.

By the time I returned to the fire, Lara was speaking to Diba.

"Diba says we will find him half a mile to the north," she said, standing and kicking her feet back into her ankle boots. "Let's go."

She picked up the rifle, and we headed in the direction Diba had indicated.

Minutes later we heard scuffling and flapping ahead of us, and then a gruesome scene confronted us. Illuminated by the low light of the rising sun, a score of vultures were fighting to get closest to the corpse that lay in the bloody dust. White-backed vultures contended with marabou storks to rip away what the hyenas had left. That had been the sound I had heard in the night, a pack of hyenas closing in on Parkes and locking their powerful jaws into his flesh and bone, tearing him apart.

The long shadows of the big birds moved in a satanic dance across the bare earth until the air was split by the blast of the rifle. Lara had fired in the air, and now the birds moved away, some perching in nearby trees, others returning to the sky to pick up the thermals generated by the heat of the new day.

A dark patch on the ground was surrounded by a collection of broken bones and sinew. Very little was left of "Honest" Ed Parkes.

Had he tried to get away or, unable to live with himself, had he sought out death as the only escape from what he had done, a way to avoid the judgement and condemnation that he knew must be coming his way? The animals that had devoured him wouldn't have bothered to judge him. We left the remains, knowing we'd be able to find the spot again.

VII

"Why did you release him?" I asked Diba.

"He wanted to die, and he needed to die," she replied. "When an old elephant knows that it must die, it leaves the herd and finds a wild place. It was the same with him. He had deserted his family; it was time."

"But we needed to hand him over to the police; he was our only witness." David was annoyed.

"Now I'm your only witness," she said softly.

There was so much sadness in her voice that my heart clenched, and I reached over and took her hand. She didn't resist. I felt her fingers gently squeeze mine.

It didn't take David long to get the Piper ready for takeoff. The engine roared, and the little plane rushed over the ground before lifting its nose and pulling into the morning sky.

David adjusted the trim and levelled off at five thousand feet. Diba sat behind us, but the noise was too great for conversation, and I'm not sure there would have been much to say.

She was a minor who had been horribly abused. The fact that her father was the leader of a militia and involved in the drug trade wasn't her crime. All her immediate family members were dead. Until now her life had been buffeted by the winds of fate, and she'd never had the opportunity to choose the course her life should take.

Once again I had a growing feeling that I had a role to play in her future. Despite what had happened to her, she had shown me signs that she still wanted and needed the affection and support that any adolescent craves. I needed to talk to David.

After maybe forty minutes, his voice came over the headphones. "If you look down, you'll see the curve of the Limpopo. We'll be back in South African airspace in a few minutes. That's Pont Drift off in the distance."

"Should we just put down here?" I suggested. "There's a police station, isn't there?"

"I have a bad feeling about it, Lara. It's a small place, and there'll be Shashe people in town. I think we're safer to head to the city."

He turned on the radio and adjusted a couple of settings. "Piper eight Charlie Delta calling Polokwane tower. Come in."

There was a momentary delay filled with the crackle of static.

"Piper eight Charlie Delta, this is Polokwane tower; over."

David gave a brief explanation of who we were and our ETA. He also told the tower that he only had an hour's experience on the Piper. The tower identified our runway and said they'd put the fire crew out on the tarmac in case of mishap.

"Please contact the Polokwane police department for me, and get them to let Chief Inspector Olivier know that we're inbound; over."

"Roger, Piper eight Charlie delta" the tower replied. "Raise us again when you have a visual of the runway. Over and out."

As it turned out, David made a perfect landing on runway two and taxied toward the terminal. As we got closer, I saw the square shape of Coby and the tall elegance of Lilitha by his side. They whisked us into a police van, and we sped off to headquarters. We took showers, and Lilitha found some clothes for us to change into. They didn't fit well, but we didn't care. After we'd had a meal in the canteen, she showed us into a large interview room where Coby sat finishing off what looked like an apple pie. He had a thin moustache of whipped cream that he removed with the back of his hand. Lilitha rolled her eyes and shook her head.

"What?" Coby said. "A man has to eat."

Diba looked pretty calm, but I could tell from the way her eyes darted from Coby to Lilitha that she was tense.

"Where to begin?" Coby said, placing his massive slab hands face down on the table.

We began from our departure from Polokwane, which felt like a lifetime ago but in reality, had been just a few days.

David and I took turns giving a brief outline of everything that had transpired since we last saw them. Diba sat quietly throughout.

Coby listened intently, occasionally raising his eyes to heaven or whistling softly. When we were finished, he rocked back in his chair.

"So, the boy's death has brought the whole house of cards crashing down," he said.

"The Congo militias will still need cash, and South Africans will still want drugs," I replied, "but Ed Parkes won't be part of it."

"What you have discovered will set their network back years," Lilitha remarked.

"I will brief the Botswana Defense Forces," Coby said. "I imagine they will want to act quickly. There may still be a chance of apprehending Kumalo. Can you give me an idea of where we can find Parkes's remains?"

"It should be easy enough to locate the downed Beechcraft. It's close to there, but I'll draw you a map.

"We need to get back to Cape Town. Lilitha, you have to come too. We still have to construct a case, and we will need evidence and witnesses."

Coby looked directly at Diba. She held his eye without blinking until he looked away.

CHAPTER 13

I

Diba looked lost in the bustle of the airport in Johannesburg, and she didn't touch the food I ordered for her. We were all walking to the gate when she gave a small tug on my arm and leaned in close.

"I need to talk to you," she whispered.

I sat beside her on the flight to Cape Town, which was half empty. David and the detectives were several rows away. When the plane was airborne, she turned to me.

"My father spoke to me before he died," she said.

I nodded. "I saw you talking."

"He forbade me from returning to the resistance. He said he wanted me to start a new life. He said you were a good person and that I should ask for your help. That was his dying wish. I cannot disobey."

Tears fell from her beautiful brown eyes and plopped onto the oversized blue jeans she'd been given at the police station. Her hand lay on the armrest between us. I covered it with mine.

"I will help you," I said, not quite knowing what that might mean but certain it was part of the future.

I looked at her sitting beside me, the girl who would have killed us at a word from her father. *Perhaps it's because the human heart isn't properly connected to the human brain*, I thought, *but I love you little girl.*

Back at the Cape Grace, I lay in the oversized whirlpool bath in our suite, floating weightless and allowing the jets of warm water to caress my bruised body while the scent of rosemary oil soothed my mind. I had so much to think about, but I was so tired.

I heard the rumble of David's voice as he spoke on the phone in our bedroom. Every so often I picked up a scrap of conversation that let me know he was talking to Pius Croken.

I got out of the whirlpool and stepped into the shower. I ran the water hot till it hurt and then turned the hot off and stood in the stream of cold water until I felt that I could remain fully awake at least for the next couple of hours. I'd checked Diba into the adjacent room and told her we'd pick her up for something to eat at 7:00 p.m. That gave me an hour to speak to David.

I was nervous. I wanted what David and I had together, but something in the centre of me told me that Diba had to be part of our life too. I knew I might not be able to have both, and if I had to choose, I didn't know which way I would go.

I wrapped myself in a bathrobe and walked into the bedroom as David finished his call.

"That was Pius," he said. "I gave him the broad strokes. Mostly, he's relieved we're safe and in anguish over his part in sending us into danger. But he's pleased with the results. He wants to see us tomorrow."

"Can I speak to you, David?" I asked as I sat on the edge of the bed and looked up at him. Judging from his face, he expected something bad.

I smiled at him. "It's OK; I'm not going to expel you."

He came and sat beside me.

"I think we both know now how we feel about each other," I said.

"Yes, we do," he replied. He made to put his arm around my shoulder, but I shrugged him off.

"David, I have to talk to you about something that is important to me."

"Of course." Looking serious, he sat up straighter.

"But it's something that could come between us." I kept my voice steady even though I was close to tears.

"Go on," he said, nodding.

"I've told you that Alex will always be part of my life," I began.

"Yes, and I've told you that I want him to be."

"No, listen, David, please just listen." I was finding this very hard. "It's Diba. I need to talk to you about Diba." I told him about Joca's last words to his daughter and how I felt about helping her. He listened carefully, nodding occasionally.

"That's it, nothing important really," I said in conclusion, ending with a little laugh that turned into a sob.

He stood up and walked to the big window. The last rays of the sun cast his shadow across the room. He didn't say anything for several minutes, and I was glad that he was thinking carefully about what I'd offered him. He deserved to be happy, and maybe I had just dashed that possibility. Finally, he turned and walked back to me. Sitting beside me on the bed, he took my hand and looked at me, his brow wrinkling. I marvelled again at how blue his eyes were. I'd miss them, I thought.

"Diba is fifteen, right?"

"Yes, that's what she told me."

"And you want us to adopt her?"

"If the authorities will let us, yes, I do"

"Lara, I'll be sixty years old before long. I'm not sure I can offer her the sort of support she needs, and in any case, I don't think she trusts me."

"She doesn't have much reason to trust anyone, particularly men. But you're special, David, and you've spent your life working with children. If anyone can win her trust, it's you."

"What would this look like?" he asked. "I mean, where would we live? Where would she go to school?"

"David, these are just details, and you know we can work them out if we make the commitment."

He stood up and walked back to the window. "What will you do if I say no?"

I'd hoped we wouldn't come to this, but I suppose it was inevitable.

"I'm not sure," I admitted.

He was quiet for a while.

"Do you remember what I told you back on Bloubergstrand when you said that Alex will always be a part of you and that he would be a part of our relationship if we were serious about each other?"

"Tell me again," I said.

"I told you that it was you I loved and that Alex's life and death have shaped you and made you who you are, the person I want to live with. You have the best instincts of anyone I've ever known. If you believe that Diba has to be part of your life—our lives—then I can't second guess you. I just don't want to let either of you down."

I jumped up and ran to him. He turned, and I put my arms around him and buried my head on his shoulder. I squeezed him hard.

II

Malcolm gave us a table overlooking the harbour. David had ordered a bottle of prosecco, and the waiter was peeling back the foil.

"Would you like to try some?" I asked Diba. "Or you can have a Coke or some milk."

"I'll try a little bit," she said. "I know about alcohol. We would drink letoko in the bush."

"What's that?" I asked.

"It's made from plantain," she said. "It's rough. The slang name is 'petrole.'" She smiled. "It was horrible, but it helped us forget."

The waiter raised one eyebrow a fraction but pushed out the cork and poured three glasses.

"Diba, Lara has spoken to me," David began. He was being a bit headmasterly, and Diba froze and stared at him.

"It's alright," I said. "He's British, and he gets very formal when he's feeling an emotion. I'm not like that. I'm Colombian, so I yell or cry."

That made her smile, and it seemed to make things easier for David too as he continued.

"Look, Diba, what I don't want to do is make promises to you that we can't keep. I think that's happened to you a lot in your life. For example, I don't know what the police will do. They may want to press charges. Even if that goes well, I don't know if we'll be allowed to adopt you, But even if it turns out to be possible, is that really what you want?"

"I want that more than anything else in life," she said. "My father made mistakes, but he was a wise man. He told me to turn my back on the past and to ask you for help in building a future. That was his dying wish."

The softness of her voice and the way she stressed certain syllables gave her a quiet power that was compelling.

There was a significant pause before David spoke again.

"Lara and I will do everything in our power to make that happen," he said. "And even if things are complicated and we encounter setbacks, we'll be there for you. I feel like I'm too old to be a good father, Diba, but I'm going to give it everything I've got."

I was almost in tears again, but Diba looked very matter of fact.

"You're not much older than my first father," she said. "And when you're too old to tie your shoes and feed yourself, I will be there to help Lara look after you."

I looked at David, and we burst into undignified laughter.

A sly smile crept across Diba's face. *Still waters run deep,* I thought.

III

We were all exhausted, but we were in demand. On top of our appointment with Pius in the afternoon, Coby called to say that he wanted all three of us at the Central Police Station at 9:00 a.m.

We weren't at our sharpest as I parked the Land Cruiser in the station parking lot and checked in at reception.

The same female officer greeted us. Our fingerprints and DNA were already in the system, but Diba had to give hers. Once that was done, the officer took us up to the fourth floor and ushered us into Coby's office where he sat sipping coffee from a paper cup and sharing a joke with Lilitha.

"Come, come." He stood, waving his great bear-like arms at us.

Diba looked a bit nervous, but she took a seat next to Lara.

"Before we start I want to congratulate you and thank you both for what you have accomplished. If I had known what you were heading into, I never would have allowed you to go."

"If we had known what we were heading into, we would never have gone." Lara offered Coby the hint of a smile.

He smiled back. "But the fact remains that you're here, and it seems that you have made a remarkable breakthrough in a number of areas but specifically relating to the death of Tom Parkes. We have to be scrupulous in combing through what you have learned and in building a case that we can bring to the prosecutor. That's what we're going to do this morning."

It was a hard slog. Lilitha kept stopping us and asking us to go back over things that we felt we had already covered. But she was right; the second time around we often remembered more details.

We told them what we had found at the Shashe main camp, including the Russian heavy machine gun, and we described the bush camp and what we'd learned there. We also related the story that Joca had told us about his motivation. It was hard for Diba to hear us talk about her dead father even though the character we described was that of an honourable man who had committed his life to the protection of his people. His methods had been violent and illegal, but he wasn't motivated by greed or avarice.

"Sounds as if you quite liked the guy," Coby remarked.

I looked at Lara.

"We did," we said in unison.

"And then we come on to Honest Ed Parkes." Coby folded his hands and waited for us to tell him what we knew.

We recounted all we had learned at the bush camp about his involvement in the drug smuggling operation, and I spoke about the conversation that I had with him by the waterhole when he was in despair. I confirmed that he had confessed to arranging the murder of his wife and went over what he had told me about the circumstances of Tom's death.

Lara described how we had found his body. When Lilitha asked how he had escaped, I said I hadn't secured him properly. I saw no point in involving Diba to a greater extent that she already was.

"We'll need to connect with Dr. Naidoo soon," Coby said, not looking particularly pleased.

"She'll want to hear all about this, and I suppose you'll have to report to the headmaster," he added with a note of scorn.

"This afternoon, in fact," I said.

"DCI Olivier asked me to make some inquiries with the Department of Justice about how we should approach the girl's involvement," Lilitha said. "Diba is not a citizen of this country. She's also a minor. These facts count in her favour. The prosecutor's office told me that she cannot be charged with conspiracy to traffic drugs or conspiracy to murder in South Africa. By the letter of the law, we should inform the authorities in the DR Congo and give them the opportunity to extradite her. The police in Botswana may also hold an interest, but I'm told that there is a degree of discretion in our approach. If you can give me details of what you intend for her future, it would be helpful in deciding the best course of action."

"Excuse me, ma'am. If I may speak, I can tell you what I plan for my future," Diba said.

Lara looked at me and smiled. I'd seen that smile on the faces of hundreds of proud parents.

Diba went on to lay out her ambitions and her timeline. Some of it we had talked about at dinner the previous night. Other parts we were hearing for the first time. She spoke with such calm certainty that even the hard-boiled chief inspector nodded silently as she laid out her vision for her future: finishing her schooling, training to be a doctor, and then working with the poor and marginalized in DR Congo.

"If Ms. Rios and Mr. Mallory will take my hand and walk with me, I know I will succeed."

Lilitha shed a tear. Coby passed her the box of tissues and cleared his throat as a diversionary activity. I could tell he was moved.

"Well, let's see if we can play a small part in getting that dream off the ground," he said.

IV

The morning sun was sending cheerful rays lancing through the big windows in the headmaster's study. They lit up the golden surfaces of the wood panelling and danced across the oak table at which Dr. Pius Croken and Dr. Naidoo sat. A soothing aroma conjured from beeswax and old books enveloped us as David and I crossed the room.

They both rose to greet us. Pius spread his arms and enfolded us in a bear hug. Dr. Naidoo shook David's hand but held me in an embrace that went on for several seconds longer than seemed quite appropriate.

"I'm so happy to see you both back here." Pius couldn't hide his genuine pleasure and relief. It was written all over his wide sun-tanned face. It was easy to see how his innocent and open take on life made him popular with the students.

"I felt terrible when I realized my stupidity had put you in such terrible danger," he said.

"How so?" David replied, although I knew what Pius was going to say.

"I completely misread Stephen Kumalo. I had total faith in his loyalty, and that almost got you killed. As for my Shelburne board, well, some heads will roll there."

"He fooled us too," I said. I remembered the sound of Stephen's children playing in the background when he spoke on the phone. His affection for his family was genuine.

Pius shook his head. "He seemed like the perfect employee and a devoted father."

"People commit evil acts and yet still retain the ability to love," I said.

"I don't think Stephen was doing this for himself; I think he was doing it so that his children could have the advantages that he saw others enjoying." There I was again looking for the good in someone who would have ended my life if he'd had his way.

"You're too charitable," Dr. Naidoo said over the lip of her teacup.

I shrugged. "I find it easier to live in this world if I can understand what makes people act the way they do."

"Has he been found?" David asked.

"He has not, and I know that is causing the police concern," Pius replied. "The DCI tells me that the Botswana Defense Forces surrounded Shashe yesterday, took several people into custody, and found large quantities of cocaine and armaments sufficient to sustain a small war. There was no sign of life at the bush camp. Stephen has vanished, and the authorities advise that he is desperate and dangerous."

"He will contact his wife," I said.

"Maybe so," Pius replied. "The police have his house under observation."

Dr. Naidoo placed her cup back in its saucer and pushed it an inch away from her. "Shelburne's focus is on finding the truth about Tom Parkes' death. You've dug up a lot more, but that's for the government of Botswana to sort out. The police are building their case, but they are missing important witnesses. I believe you killed the best ones." She looked at me. Did she wink at me? I couldn't think of a response. "We still do not have the key piece of evidence in Tom's death."

"The source of the diatoms," I said.

"Precisely," she replied, nodding. "The humble but oh so diagnostic diatom Cyclostephanos dubius. We need to visit the lake where Parkes said his son died and collect water samples."

"DCI Olivier tells me that if we can make that link then he will put the case forward to the public prosecutor," Pius said. "If that happens, I believe the Shelburne community will have what it needs to heal and move forward. And your job here will be done, and very well done too."

"You said *we* need to visit the lake," I said to Dr. Naidoo. "Surely this is a job for the police?"

"Not at all, Lara. This is a job for my department and the university labs. I said *we* because I thought it might be a good opportunity for us to spend some time together." She raised her eyebrows interrogatively. David wasn't included in the question.

"When do you want to go?" I asked.

"I have the technicians booked for tomorrow morning," she said. "I can pick you up."

I nodded. "Let me talk to David and then I'll call you."

She stood to leave, and Pius ushered her to the door.

"What was all that about?" David asked.

"I think she has a crush on me," I said.

"Good God," he replied, though mercifully we couldn't continue the conversation as Pius returned, and we had something important to discuss with him.

He sat down and put his hands together as if in prayer. Evidently, it was his characteristic gesture when he sensed that a confidence was to be shared. He probably used it when parents came to tell him that they were getting divorced or when a teacher came to his office to tell him she was pregnant. He was a good listener.

"We've got something to ask you, Pius," I began. "It's something that's very important to David and me." I was finding this more difficult than I had expected.

Pius nodded, encouraging me to continue.

"We have made a commitment to the girl that we rescued from Shashe," I said. David, Diba, and I had agreed to use that verb. "She's a remarkable young woman with no supports now that her father and brother are dead. We want to be that support for her." I looked over at David.

"Lara and I have spoken with Diba—that's the girl's name, Diba—and we've made a plan," he added. "We're going to start an adoption process, but that will take quite some time, and it might never be approved, as I'm over the age they normally consider for an adoptive parent."

I reached over and took his hand. "In the meantime, we have applied for guardian status, and it looks as if that will go through quite quickly," I said.

"That's a big step, Lara, but I would say that the girl is exceptionally lucky. What part can I play?" Pius sat forward, keen to engage.

"Diba says she wants to study medicine in the US, but she's young, and that could change. We want to be part of her life, but we also think she should finish her secondary education in Africa. That way she can keep her options open."

"So, Lara and I are wondering if she could enroll as a boarding student at Shelburne," David said, jumping in. "She would come to us in Florida every long holiday, and we would come to Cape Town twice a year. That way we think she would have the best of all possible worlds. Up until now she has had precious little go her way."

Pius was silent for a moment, allowing space in case we had anything more to add.

"Is this what she wants?" he said at last.

"She says she does, although she doesn't really know what life is like here," I said.

"If a student wants to be here, there is almost nothing we can't help her achieve. But if it's the parents' idea, and the child thinks she's being sent away or punished, it can be very difficult."

"That's why, as well as the usual admissions tests and tours, I insist on an interview with every applicant without the parents present. I know you both, and I believe your motives for wanting to help the girl, but I'm not changing my approach."

"We wouldn't want you to," I said. "You're the professional here, and you know your school better than anyone. If this isn't the right place, then perhaps you could advise us."

"Is the girl here?" he asked.

"We left her sitting in the lobby," I said, wondering if I sounded like a negligent parent.

Pius led us from the room. As we approached the lobby, we heard peals of youthful laughter. Diba was sitting where we'd left her, but she wasn't alone. I recognized Kristy and Aphiwe and a couple of other boys with them. They couldn't have been together for more than a few minutes, but they were giggling like old friends.

In a heartbeat I saw Diba almost as if for the first time. She was an adolescent girl with all the social and emotional needs of any other child her age. Given the right conditions, she could develop into a happy and confident young woman. The dark misery of the past five years would never leave her, but she could move beyond it, maybe even harness it, and build a life for herself.

I have times—many times, if I'm honest—when I'm consumed with the immediate, the urgent, but occasionally, there are moments when I realize I'm in the presence of something with enduring importance and transcendent truth. This was one of those moments, and I knew that the commitment that David and I were making to Diba was like a pebble being tossed into the millpond. The ripples would spread in every direction and lap against many shores.

The students rose as we approached; Pius greeted them and then introduced himself to Diba. He explained that he wanted to have a conversation with her, and the two of them returned to his office. The students said they had to go to class, but Kristy hung back.

"I'm glad to see you both back at Shelburne," she said in her best guardian manner. Then she lowered her voice. "Have you found out anything about Tom?"

"We have," I said.

"Not good?" she asked, raising her eyebrows.

I shook my head slowly. "No, not good."

V

Lara and I sat in the lobby for the better part of an hour. We thumbed through the school magazines and yearbooks and surveyed the gallery of past headmasters.

Finally, Lara broke the silence. "I'm actually nervous about this," she said, smiling. "We're sitting here like a married couple worrying about whether our daughter is going to be accepted into school."

"I've always been on the other side of this situation," I said. "I'd forgotten how it feels to have someone sit in judgement on a person you care about."

Before we could say any more, Pius and Diba appeared. They were smiling and laughing as if they'd known each other for years. We jumped to our feet.

"This is a remarkable young woman you have brought to campus," Pius said.

"We agree," Lara said, an unmistakable note of pride in her voice.

"Diba has told me about herself and about her schooling at the mission school in Bukavu. The sisters did a good job, but they had a clever girl to work with. With some extra tutoring in a couple of areas I think Diba will do well to join year eleven. We're halfway through the year, but I believe she can do it."

"So, you're accepting her?" I asked.

"Diba has convinced me that she is ready to take on this challenge. So, yes"

Lara stepped forward and hugged Diba, a tear glistening in the corner of her eye. Seconds later, I joined her. Pius stood quietly till we were done.

"And what's more," he said, "we have scholarship money left in the admissions budget for students who bring us the greater diversity we seek, and I would say that Diba certainly qualifies." He gave Diba a knowing smile, which she returned.

The next hour was filled with formalities. We signed a contract for the current academic year and discussed how we would like to pay the balance of the tuition after the scholarship had been credited. We also signed a waiver that absolved the school of responsibility in case of misadventure, but, as I well knew, it was worth nothing if the school had been negligent. Pius also introduced us to Monica Gonzalez the housemistress of De Beers House where Diba would be living, and we went for a visit. The girls shared large double rooms that were luxurious even by the standards of elite independent schools. Diba's eyes widened as she took in the details of her new home.

That night the three of us ate in the suite again. It was a celebration full of laughter and talk of the future. There were poignant moments too when Diba talked about her father.

I asked if she would like to talk to someone about what she had experienced in the bush wars. Perhaps a therapist would be the right approach. She looked up at me calmly and held my eye.

"Yes, I would," she said. "I would like to talk to you and David about it."

"That's not quite what I meant—"

"I know what you meant," she said, "and my answer stays the same. My father knew that he was putting us in harm's way by asking us to live a life no child should experience. He used to say, 'There is pain that uses you, and there's pain that you use.'" She smiled sadly. "Archange and I would tease Father about his sayings, but we knew they usually contained an important truth. I'm going to make sure I use the pain I have felt to keep me focused on what I must achieve if I'm to honour and justify the sacrifices of my family and my people."

She raised her water glass to us, and we returned the salutation.

"And you will," I said. "And you will."

CHAPTER 14

I

The Land Cruiser sped eastward along N2. Diba sat beside me, and we maintained a safe fifty-metre gap between us and Dr. Naidoo's maroon Mercedes ahead. We picked up R310 and headed north through Stellenbosch. Ten minutes beyond that the Mercedes signalled right, and we turned onto R45, which was signposted for Franschhoek.

I'd called Dr. Naidoo earlier the night before and told her that the two of us would love to come along and watch her team at work. Her tone suggested that wasn't quite the arrangement she had hoped for, but she acceded, and she'd swung past the hotel to pick us up before the sun rose. She was further miffed when I insisted on taking two cars, but I held my ground.

I had encouraged David to stay at the hotel. He had some work phone calls to catch up on, and, more importantly, he looked tired, and I thought he would benefit from a day off. But I could tell that after everything that had happened recently, he wasn't keen to let us go without him.

The sun was gaining height in the eastern sky as we approached Franschhoek. We drove past vineyards that ran back up the valley's gently sloping sides. The young vine leaves were a startlingly bright and vigorous green. Soon the fruit would begin to form and ripen in the strong summer sunshine, growing plump and heavy for the March harvest, followed by the transformation into world-class wine.

We drove along the town's main street. Its restaurants and gift shops were newly opened for the day but already busy with tourists from all over the world looking to buy things they didn't need. In a few days, newly purchased tanzanite jewellery and organic biltong would be packed in suitcases and put in the cargo holds of airplanes whisking the travellers homewards to Tokyo, Bahrain, Frankfurt, and Miami.

The stores thinned as we drove out of town, and the road turned south and became steep and twisty as we climbed over the Mont Rochelle Nature Reserve before dropping into the steep-sided Theewaterskloof Valley.

The Mercedes signalled again, and we turned right off the asphalt highway. Our tires scrunched on the crushed-rock surface of a private road, and in a hundred metres we arrived at some grand gates and a deep-blue wooden sign proclaiming in gilded letters that we had arrived at "Die Leeukuil."

There was a gatehouse and a sign ordering visitors to check in but the small stone building was empty, and the black wrought-iron gates were open, so we moved slowly ahead.

The road wound upwards through woodland. Yellowwood and white pear trees cast morning shadows on the tree ferns sprouting in grassy glades. Two small klipspringer antelope caught sight of us and froze before bounding away into the forest. A family of baboons sat beside the road happily engaged in social grooming. The natural world was getting on with its business unfazed by the murder and mayhem that had been dreamed up by human minds in that beautiful place.

The road leveled out, and around a final bend the forest opened to reveal a parklike vista of trimmed grass and ancient trees. Loose-limbed well-bred horses cantered around in paddocks fenced with white posts and rails. A hundred metres later, we caught sight of the house itself. It was obviously old. Its white stucco walls were punctuated with deep windows. There was a classical pediment above the massive main doors, and the roofs were thatched.

As we drove closer, we saw the reed-fringed lake. A dazzling blue-and-orange bird crashed into the smooth plane of the water and emerged the next second carrying a small silver fish writhing in its beak.

An elegant pale-blue European convertible that could have rolled off the set of a 1960s Bond movie sat in the shade of a giant willow, and we pulled up beside it.

One of the massive main double doors was open, and we walked from the bright day into an expansive entrance room dimly lit and floored with large worn flagstones. It had the feel of a place that had been welcoming visitors for hundreds of years.

A wide formal staircase in white marble rose from the centre of the space up to a second floor where it divided and headed off left and right to a gallery and a third story.

I heard the clacking of dog claws on stone and looked up to see a gorgeous Irish Setter gracefully descending the stairs. It headed over to us, tail wagging, and sat in front of us looking up questioningly. Diba knelt down and patted it. The dog wiggled closer and licked Diba's ear.

"You make friends easily," Dr. Naidoo said, smiling.

"I was brought up around all kinds of animals," Diba replied. "I think they can tell that I respect them."

The three of us moved toward a door on the left side of the room through which we could see another door open to the outside. The sound of voices drifted into us. We headed in that direction and stepped out onto a large gravel parking area on the side of the house where a white van with University of Cape Town markings was parked beside a police car. Dr. Naidoo spoke briefly to two young technicians and then returned to us.

"We're going to use a boat to collect water samples from different locations and different depths," she said. "Will you come with us?"

"I'd really like to look around the grounds, if that's OK," I offered weakly, noticing the smallest of frowns cross her face.

"I'll come down to the dock with you," Diba said, and she and the dog took up the rear as the small group carried their equipment, which consisted of bottles, nets, and a laptop computer, down to a wooden jetty that ran perhaps forty feet out into the lake.

One reason that I had declined to go along was that I didn't want to encourage Dr. Naidoo's attentions. I suppose it should have been flattering that such an accomplished woman had taken a shine to me, but I could only see it as an unhelpful and unwanted complication in what was already a pretty intense scenario. But the main reason I wanted to remain onshore was that I needed to explore the house and the grounds. I know it sounds a bit crazy, but I felt that we had developed an almost intimate relationship with Ed Parkes, and I wanted to try and understand him better. He had obviously loved this place; perhaps it would reveal things about him that would help to explain his behaviour.

Lost and Found

One can live with a person for years, and the daily routine and the playing out of well-rehearsed roles can mean that one never really knows them on more than a superficial level. We had only interacted with Parkes for a matter of hours, but in that time he had propositioned me, advocated for killing us, had his wife executed, and walked away into the night toward what he must have known was a certain and horrifying death.

Perhaps I was motivated purely by morbid curiosity, but maybe something would be revealed that would be helpful in settling the case.

I looked back toward the lake. Diba sat on the dock paddling her feet in the water with her arm around the dog as one of Dr. Naidoo's assistants untied the boat and pushed off. Diba turned to see where I was. I waved at her, and she waved back. She looked very happy.

I walked up a gently sloping gravel path leading up a low hill behind the house. The sea lavender was in full bloom, and insects of all kinds hummed around the large purple flowerheads. I stopped to inspect the pink carpet of wild geraniums and realized I was looking at a big brown hare not four feet from me. I wouldn't have noticed it if it hadn't blinked its beautiful orange eyes. It twitched its nose slightly and flattened its long ears against its back. Maybe it knew it had been spotted, but it wasn't going to throw away its well-tried strategy of hiding in plain sight. I continued up the hill.

Just below the crest of the hill I found a large stone building almost hidden by trees. The stone was coated with moss and lichen and overgrown with creepers. There was a big double door on one gable end. As I drew near, I saw that it was made of unvarnished wood. It looked heavy and solid, oak maybe. A huge circular iron handle turned easily in my hand, one of the doors creaked open, and I stepped inside. The door swung shut behind me.

It was dark, and it took several seconds for my eyes to adjust. The only light came from a skylight up in the ridge of the roof. It was dirty and covered with mould. Even after standing quietly for a minute, I found it hard to make out what, if anything, was inside the building. In the gloom my other senses were heightened. I smelled decay and something putrid, like old food.

I heard a sound, but it was so faint it was more of an impression of a sound. I couldn't make it out, but I was certain I wasn't alone in the building. A large part of me suggested that I back out of that place, but I have a stubborn streak, and I wasn't giving up yet.

I pulled out my phone and flipped on the light. As the beam swept the walls and the floor, I saw that I was standing in what looked like an abandoned squat. There was a thin mattress on the floor with a stained yellow sheet balled up to form a pillow. A propane gas burner sat on an upturned metal pail, and a dirty frying pan lay beside it. A plastic bag hung from a nail in the wall. I shone the light inside and found cans of sardines and corned beef, a bottle of hot sauce, and at least a dozen chocolate bars. I put my hand on the frying pan. It wasn't hot, but it was warmer than the air, suggesting it had been used recently. I moved deeper into the building, the leather soles of my shoes grinding on the dirt and grit covering the concrete floor.

Something brushed against my face. I screamed and lurched backwards, bringing the phone light up in front of me. A rope with a noose in the end swung slowly to and fro in the white light. It was suspended from a pulley screwed into one of the ceiling beams. The floor below the rope was covered in dark, irregular stains. As I shone the light downwards, the stains turned from black to crimson. It could only be dried blood. I was standing on a killing floor.

The staff probably used it to butcher the sheep I had seen grazing beyond the lake. Behind the dangling rope I saw stone steps leading down to a basement.

Ignoring the screams of warning from my frontal lobe, I took one cautious step downwards and then another until I found myself at the bottom of the stairs and in another space with no windows. Save for my phone's light, it was pitch black. It was also cooler down here, telling me that I was underground. I had pointed the light at the ground to guide my steps, but I moved it upwards and then gasped as the beam was reflected in dozens of pairs of tiny shining eyes. I took a step back, waited until my heart rate returned to something closer to normal, and then slowly moved the light around the walls.

Cages, some glass enclosures, and some made of fine mesh lined the walls. I slowly approached the nearest, focusing the light on the leaf litter in the bottom of the cage. In that instant a gaping mouth filled with fangs launched itself toward my throat. I screamed, reeled backwards, tripped over a box, and fell heavily to the floor. I had dropped my phone, but I grabbed it and scrambled to my feet. My heart was thumping as I shone the light back on the cage. There, digging itself back into the leaves, causing the faint rustling noise that I had heard, was a large black snake. The front pane of the Perspex cage dripped with the venom that had been intended for me.

Breathing rapidly, I inspected the other enclosures. They all contained snakes of different sizes and with different markings. The final cage contained several grey mice that sat there frozen in the beam of light from my phone, presumably food for the snakes.

I wondered if anyone was still caring for the snakes now that Parkes was dead, and the estate was working with a skeleton staff. I knew that snakes only needed to eat every couple of weeks, so even if no one had fed them recently, they'd be fine.

I selected a cage in the middle of the room and shone the light on it. A bright green snake, perhaps three feet long, was entwined around a branch that had been stuck into the sand on the bottom of the cage. About a foot back from its mouth, its body was distended with some partially digested meal. Someone was still feeding them. I wondered if that person was there in the dark with me now.

It was definitely time to head back to the light. Like a modern-day Proserpina returning from the underworld, I climbed back up the stone stairs. I had just placed my foot on the top step when I felt rather than saw or heard a movement behind me. I started to turn my head, but I didn't get far before a hand reached around and covered my mouth and nose. I smelled something like disinfectant, and my head filled with bursts of light. I slumped forward onto the filthy floor, and everything went blank.

II

Lara and Diba left early, and I took my time getting ready for the day. The leisurely pace felt like a luxury after the intensity of the past few days.

I walked along the waterfront and ordered a decaf coffee at a small bistro with tables outside that overlooked the harbour.

I wasn't crazy about the idea of them going off without me, but I rationalized it by telling myself that it would be good for them to spend some time alone together. Also, I didn't want to look as if I was hovering over them, a tendency I knew I had developed over the years.

I waited till it was 9:00 a.m. in the UK and then called Jessica. She was heading out to an early chemistry and materials lecture, so we only had a few minutes, but she sounded really happy. It wasn't the right moment to tell her what had been happening with Lara and me or the decision we'd made about Diba, so I told her about some of the people we'd met and the animals we had seen. I'm sure I left her thinking it was another one of Grandad's luxurious foreign junkets.

I really wanted to speak to Emy. Her friendly, caring voice always gave me a lift, but the time difference between Boca and Cape Town meant that she wouldn't be in for a few hours yet, so I contented myself with checking the emails she'd sent, telling me about the inquiries that had come in. These included a lawsuit alleging racial discrimination at a prominent school in Los Angeles, an allegation of sexual assault at an elite school in Chile, and a messy situation involving a new young headmaster at an international school in Singapore.

I called the school in Singapore and spoke to the board chair. It was evening there, but he was desperate to talk, and we sorted out the problem in the course of our twenty-minute conversation. The head had shown exceptionally poor judgement, and if that had happened once, experience told me it would happen again. It was a straightforward personnel issue; the head had lost the board's trust, and he had to go. The trick would be managing the communication, and they asked me if I could consult on that piece.

I had been thinking we would all need a break when the Shelburne case was over, but a few phone calls wouldn't hurt, and the money was attractive, so I agreed. I'd call Los Angeles and Santiago later and tell them I was overcommitted.

Back in the suite I called Lara's cell. There was no answer, and it went to voicemail. That rarely happened. When I called ten minutes later, and the same thing happened, I started to get anxious. I had Dr. Naidoo's number. She answered but said she was in the middle of the lake working and wouldn't be back on shore for at least an hour.

There was a car rental desk in the hotel lobby, and within ten minutes I'd given in to my anxieties and was sitting behind the wheel of a dark blue Range Rover heading east.

Just outside the city limits, I approached a roundabout too fast and had to brake sharply, causing the cars behind to sound their horns. I realized that, in my anxiety, my mind was elsewhere, and I needed to refocus on driving. In all likelihood Lara was fine, and there was a simple explanation for her not answering her phone, but my relationship with her had deepened to the point that I didn't want to contemplate life without her. She was what gave things meaning, the silver behind the glass.

Surely, I was panicking unnecessarily. There were three of them at the site, and there would be others from the university. It would be OK. In fact, Lara would probably be unimpressed that I had driven up to check on her. But she always answered her phone.

I took two deep breaths, exhaled slowly, gripped the steering wheel more firmly, and concentrated on the road ahead.

After a while the English voice on the GPS guided me to the turn off for Die Leeukuil. As I came to a halt in front of the big house, I saw Diba chatting with Dr. Naidoo on the dock, but there was no sign of Lara.

III

He came like a shadow emerging from the darkness. My skull was pounding with the worst headache of my life, and I struggled to focus my eyes on the figure in front of me. Even before I could make out the details, something about the stance and the set of the shoulders told me who I would discover when my senses came together. When they did, sure enough, Stephen Kumalo's face swam into view.

In place of the snowy-white shirt and tie, he was wearing a tattered and stained T-shirt. His pressed grey trousers had been replaced by cargo shorts, and he wore flip-flops instead of shoes.

His appearance was different, but his face bore the same proud, almost haughty look that had been there from our first meeting.

"Ms. Rios, I apologize for the discomfort you must be feeling." His brow furrowed and he appeared to be genuinely distressed. "I had intended to kill you outright once I realized that it was you who had entered my . . . my lair." He smiled sadly. "You will remember that at Shashe I expressed my strong opinion that you and Mr. Mallory should be eliminated before you could do us any further damage. It appears I was correct in that opinion, but as you know, Mr. Joca's view prevailed, and now look where we are."

He chuckled and then looked away at the blank walls as if considering a vision that only he could see. "I believed that all is lost for me, and I was in despair wondering what my next move should be. Should I run? Perhaps kill myself? Nothing seemed quite right, but now with your arrival, I see the possibility of an amusing endgame. 'Revenge' would be an inadequate word and 'payback' too coarse a term, but perhaps we can construct something that will give a sense of meaning to the relationship we have built over the past few weeks. We will compose a beautiful coda, a final movement to our little quartet. You, David, and Diba will play the melody, and I will provide the continuo. It will be a thing of beauty."

He seemed to have lost touch with reality, and his controlled aggression terrified me.

"What about your family?" I hardly recognized the harsh rasp that croaked out of my aching throat as I spoke the words. "The first time we met you spoke about them, and I could tell they meant everything to you. Surely you have something to live for?"

Stephen nodded sadly. "You're quite correct, Lara. You're an empathetic woman, and you can sense emotion. My family is the reason that we're here now having this unusual conversation." He giggled in a way that disturbed me.

"Working at Shelburne was a mixed blessing for me. It was a good job with real responsibility, and it paid well, but it didn't pay enough. Every day I saw what real wealth could buy for the children of Shelburne. They had the best teachers and the best facilities, and when they graduated every door was open to them. It would never be that way for my babies. The colour of their skin was no longer the barrier; it was the colour of my money. I was determined that my children would have those opportunities, so I searched high and low for ways to make it a reality. Can you guess what I found?"

His tone had become light and pleasant as if we were discussing the weather over a cup of tea.

"You found Ed Parkes," I said.

"Oh, Lara, how I wish we could have been friends. You're such an intuitive woman and so clever. If only things were different." He sighed. "You're correct, of course. My role at Shelburne required that I sat in on board meetings and attended school functions, and soon I became aware that Parkes was involved in something highly lucrative but over which he had lost control.

"Perhaps you have come to know me well enough to know some of my skills Lara." He spoke with an assumed intimacy that chilled me. "I'm very organized, I see into people's hearts, and I will not be outworked. I told Parkes what I suspected about his activities. He thought at first that I was trying to blackmail him, and when he realized I wanted to partner with him, he was so relieved that he fell into my arms, so to speak."

He knelt next to me and ran the back of his hand down my cheek. I shrank away in disgust and terror.

"You're a very attractive woman, Lara. I hope you know that. David is a lucky man to have your love."

"What will happen to your wife? Your children?" It was the only thing I could think to say that might cause him to back away.

"It's kind of you to think of them, Lara. They'll be fine." He stood up. "I've made a lot of money, and I have made provision for them in a blind trust managed at several removes. Elsie will be able to hold her head high in any company, and little Stefan and Lola will have access to everything they need to get ahead."

"But you won't be there to see them grow," I said.

"Well, it doesn't seem likely at this moment, does it? But you can never tell, Lara. I'm a very patient man, and I'll be there when the final card is placed on the table. Then we'll know."

He took my hand, raised it to his lips, and gently kissed it, his lips lingering on my skin. His face was lined and dirty, but his eyes still shone with the predatory satisfaction of a big cat that had its prey at its mercy.

"This is quite intimate isn't it?" He smiled. "But you know what makes it truly intimate, almost conjugal?" I could only shake my head in despair.

"The fact that I'm telling you everything. That I'm confessing my sins to you. That I'm laying my life before you and giving you the knowledge and the power to destroy me. I'm submitting myself to you."

"But I have no power. You plan to kill me, so it's not intimate; it's insane."

He pouted and shrugged. "I disagree. Yes, surely my intention is to design a dénouement that will bring the greatest suffering and regret to you and

David as a special thank-you for ruining me, but that process could be quite thrilling. You and I could become very close before I finally release you to death, a death that you will be begging for by the time I grant it."

"And David?" I had to ask.

"Well, obviously, he has to live. Anything else would be far too kind. He has to live with the certain knowledge that he and he alone brought you to your death. He will suffer every day for the rest of his life. I aim to create a living purgatory for him. Drugs, madness, suicide; he can choose his own road to hell."

He made a small gurgling sound that made my skin crawl. He frowned at me. "Oh dear, Lara, I'm a man who needs to be organized. I like to plan things out in advance, taking care of all the details, and here now we have to come up with something 'off the cuff,' you might say. It's all a bit spontaneous. I don't do very well with 'spontaneous.' It makes me quite nervous." He smiled sadly. "But we'll make the best of it, you and I, won't we? I'll do my best to come up with something original, and I know you'll play your part. It has to be something worthy of us all. Something truly unforgettable. I'm thinking of a simple structure, perhaps three movements, like a concerto. We'll start off with something engaging, move into a slower and more lyrical passage, and then finish up with something explosive and truly memorable."

He looked around as if searching for inspiration. "We must adapt to the resources at our disposal, Lara. 'To a hungry person even bitter food is sweet,' as my mother used to say."

He moved closer to me and pulled me to my feet, then pushed me roughly past the dangling noose and back down the stairs to the basement. I stumbled over the bottom step and fell to the floor. He took a piece of cord from his back pocket and wound it around my feet, tying it so tightly that my ankles pressed together painfully. Then he bound my hands behind my back.

"Are you an animal lover, Lara? Parkes was. He built up quite a collection of wildlife here at Die Leeukuil. That means 'Lion's Den' by the way. Quite appropriate really. The house is up for sale now, and most of the larger animals have been reintroduced to the wild, but the snakes remain. They live in the upper part of this building. Perhaps you already made their acquaintance?"

I didn't say anything. My mind was blank. I'd told David that I didn't fear death anymore. It appeared that I'd soon get a chance to see if that assertion was true. What I certainly did fear was pain, and I had a pathological dread of snakes.

He disappeared from my view, and I heard his footsteps grating on the flagstones. He reappeared a moment later and placed three cages on the floor in front of me.

"I have three new friends to meet you, Lara. It's dark up there, and the cages aren't labelled, so I'm not sure what we've got." He rubbed his face with both hands. His skin was grey beneath the layer of dirt, and I could see that he was exhausted.

"I'm no expert on snakes," he said, "but I know that all the snakes Parkes collected are among the most poisonous in Southern Africa. The lab at the university hospital would visit here regularly and milk them for the production of antivenom. I know that he kept a puff adder in one of the cages. I'm told they're bad tempered snakes, and their bite produces very painful symptoms, not necessarily fatal but very painful. Then there's a boomslang, a pretty little green tree snake."

I thought that the boomslang and I had probably already met.

"They are nervous little things, and I'm told their venom causes mental disorders as well as internal bleeding. Isn't it strange how something so delicate and pretty can produce such awful outcomes? And I know there's a black mamba up there. You may have heard of them. They deliver multiple bites in quick succession, and the neurotoxin they inject is particularly potent. If you do get bitten, and you find your eyelids drooping a few minutes later, it's probably the mamba.

"I hope it doesn't go that way because you'll likely be dead before we can develop our plan further. As I said, I've chosen three at random for you, and I don't know which they are, but I thought I'd leave you down here with them for a while and see how you get along. Being cold-blooded, they like to find warm places, and I think you're the warmest thing in this part of the building, so you'll likely find them snuggled up with you quite soon. I'll put the kettle on and make some tea, and I'll bring you a cup down in an hour or so. Hopefully, you'll still be able to swallow. Do you take milk?"

He carefully unlatched the three cages and then backed away up the stairs, closing the door behind him and leaving me in complete darkness.

IV

"Hi, David," Diba called out to me. She was trying hard to call me "David" instead of "Mr. Mallory" or, more usually, nothing, but it still sounded a bit forced. She ran over to me, a spectacular Irish setter trotting along beside her.

"We have had a really interesting day. I'm so glad I came. Dr. Naidoo has spent hours telling me about the ecology of freshwater systems and about the different kinds of diatoms and how they can be diagnostic in a case like this." She was gushing with teenage excitement.

"That's fabulous. Maybe there's a career here for you," I said. "Have you seen Lara?"

"Oh, wow. Not for a while. She went for a walk. I think I saw her heading up that trail." She pointed. "Have you called her?"

"She's not answering, which is unusual, but maybe her phone's battery is dead. Probably no reason to worry. You have a new friend?" I said, nodding at the dog.

"Isn't she beautiful?" Diba knelt and held the dog's head between her hands. "She used to belong to one of the chefs, but the staff have all left, and she's been abandoned. The tag on her collar says her name is Molly. I think she likes me."

There was little doubt of that, and I could tell by the look in Diba's eye that she was sizing me up to see if this was the right moment to ask if we could keep her. I didn't want to deal with that now, so I gave the dog a pat and changed the subject.

"Look, why don't you finish up with Dr. Naidoo, and I'll scout around, see if I can find what Lara's up to."

"OK. Give me a few minutes, and I'll come and join you."

She ran back to the dock, the dog bounding along beside her. Diba was finding her voice.

V

It didn't take long for the snake to find me. I heard it moving across the dusty floor, and then I saw its shape, a softer black gliding against the hard black of the ground. I didn't know whether I should try and wriggle away across the floor or if that would alarm it and make it more aggressive. The alternative was to lie there quietly and wait for the snake to find me and explore me.

It was with me before I had a chance to think it through, so I lay as still as I could. I felt a gentle poking pressure on the front of the cotton blouse I was wearing. The snake found a gap between two buttons and moved forward. It felt cool and smooth as it worked its way under the fabric. I sensed that it was fairly small, and soon it was curled into a ball beneath my breasts and above the waistband of my jeans. I breathed slowly and tried not to descend into panic.

As I lay there in the dark, a powerful image of Alex came to me. When he was very young, I would go to his bedroom at night just to watch him sleep. He always slept with a smile on his face, and sometimes I would lie beside him, trying to imagine the beautiful dreams he was having.

Years later he had managed to keep that smile going through what we both had known was a death sentence. Thinking of him gave me strength, and I closed my eyes and tried to accept whatever fate might be about to befall me. The idea of escape and rejoining a life with those I loved seemed like a distant dream at that moment. Surviving the next few minutes was all I could aspire to.

I was gently exhaling as the snake nestled close to my heart when I heard a scratching sound coming from the other side of the room. Snakes don't have ears like ours, but they can pick up vibrations through the ground, and my snake had obviously sensed what I had heard. It tensed and then slowly moved its head around, looking for the gap in the shirt fabric. My warmth had made it more active, and now it was on the hunt for food.

There was perfect silence for several minutes after the snake left me. That silence was broken suddenly by the screams of a small animal as it fought in vain for its life. The screams faded as quickly as they'd begun, and I pictured the snake dislocating its jaw and wrapping its distended mouth around the prey. Would the activity excite the other snakes? Stephen had opened three cages. Would the others now come and find me? I decided it was time to try to move. I wriggled sideways until I found a wall. I pushed my back against the stone, pulled my knees under me, and flexed my quads until they burned. Seconds later I was panting, but I was upright.

From where I stood I saw a line of grey light seeping in from what was probably a doorway. I hopped in that direction but fell over something embedded in the floor by what I was now certain was a door to the outside. I went down hard and lay there for a moment to recover. Reaching out to examine the obstacle, I found what felt like an old-fashioned metal boot scraper. The blade was meant to remove mud, not to cut through rope, but I didn't have a lot of choices, so I began to work my wrists across the top of it. After a minute I was breathing hard, and I paused, wondering if this was having any effect. I brought the rope up to touch my lips and I could feel that it had begun to fray. Encouraged, I went at it harder, and within seconds I felt my bonds give way. My hands were free, but they were numb from the restricted blood flow, and it took me what seemed like an eternity before I got enough sensation back in them to allow me to undo the tether around my feet.

I had just finished working on the last knot when I heard footsteps approaching on the gravel path. Stephen was returning.

VI

In my heart I knew that David was trying his best to build a relationship with me, but he was a formal man, and it's hard to build a relationship if you're not willing to show something of yourself. He knew I had watched my real father die in my arms only a few days ago. Other people would have found a way to confront that reality and use it to get closer, but not David. He was kind and respectful, but I didn't know him the way I knew Lara.

She wore her heart on her sleeve. She'd sat with me after dinner the evening before and told me about her life and the death of her son. She was very direct and said I was not a substitute for Alex, that no one could ever be, but she had love to give, and she wanted to give it to me. She told me that she had been the one with her hand on the trigger, that she'd been the one who had shot down the plane, and I could tell that her love was tinged with guilt.

I resolved never to use that against her. My father had given me his dying wish, and my life from this point forth would be with Lara—and David, if he would allow it.

VII

I tried the handle of the door. It was locked, and there was no key that I could feel on the inside.

I pushed on the door, and it gave slightly, a ray of light shining through the crack I had created in the old wood door. I heard a key turn in the lock at the far end of the building. I didn't have long, and the time for stealth was past. I took a couple of steps back and ran at the door, leading with my shoulder. I bounced off it and landed on my back, but I could see that the wood was splintering. I tried again, and this time two of the central planks exploded outwards, creating a space big enough for me to clamber through. The light outside was blinding, and I had to stand there for a second, shading my eyes.

Stephen was standing ten feet from me. His arms hung by his side. In one hand he gripped a small gun unlike any I had seen before. My heart sank.

"Dear, Lara," he said nonchalantly, "I hoped this would be your personal purgatory, a place for punishment or purification, but you have outwitted me."

He smiled in a way that made my blood run cold.

"Of course, this was never meant to be the final act. It was too private; there was no audience, and we were missing the most important spectator of all. But not to worry; David is close, and I don't think we will have to wait too long for him to take his seat."

He raised his right arm, pointed the gun at me, and squeezed the trigger.

VIII

I'd been walking the trails for several minutes when the dog found me. A moment later, Diba jogged into view.

"Any sign?" she asked.

"Not yet but with you and the dog along, I'm sure we'll sniff her out in no time. All finished with Dr. Naidoo?"

"She's gone back to Cape Town with the techies. She said she'll call tomorrow."

We continued on a trail that led uphill toward a low stone building. We were probably a hundred metres away when a crash like the sound of splintering wood came from the building. The dog froze and then dashed toward the noise. We looked at each other and then ran after her. We were maybe fifty metres away when we caught up with the dog, who had frozen again and was pointing her nose toward the rear of the building. We looked in that direction and saw a dreadful tableau unfolding before us. Lara and Stephen were facing each other maybe ten feet apart. As we watched, he raised the weapon in his hand and shot Lara, who crumpled to the ground. It was virtually point blank; she had to be dead or dying.

Stephen moved over to her body and picked it up, carrying it over to a nearby Nissan pickup and dumping it in the back. He secured her wrists to a tie-down and then turned and looked straight into my eyes. I was close enough to see him raise his eyebrows and observe the smirk on his face. He was taunting me. Seconds later, he drove off in a cloud of dust.

"Come, we must get to the car!" Diba was tugging at my sleeve. I didn't question her. She had a natural authority that worked in that moment. I ran faster than I had in a couple of decades to try and keep up with her.

"He'll have to go through the main gate!" I said, panting. "We can cut him off there."

"No, there are two entrances to Die Leeukuil. He's heading for the service entrance," Diba replied as we threw ourselves into the Range Rover. The dog stood looking puzzled as we drove off in a cloud of gravel and dust.

"Turn left here," Diba said in a calm, clear voice.

"How do you know your way around here?" I asked, realizing I knew the answer before I had finished the question.

"I've been here before," she said quietly.

CHAPTER 15

I

We caught up with the truck just as it turned onto the asphalt highway. Stephen wasn't driving fast; it was almost as if he wanted us to catch him. I pulled up to the back of the Nissan, and from the high vantage point of the Range Rover, we could see Lara's body slumped in the back. Her eyes were open but unseeing, and her lips were slightly parted. Blood was seeping from a wound in her shoulder. She had to be dead. Stephen wouldn't have made a mistake with his aim from that range.

"She is sleeping," Diba said, and at first I thought she was speaking figuratively.

"Surely she's dead," I replied.

"No, just sleeping," Diba insisted. "Stephen shot her with a tranquilizer gun. We used to carry them in the bush for when we met enemy soldiers whom we needed to interrogate before we executed them."

I grasped at this shred of hope.

"How can you tell?" I asked.

"I saw the gun he used. But she is still in great danger. There are no tranquilizer darts designed for humans, so he will have used one designed for a large mammal. Humans can react very badly. Several of the fighters we tranquilized didn't survive. If the dose is even slightly too great, it can cause respiratory failure."

My heart sank.

"But look," she said excitedly. "Did you see her eyes roll just then?"

"No. Are you sure?"

"I'm sure. This is a good sign. She will live."

At that moment my cell phone rang, and the Range Rover's hands-free display blinked to life, displaying Lara's number. I touched the button on the steering wheel to accept the call. No one spoke for several seconds, and I wondered if the call had dropped.

"Good afternoon, David. I hope that your day is unfolding nicely," Stephen said in his usual clipped and elegant style. It seemed incongruous juxtaposed with the brutal scenario playing out before us.

"What do you want, Stephen? You have no hope of escape."

He laughed. "I haven't the least interest in escaping. I have not even considered my fate in designing the entertainment that we will enjoy together this afternoon. It's all about you and Ms. Rios. I'm not sure exactly how things will turn out beyond knowing for certain that they will go very badly for dear Lara and thus, because you love her and are responsible for the fate that awaits her, even worse for you."

The pickup hit a deep pothole, causing Lara's body to be flung in the air and crash violently back onto the metal truck bed. I saw her blink as a grimace contorted her face. She was alive.

That changed the calculus in how I should respond to Stephen. If she'd been dead, I could have run him off the road, but now my options were different, and I decided to let him call the shots.

"What's the game, Stephen? What do you want from me?" I tried to appear calm, but my gut was churning. I would have to live by my wits over the next few hours if Lara was to stand any chance of surviving the mess I had landed her in. My life to date had been characterized by measured, intentional decisions, and I wasn't sure I had the skills to save her. The sight of her bruised and bloody body in front of me was almost more than I could bear.

"My dear David, I'm so glad that you're seeing things from the proper perspective. We're going for a drive down the Cape Peninsula to the beautiful little town of Hout Bay. Do you know it? There are some great seafood restaurants there. Unfortunately, we're not going to be able to patronize any today, but maybe years from now you'll go there again. You can have an elegant lunch and relive the memories of what unfolded on this day, though I fear those memories will put you off your food." He chuckled. "And I know what you're going to say next; you're going to ask me why you don't just call in the police and have them intercept our little convoy. Am I right?"

He was, but I didn't respond.

"Ah yes. I thought I was. Well, the thing is, Ms. Rios is not dead, but she will be if there's any interference. I will turn around and put a bullet in her head. You will have a perfect view. Maybe some of her brains will spatter your elegant vehicle. But that, my dear David, is a call that you will have to make—and live with."

II

My brain raced back to the clearing in the centre of our village five years earlier when the Hutu militia put a gun in my hand and forced me to shoot my mother. They made her kneel in front of me. Though they had beaten her badly, she smiled up at me, her eyes speaking the love that her swollen lips could not. She nodded gently, granting me permission and forgiveness in one gesture. I pulled the trigger, and her body slumped onto the dusty ground. A dark pool of blood grew like a morbid halo around her head, and a fly settled on her cheek.

I looked ahead through the windshield and saw the woman whom I already respected and who I knew I would come to love. She was bleeding and bruised, and I felt anger more than dread.

I pulled myself away from that dark dream that still haunted parts of every day. I looked across at David and saw a good man who was out of his depth. He was wise and accomplished, but he had no experience of the madness and desperation that pulsed through Stephen Kumalo and threatened to take Lara's life.

I had lived in the bush with my father for five years. We had hunted and been hunted. I had learned how to live with fear and not let it paralyze me.

I will always remember what my father said to me on one occasion when we were hiding waist deep in muddy water in the reeds of an island in Lake Kivu. The militias were all around us and closing in, and our troops were in despair. "Courage is contagious, and hope can have a life of its own," he whispered to me. As he always did, he found a way out for us, and his mystique grew even greater.

I had to be part of saving Lara. I ran my hand over my left ankle and caressed the leather sheath and the bone handle of the skinning knife that I carried everywhere with me. Lara had taken it from me at the crash site but had returned it to me during our conversation last night.

I had decided that it wasn't going to be part of my Shelburne school uniform. Abandoning it would be the symbol of the change in my life, but for now I was glad I was still wearing it.

We turned onto a wider busier road, but Lara was hidden from view in the truck box and attracted no attention. We motored on for perhaps forty-five minutes before Stephen indicated a left turn and pulled across the highway onto the road leading down to Hout Bay harbour.

It was the end of the afternoon, and a steady stream of cars was heading in the opposite direction back toward Cape Town. The parking lot behind the harbour was emptying fast. Stephen slowed and drove carefully along the dock, almost to the very end where there were no tourists and no prying eyes. He pulled into a space beside where a large fishing boat was moored, its engine idling. Wisps of smoke puttered from the exhaust pipe above the cabin roof. David's phone rang again, and we both knew who was calling.

III

The sun shone from a cloudless sky, and the road was smooth and empty as our little convoy drove south. Anyone watching would have seen nothing untoward. Only the four of us knew the deadly drama that was playing out. Stephen might be mad, but he knew how to serve up his revenge in the cruellest way.

After what seemed like both a millisecond and an eternity, he pulled into Hout Bay. He drove slowly along the waterfront and parked. My phone rang again.

"We're getting near the final act, David. Are you getting excited?" He laughed. "Lara and I are going for a boat ride. We're going to feed the sharks off Duiker Island. There's a large colony of fur seals there, and that attracts some of the biggest great white sharks in these waters. It's a popular tourist attraction, and if we spill just a little blood, I think we can be guaranteed an impressive spectacle for everyone. We have this nice little fishing boat captained by an old friend of mine. We worked together on, how shall I put it, some import-export deals, but unfortunately, there's no room for you on the boat, David.

"Now don't get me wrong; you simply have to see this. After all, what would be the point if you couldn't witness exactly what's going to happen?" He chuckled again, and my blood ran cold.

"If you look across the harbour, you will see the South African Maritime Safety Authority station. When I give you permission, you will go over there and tell them everything that's happening. They will chase us, but they won't quite catch us in time. You see, I don't want to escape. I want the opposite. I want to be with you forever, to be part of your nightmares from this moment until you take your final breath."

I heard a quiet click, and when I looked across at the passenger's seat, Diba wasn't there.

"Why should they believe me?" I asked.

"No worry on that score, David. I'll have Lara in plain view, and she does look a bit banged up, I'm afraid. I'm sure they'll believe you. Now sit tight until I get Lara on board and then I'll get back to you."

I sat there while Stephen and a huge, swarthy man in shorts and a filthy T-shirt bundled Lara out of the truck bed and down the sloping wooden gangway onto the fishing boat. It took them a couple of minutes because Lara kicked at them and made at least one good connection. They sat her on the bench behind the cabin superstructure and secured her hands to a ring bolt. She seemed much more alert now, and the terror written plainly on her face sliced through my heart.

Both men stepped inside the cabin, and the boat's engine roared as it pulled away from the dock.

The phone rang again. It was Stephen ordering me to contact SAMSA.

Where was Diba? How had she gotten out of the car without me noticing? I guess I had been fixated on the phone call. I couldn't wait for her to reappear. I put the Range Rover in gear, spun the wheel, and gunned the engine. The tires squealed as I raced around the waterfront to the SAMSA station.

I explained myself to a young officer who looked sceptical but whom I persuaded to step outside with me. He looked in horror as the fishing boat passed with Lara battered and in chains.

Ordering me to stay where I was, he ran back into the station, speaking into a walkie-talkie as he did so. It couldn't have been more than a minute later that he reappeared with two colleagues and waved for me to follow them as they ran. A minute later, the two massive outboard motors of the coast guard vessel started up, and one of the officers, a youngish woman in a white open-necked shirt and blue fatigue trousers, cast off the line just as I jumped on board. I looked around again for Diba, but she was nowhere to be seen. Where had she gone? A momentary anxiety crossed my mind but vanished again in an instant. There was something more immediate to worry about.

IV

When Stephen pointed the gun at me and pulled the trigger, I knew I was going to die, so as I began to wake up, my first impressions were that death was a lot dustier and bumpier than I had imagined. It wasn't for several minutes that I realized I was alive—in a very bad place but alive.

It took me a few minutes longer than that to figure out that I must have been shot with a tranquilizing dart. My shoulder hurt badly, and it wasn't helped by the fact that I was chained to the bed of a truck and bouncing along a rough road.

I like to think that I have been in control of most parts of my life. Watching Alex die and knowing that I couldn't stop the cancer spreading was really the first time that I had felt helpless, but my current predicament looked like it would be another. I felt small and alone. Stephen wasn't rational, so there would be no way to bargain with him. He held all the cards.

As the truck rounded a bend and started up a short hill, I saw a vehicle behind us. When we pulled up at an intersection, and the Range Rover came closer, I saw David at the wheel with Diba beside him. For a moment my heart leaped with hope. Then the reality of the situation sank in. Stephen's plot involved all of us, and any attempt to rescue me would likely put them both in grave danger.

After maybe an hour of driving and just when I thought I would scream if the pain in my shoulders and chained wrists didn't stop, I sensed the quality of the light changing. Moments after that I smelled the ocean and the fishy diesel smell of a harbour.

The truck pulled up with a jerk, and I felt the suspension relax as Stephen got out. Moments later two pairs of hands dragged me over the side of the truck bed. My arms were pinned to my sides, but my feet were free, and I delivered a few kicks, to little effect.

Lost and Found

Stephen's accomplice swore at me, and Stephen laughed.

"You have hurt Stefano's feelings, Lara. He sees himself as a bit of a ladies' man. Save your energy; you will need it later when you go swimming with the sharks."

He pushed his face to within inches from mine. His breath was rank, and drops of spittle sprayed from his lips as he spoke. "Are you a good swimmer, Lara? I hope so; it will prolong the show." He pulled away, his face contorted into a sneer.

The engine revved, and I felt the boat move forward, but it travelled slowly, as if it was a pleasure cruise around the harbour, and we had all the time in the world.

At least I was sitting upright now, and I could see most of what was going on. I heard tires squeal. Looking around I saw the dark blue Range Rover hurtling along the harbour road until it pulled up outside some kind of military office. I also realized that to get out of the harbour, the boat would have to pass close to where the Range Rover was stopped. It was torture to be so close to David and to freedom but to know that escape was an impossibility.

Just as the boat turned and headed for the harbour mouth, David and some uniformed personnel jumped aboard a patrol vessel. I heard its engine start, followed by some shouted commands, and then the engine of our boat revved loudly, drowning out even the persistent squawking of the gulls hanging in the clear blue sky overhead.

V

The SAMSA boat remained perhaps a hundred metres behind Stephen's boat. In a horrible irony, the name *Lucky Girl* was painted in green across the white stern of the boat that Lara was on. One of the SAMSA officers who had introduced herself as Zephyr Rodrigues approached me.

"We're going to have to take some kind of action," she said, "or there's not much point in us being here. My colleague, Sam, has sniper training. He can try and pick off the men."

"It's too risky," I said. "Please wait until we find out what they plan to do. Then we can formulate a response" I was terrified of taking any action that would harm Lara, but Zephyr was correct; at some point we would have to act.

Now that we were out of the shelter of the harbour, the two boats were ploughing through the big Southern Ocean swell, and I saw that we were heading for a group of low rocks sticking out of the ocean to a height of perhaps twenty metres. A tourist boat was already in position, rocking in the heavy swell. Colourful plastic ponchos protected the onlookers from the spray, fingers pointed, and camera lenses focused.

The rocks were covered in seals. Some were lying lazily on their sides, a flipper extended skywards; others were barking and pushing each other. Every so often a few of them would slip off the rock into the dark green water to hunt for the sardines and mackerel that abounded in those cold waters. As I watched, a group of three seals shot out of the water and landed ten feet up the rocky slope. They were agitated, and soon the whole colony was baying in fear and annoyance.

Then I saw why. A sleek dark fin cut the ocean's surface a few feet off the rocks, and a cruel mouth filled with razor sharp teeth appeared in a patch of pink-stained water. The tattered remains of a fur seal were flung in the air before falling back again into the gaping maw of the great white shark.

This must have been what Stephen was looking for because he shouted to the man at the wheel, and the *Lucky Girl* turned a few points to starboard and headed for the spot marked by a scum of pale pink foam.

Stephen emerged from the wheelhouse, unlocked Lara's chains, and held her in front of him, a gun to her head.

"Are you ready David?" he bellowed across the space between the boats, which was now no more than twenty yards. "I want to be sure you're paying attention. I don't want you to forget any of the details of what's happening here. Smell the air and feel the sun on your back, but know that the water is brutally cold. Imagine the fear in her heart as she flounders in the surf waiting for the killing machine to tear her apart. This is not a good way for a human being to die, and you're responsible for bringing her to this, David. My revenge is that you will have to live forever with the memory of her screams tearing through every day and night of your life."

He pushed Lara toward the side of the boat.

Zephyr touched my arm, and I saw that her colleague, Mike, had a sniper rifle at his shoulder, but surely the rocking of the boat would make any shot highly speculative. He was as likely to hit Lara as Stephen. I looked at Zephyr, and she could read my wordless despair.

"We have to do something now," she said, and I knew she was right. It was time to roll the dice. I was about to say something in agreement when I caught the faintest unexpected movement on the other boat. Then it came into focus. Someone was inching across the roof of the cabin, and it only took me another second to realize it was Diba. How in the name of God had she gotten on the boat?

"Wait!" I said, louder than necessary.

Mike looked over at me and lowered his rifle.

"Just give me a minute to reason with him." I had to distract Stephen and buy Diba a few seconds to do whatever it was that she planned, and I knew he could hear me, as the boats were closing in on one another.

Stephen laughed. "I'm past reason, David. You can save your words for the eulogy. I wonder how you're going to put a positive spin on your girlfriend being ripped apart by a giant shark. I only wish I could be there, but I doubt I'll be invited."

With that he took the gun and clubbed Lara over the back of the head. She didn't pass out, but blood welled from the wound.

"It always helps to have a bit of chum in the water, David." Stephen chortled as he pushed Lara to the edge of the boat.

"Goodbye, Lara!" he shouted, but the final syllable of her name came out as a scream. I watched in disbelief as the tip of a marlin spike poked through the front of his chest. Surprise on his face, he scrabbled futilely at it as pink bubbles frothed from between his lips. He released his grip on Lara and sank to his knees.

The commotion attracted the other man, who emerged from the wheelhouse. Diba dropped silently from the roof behind him and in the same motion drew a knife across the man's neck. A gaping red mouth opened in his windpipe, and arterial blood sprayed in every direction. He was dead before he hit the deck.

Stephen found the strength from somewhere to regain his feet, and Lara cowered as he grabbed for her. She sidestepped him, and his forward motion caused him to fall across the boat's narrow coaming. His hands grabbed for purchase on the slippery fibreglass, but the motion of the next wave tumbled him overboard. With the blood pumping from the massive wound in his chest, it was only a matter of seconds before the sharks found him.

He disappeared below the surface and then reappeared a few seconds later. Our eyes locked for a split second before he was pulled down into the cold green waters for a final time.

Diba went to Lara, and they held each other for a few seconds before Diba said something to her, and they both ran into the wheelhouse. The boat was drifting toward the rocks where the Southern Ocean surf was breaking in huge plumes of spray.

It took them only a few moments to figure out the controls, rev the engine, and steer the boat away from the rocks.

The tourists in their multicoloured ponchos looked on in disbelief. They had gotten rather more than they had bargained for.

CHAPTER 16

I

When I killed in the bush with my father and brother, I was a different person.

I was killing to survive, killing for revenge. I believed the lives that I took had little value, and I also held my own life to be of transient value. If I'd died, few people would have mourned me. I operated on a different plane of existence. Perhaps I had forgotten how to be human. Maybe that's what I had to do to survive.

Since I had found Lara and David, I had been able to imagine a life with meaning and hope. More than anything I wanted to put the old ways behind me and live the life of a normal teenager. I wanted to be silly with friends and play sports and wake up late on weekends. I wanted to learn the skills that would allow me to go back and help my people.

But within days of daring to imagine that life, I had been required to use the skills from my old life to kill two more people. I couldn't see how I'd had a choice, but maybe I had.

Maybe I should have stayed in the car with David and let the SAMSA officers deal with it. That's what a normal teenager would have done. But if I hadn't acted, I'm certain that Lara would be dead, David would be broken, and the future would look very different.

I had to find a way to put my old life behind me, but perhaps it wasn't going to be so easy.

Lara lay beside me on a lounger by the pool. I reached out and took her hand. She had been in the hospital for two days to get a couple of wounds stitched up and to be monitored for possible head injuries. The tests had all come back negative, but she was bruised and banged up and moved like an old woman.

The hospital had recommended aqua therapy, so that was why we were at the pool. We'd swim a length of breaststroke and then flip over and do a slow length of backstroke. Lara grimaced a lot, and I knew it was hurting her, but I was learning that she was tough.

"Do you want to do another length?" I asked. Her head jerked slightly, and I realized she had been asleep.

"What? Sorry. I must have dozed off. The painkillers are making me really dopey."

"I think you should go and have a long, hot shower. I'll come up in a while, and we can get some dinner sent up. David called to say he'd probably be late. The debrief with Dr. Naidoo and the police is taking longer than he thought."

"Poor David." Lara turned to me. "This has been very hard for him. I know he feels responsible for everything that happened. It's not really his world. He's used to feeling competent and in charge, and over the last few days both those things have been questioned."

"I know," I said. "I've been thinking a lot about that. Our worlds have been turned upside down. A teenage bush warrior trying to be a private school girl. A retired headmaster battling international drug cartels, and you, well, where to start?"

Lara was quiet for a moment, and I knew that she was wondering whether our relationship was strong enough to bear what she wanted to say.

"You probably won't understand this," she said, "but the most difficult part of the last few weeks for me was not what happened with the snakes at Die Lieukuil or even on the boat; it was shooting at your aircraft. I couldn't control anything that Stephen did to me, but I made the decision to shoot down your plane knowing it could kill you all. I wanted to kill you all. I even practiced so that I could kill you all. I killed your father and brother. I feel as if I gave away a bit of my soul by doing that." She broke into tears.

I wanted to say that I understood completely, to tell her that I had given away almost all of my soul and hoped only that there was a fragment left that she and David could help me cherish and nourish back to health, but I couldn't say that, not yet.

"You have a great soul, Lara, and in time you will come to know that what you did was the only thing you could have done. Sometimes there are only bad choices, and we have to opt for the one that is least bad. You didn't go looking for any of this."

"And look," I gave her hand a squeeze. "It brought me into your life, and you and David are helping me to create a new life out of my chaos, so it's not all bad."

"I'll try and focus on that," she said, smiling through her tears.

"Help me out of this lounger, will you? I feel like I'm ninety years old."

I took both of her hands and pulled her gently to her feet. As we walked into the hotel, she leaned on me as I knew I would lean on her in the future.

II

The funeral for Tom Parkes and his mother was held in the Shelburne Chapel.

Lara and I sat beside Pius in ornately carved stalls behind the choir. Members of the board sat on either side of us while opposite us across the aisle were some familiar faces.

Coby had squeezed himself into a suit that threatened to burst its seams with every movement he made. Dr. Naidoo sat next to him looking regal in a black silk dress and wide-brimmed hat. Even Ed Parkes's widow, Lena Michaels, was present wearing an inappropriate pink sheath with a plunging neckline and fidgeting with her clutch purse. Her surviving stepson sat beside her looking as if he'd rather be anywhere else.

Diba sat with her classmates for the first time. She was wearing her new school uniform, and she really looked the part. Over the massed heads of the student body, the two coffins looked small lying side by side in front of the altar. The organ played gently as the chaplain and the acolytes processed up the aisle.

The stalls weren't built for comfort, and something about their construction made me sit up straight. Dozing wouldn't be an option. Nonetheless, I fell into a reverie, thinking of my interview with Coby and his colleagues. Diba had killed two people, but there were two hundred witnesses on a tourist boat who could testify that it was in self-defence and to prevent a murder. Coby wasn't interested in investigating further. Of course, there were forms to fill in and statements to make, which took several hours, but afterwards Coby had insisted on buying me a beer.

"They were both bastards," he said, wiping froth from his lips with the back of his hand.

"They're both dead, and a judicial inquiry is a lot cheaper and quicker than a jury trial. It's the right outcome."

"What's the process for dealing with Tom and Sarah's murder?" I asked.

"Same thing," he said. "There will be an inquiry, and the verdict will be murder, but because the principal players are all dead, it will stop there."

"That should offer some closure for the school, but I feel terrible for Sam," I said.

"The rest of his family is dead, and the father he worshipped turned out to be a villain."

"He'll need a lot of help, but the school is a tight-knit community, and they have the best resources. He'll get counselling and support from his friends," Coby assured me.

"If he can afford to stay at the school," I replied.

"Fair point," Coby said, downing the rest of his beer in one swig. "But you know, shit happens. You can't protect people from that. You just have to try and give them the strength to survive it."

Coby had a comfortingly simple outlook on life. I was almost envious.

"Before I go, I wanted to say that it has been an honour to work with you and Lara. When I first met you, I thought you were a stuck-up British know-nothing. But I was wrong. You pulled it off. Of course, I'd attribute that mostly to Lara, who is obviously the brains behind the operation." He aimed a fake matey punch at my shoulder. "But seriously, what you did was brave, and you both have my respect."

I wasn't good at receiving compliments. I looked at the floor. "That means a lot, Coby. Thank you. I wonder if it wasn't just dumb luck, but it looks like it turned out OK."

He rose, shook my hand, and walked out into the soft early evening light.

The procession had reached the altar, and the chaplain was perched in his pulpit saying something I couldn't quite hear. It was warm in the chapel, and my mind wandered to the conversation I'd had with Dr. Naidoo the day before.

She'd sat back on the sofa in her office with her legs crossed sipping tea from her fine bone china cup. She had been able to show that the lake at Die Leeukuil was the source of the diatom *Cyclostephanos dubius,* thus proving beyond a reasonable doubt that young Tom had died there.

She asked after Lara's condition and said she hoped to see her before we headed home. I suspected that Lara would prefer it if that didn't happen. She offered to keep an eye out for Diba as she started at Shelburne, and I said we'd be grateful for that. Whatever Lara thought of Dr. Naidoo, she was a clever and powerful woman and a good person to have on our side.

The congregation rose to sing a hymn. One of Tom's classmates gave a touching eulogy that had most of us in tears. Then Sam left his stall beside his brightly coloured stepmom, shuffled to the front of the chapel, and spoke about his mother. He'd spent the last few years giving her a hard time, but he got this just right. Maybe it was a chance for him to atone, but whatever his motive, he did a good job.

Pius was last to speak. It was easy to see why he was so well respected in the school community. He hit all the right notes, and when he was finished, the school was finally ready to move past the tragedy and look to the future.

The three of us had met with Pius the previous evening. The setting sun shining through the tall windows of his office brought a restful warm orange glow from the polished wood panelling as we talked quietly. It was as if we were all drained of energy, worn from interacting with evil, exhausted by the unexpected twists and turns of recent events.

"Speaking for the Shelburne community, I want to thank you both for what you've done for us," Pius began. "If I had known the peril that I was putting you in, I never would have asked you, but what you have done has allowed the school to bring closure to this horrible passage in our history. You have made it possible for us to heal, and for that you have our eternal thanks."

"If I had known what we were getting into, I wouldn't have taken it on," I said, only partly joking.

"Diba tells me that you're heading back to Miami on Friday," Pius said. "I want you to rest assured that her wellbeing and happiness will be my personal concern. I have every confidence that she will make us all proud."

Diba was sitting on the edge of her chair. It remained to be seen how she would deal with the trauma that had characterized her early life, but in the short time I'd known her I'd realized she had a depth of character and a determination to succeed that I was pretty sure would carry her through.

The beautiful Irish setter, Molly, sat by her side. Pius had said that the school would give the dog a home as long as Diba cared for it while she was at Shelburne.

"We'll be back next month to travel with Diba for the long holiday," I said. We want to do tourist things together. I'd promised Lara that she could do some of that on this trip, but other stuff kept getting in the way."

Lara gave an inelegant snort at that, and Pius broke into his baritone guffaw.

III

The service was over, and the two coffins borne by the student guardians led the procession back down the aisle. Two freshly dug graves had been cut in the emerald-green turf of the school cemetery. At a word from the funeral director, the pallbearers lowered the coffins. The lilies and roses on the casket lids fluttered in the light breeze as the coffins came to rest on the thick black tape stretched over the graves.

The college chaplain, an athletic-looking young man with ginger hair, began to speak. "We have entrusted Sarah and Tom to God's mercy, and we now commit *their* bodies to the ground: earth to earth, ashes to ashes, dust to dust: in sure and certain hope of the resurrection to eternal life through our Lord Jesus Christ, who will transform our frail bodies that they may be conformed to his glorious body, who died, was buried, and rose again for us. To him be glory forever."

There we stood, witnesses to the last act of a family who had lost everything. Beyond the deaths of Ed, Sarah, and Tom, the Parkes family name had become a byword for insults and jokes.

Ed Parkes's assets were tied up in the courts and would eventually be distributed to those he had swindled. Lena Michaels and Sam would have nothing to live on, though the school had waived the fees for Sam's final year at Shelburne. Sam would have to start at the bottom like most people and see if he had what it took to make a life. He'd also lost his self-respect, but that could be earned back

Lost and Found

Stephen Kumalo's family had lost a husband and a father. It turned out they had known nothing about his criminal activities, so a confusing mixture of anger and disbelief was added to their grief. I knew that Pius had reached out to the mother with an offer of employment for her and the possibility of schooling for her children. He was a man with a big heart.

When the coffins had been lowered into the graves, and the mourners had thrown their handfuls of earth on top of them, the young priest spoke the blessing. "May God give you his comfort and his peace, his light and his joy, in this world and the next, and may the blessing of God almighty, the Father, the Son, and the Holy Spirit, be among *you* and remain with *you* always."

I crossed myself, an unthinking response from my Catholic upbringing.

We stood a little way back from the graveside. David was on my left and Diba on my right. David knew that the act of burying a child was one that would bring back difficult memories, and he reached out and took my arm. The gesture felt like love.

For my part I turned to Diba and put my arm around her shoulder. To an observer we probably looked like a family, but I knew there was a lot of hard work ahead of us if that was to become a reality.

David and I had gone into this trip different people than we were now. Before, we had enjoyed each other's company. Now we had found love and, more than love, a deep understanding and respect for each other and an acceptance of our strengths and weaknesses.

And Diba, who had lost so much—her parents, her childhood—well, she had found us, or we had found her; it didn't really matter. We were committed to her and would do everything in our power to help her reach her dreams.

We walked up the hill to the main school building, still holding each other. The sun was sinking behind the ancient trees, birds flying to roost in their outstretched branches. We shared a comfortable silence that no one wanted to break.

IV

The South African Airways flight from Jo'burg to Washington was only half full. Pius had insisted on upgrading us, so when the brandy had been sipped and the dinner cleared away, Lara eased her seat back to create a narrow lie-flat bed and was asleep within minutes.

I looked out at the cold star-filled night and thought about all that had happened to us. In the two weeks since we had arrived in Cape Town, our lives had been transformed. Love and hope had been born out of pain and despair.

Lara had made me remember that there was more to me than my job. The prospect of waking up beside her every morning made me smile. The reflection I saw in the aircraft window was that of a happy man.

Our new fifteen-year-old daughter made me realize that I had responsibilities well into the future and that I'd better forget any ideas of slowing down. Lara's real estate success had made her wealthy, but I would have to keep working if I wanted to do my share.

Our flight to Miami was scheduled to arrive at noon. I'd check in with Emy in the afternoon and see what was on the books.

If I had the choice, I'd opt for something a bit less exciting than the Shelburne job next time out, but, thinking about all that had transpired, I had no regrets.

"Out beyond ideas of wrongdoing and right doing there is a field. I'll meet you there. When the soul lies down in that grass the world is too full to talk about."
Jalāl ad-Dīn Mohammad Rūmī

CPSIA information can be obtained
at www.ICGtesting.com
Printed in the USA
LVHW042058150922
728494LV00004B/155